MYLES (SPECIAL FORCES: OPERATION ALPHA)

BLUE TEAM BOOK 3

RILEY EDWARDS

Dear Readers,

Welcome to the Special Forces: Operation Alpha Fan-Fiction world!

If you are new to this amazing world, in a nutshell the author wrote a story using one or more of my characters in it. Sometimes that character has a major role in the story, and other times they are only mentioned briefly. This is perfectly legal and allowable because they are going through Aces Press to publish the story.

This book is entirely the work of the author who wrote it. While I might have assisted with brainstorming and other ideas about which of my characters to use, I didn't have any part in the process or writing or editing the story.

I'm proud and excited that so many authors loved my characters enough that they wanted to write them into their own story. Thank you for supporting them, and me!

READ ON!
    Xoxo
    Susan Stoker

CHAPTER 1

Where are you?

I looked from the picture of Delilah Watts to the map and followed the yellow highlighted route I'd taken from San Diego to Los Mochis, Mexico. And just like the five hundred other times I'd studied it, it had no answers.

Where the hell are you?

For five weeks, with the help of Tex, Garrett, Kevin, Linc, Colin, Jaxon, and Leo, I'd been able to track Tamir Cohen. Then we hit a dead end, and after two weeks with no new leads, the guys went home.

I did not.

My mission was incomplete—wouldn't be complete until I found Delilah. But to find Delilah, I needed to find the man who'd taken her—Former Israeli Defense Force commando, Tamir Cohen.

He'd been leaving us breadcrumbs.

Tiny clues that only someone with specialized training would find.

Tamir had spent years in the IDF's highly respected Shayetet 13 before he'd asked to be transferred to his dead brother's Yamam unit. Shayetet 13 specialized in recon, intelligence, hostage rescue, and sabotage, among other things. Yamam was a well-trained counter-terrorism unit. If Tamir didn't want to be found, he wouldn't be found. He'd disappear, and no one would ever see him or Delilah again.

Shayetet 13 commandos didn't make mistakes. He was leaving us a trail to follow, but that trail ended, and for two weeks, I'd been stuck in Los Mochis.

My phone clattered on the table next to the map, and my hands curled into fists when my boss, Zane Lewis's name appeared on the caller ID. Zane calling at three in the morning local time, five in the morning his time—unless he'd gone through with his threat and was in Mexico to drag my ass home—didn't give me warm and fuzzy feelings.

"What's up?" I answered.

"Tex is on the line," Zane unhappily grunted.

"Tamir Cohen called me. He stashed Delilah in a house two and half hours south of your location. The town's called Laguna Colorada just outside of Culiacán," Tex told me.

I quickly skimmed the map and found the location.

"Got it. Did he give you coordinates?"

"Sending them now," Tex returned, and sure enough, my phone vibrated with a text. "He also gave a warning."

A chill went up my spine. A warning from an IDF commando made my jaw clench.

"What was the warning?" I asked.

"To keep Delilah off radar for as long as possible. Aviv Abrams wants her dead."

"We knew that," I reminded Tex. "Did Tamir explain why he didn't kill her? He works for Abrams, and Aviv won't be happy when his head of security comes back without a trophy after being gone for months. And if Tamir thinks he's gonna bullshit Aviv into thinking he couldn't find Delilah, that's not gonna work."

"Tamir didn't exactly explain his strategy to me, Myles. He called with the location and the warning."

There were a few beats of silence while I weighed my options. Go in alone and risk an ambush or wait until Zane got a team down to Mexico to help me extract Delilah.

"I'll send—"

I interrupted Zane. "No time. I'm less than three hours away. I'll leave now and have her secure before the sun comes up."

"Could be a setup," Zane warned.

"Could be. But he's also been leading me to her."

"That could be a setup, too."

"We already went over this, Z. Tamir knew we were following him. At any time, he could've engaged with us. He didn't. He kept his distance. He's had her two months, and as of two weeks ago, she was still alive. Our options are he's killed her and wants me to find her body which makes no sense, or he's setting a trap knowing I want her, and he attempts to kill me. But again, that doesn't make sense. I've been in Los Mochis for weeks. He knows I'm here. I've been visible on purpose, trying to draw him out. If he wanted me dead, he would've tried by now."

I had to fight against the bile fighting its way up my throat at the thought of Delilah's lifeless body being dumped for me to find.

"So, now you think Tamir Cohen's some sort of good guy?" Zane sneered.

"I think you've been right all along. There's something off about a man who was so dedicated to his country, to his family's honor that he went to his father's homeland to serve in the IDF when he was born and raised in the United States, and then that same man turns into a soulless killer."

"That's not what I said," Zane corrected. "I said, I thought Aviv possibly had something Tamir wanted or he was holding something over him that made him turn. But there's no denying he's fucking turned."

"War changes a man," Tex interjected. "It can suck the good right out of our bones if we're not cautious."

"Has he?"

This was something I'd spent a lot of time thinking about. If Tamir wanted Delilah dead, she'd be dead. He would've done it immediately and been on his way. He wouldn't have taken her eight-hundred and sixty-six miles into Mexico to do the deed. Keeping a hostage was risky, and it was a risk Tamir wouldn't take for an hour—certainly not for two months.

"Are you willing to bet your life on that line of thinking?"

"Yes."

"Get on the road," Tex cut in. "I'm gonna see if I can pull satellite images."

"Appreciate it. I'll be out the door in five."

"Don't get dead."

Zane disconnected and I folded the picture of the beautiful smiling woman back into quarters and tucked it back into my wallet.

Hang tight, baby. I'm coming for you.

Five minutes later, I was out the door.

CHAPTER 2

I was cold.

So cold my teeth were chattering and my body was shaking in a way I had no control over.

This happened every night.

During the day I would try to break free through the barred windows until sweat drenched my clothes, then night would come and everything would be damp and I'd shiver until my muscles ached.

But it could've been worse, right? Tamir Cohen could've hurt me. And not just because he was huge. I knew he was IDF. I'd done his background check when Aviv had convinced him to come work for Abrams. The dossier I'd collected for the insurance company hadn't begun to touch the surface of who he really was. They didn't need much information, just enough to insure him as the Abrams head of security. But I dug until I found who he really was. So, yeah, Tamir could've killed me a hundred different ways but he hadn't.

So I was grateful.

Grateful enough to ignore the hunger pains. Grateful enough not to think about how it felt like I was swallowing glass and dirt because there wasn't any saliva left in my mouth.

But I wasn't grateful enough not to be scared. Every day, every night, every second I'd been afraid. We'd been on the move for months, never staying in the same place for two nights in a row. Throughout this Tamir hadn't spoken a single word to me. Not one. He didn't tell me not to speak or to be quiet. He didn't ask if I was hungry or needed a restroom. He simply tossed food at me and stopped every few hours when we were driving so I could go to the bathroom. Sometimes on the side of the road.

He hadn't hit me—as a matter of fact, he hadn't touched me after he snatched me out of the hotel room I was hiding in. That was the last time I'd heard him speak, as well. He'd taken the call from Evette I'd set up.

He didn't speak so I didn't speak.

It creeped me out but I stayed silent, too afraid to break the seal. Too afraid to anger Tamir. I was quietly biding my time until I could get away. But I'd waited too long and now I was well and truly screwed.

What's the saying? A day late and a dollar short.

I should've taken Zane Lewis up on his offer to help me.

I should've pushed aside my fear and asked Tamir questions. But mostly I should've found a way to escape sooner.

Now I was in what someone might consider a house. No electricity. No furniture. An empty kitchen. Bars on the windows. A door with two deadbolts I couldn't open. And since there was literally nothing in the house to steal, those deadbolts were meant to lock me in, not keep a thief out.

That scared me, too, what those locks said.

I was a prisoner.

I had a toilet and a trickle of murky water that dripped from the faucet.

And Tamir was gone. He had been for days.

I was not relieved my captor had abandoned me.

He'd spent weeks driving aimlessly around Mexico, not saying a word, freaking me the fuck out, then he dumped me at this house and left. The worst part? I stupidly walked into what would be my tomb. I was going to die in here.

Alone.

With my teeth chattering.

My belly empty.

My throat scratchy.

I was all out of hope.

I was officially one of those too-stupid-to-live women. I deserved to die in this ramshackle house in the middle of nowhere. I prayed Evette London was safe. I hoped she got everything she needed to bring down Aviv Abrams and stop his sick brain experiments. The man was insane. His plan was insane. It was worth dying to stop him.

Those were my thoughts as I drifted in and out of sleep.

Cold and alone.

I woke up when a gloved hand covered my mouth, and I was being lifted off the floor. Fear clogged my throat, so thick I could choke on it.

Tamir was back.

Not again.

Never again.

The first time Tamir took me, I didn't fight. I was too scared. I knew his past, I knew his reputation, and I knew what he did for my boss. He'd gotten me from behind, one hand around my stomach, the other on my mouth, and I knew all it would've taken was a twist, and he could've snapped my neck. So I didn't fight.

So stupid. I should've fought. I knew Aviv had sent him to kill me. At least it would've been over fast instead of taking a two-month journey only to prolong the inevitable.

This time I was going to claw his eyes out. I would not be one of those women who whimpered and begged. I would die trying to live.

In a fury of anger and fear, I kicked, I slapped, I punched, I twisted my body in an attempt to get away. I heard grunts, his and mine. I heard heavy breathing, his and mine. What I didn't feel was pain. He wasn't hitting me back.

"Settle, Delilah." A deep, rough voice broke through my haze. "I'm here to bring you home."

Bring you home.

I no longer had a home.

Aviv would never let me live, I knew too much.

I did my best to shove the man away, but I was running out of strength. The man had no such problem subduing my flailing arms and turning me so I was facing away from him. Partly because I was exhausted, partly because he was bigger and stronger. I had one last option available to me and I wasn't going to let it go to waste. I waited until his arm settled across my chest and I dipped my chin and sank my teeth into his forearm. I didn't stop when he cursed; I bit harder when his arm clamped tighter, and finally, I tasted blood. That was when I gave up the ghost. I was screwed. Aviv sent someone new, maybe this guy would do the deed here in a ramshackle house in the middle of nowhere-Mexico.

I sagged in his arms, coming to terms with my reality.

"You done?" he growled.

"No!" But I made no move to struggle.

"Evette sent me," the man started. "I work—"

"She's alive?"

"Yes."

"Thank God. Thank God. Thank God," I chanted.

The man's arm loosened and he asked, "If I let you go are you gonna fight me?"

"Yes."

He sighed.

"Are you hurt?"

Just my dignity.

But I didn't say that. I didn't say anything. I didn't know who this man was, and I belatedly remembered the lessons I'd learned over the last six months—I couldn't trust anyone. I'd hoped Evette London was alive but the truth was, I wouldn't be shocked if she were dead. I'd be sad, I'd feel guilty for the remaining time I had on this earth, but I wouldn't be surprised.

Aviv Abrams was a sick, twisted maniac. Evette London had stumbled upon something she shouldn't have, documents *I* should've never had access to but did, and I stupidly thought I had an ally. I was so naïve I thought the two of us could expose Abrams. But then, I heard rumors floating around the office that there'd been a security breach and Aviv was sending out a crew to clean up the mess, and I tried to warn Evette to back off. Unfortunately, she didn't heed my warnings and continued to dig. Fortunately, the first guy Aviv had sent to kill Evette hadn't succeeded. Tamir Cohen was sent out next, and I knew my time was up. So was Evette's.

Tamir wasn't an amateur; he'd get the job done, and he did to some degree when he took out the guy Aviv hired to kill Evette and dumped his body in a landfill. Then Tamir nabbed me, and that brought me to now—in a dilapidated house with another man holding me hostage.

"We need to leave and we can't do that until I know if you're hurt."

Again I remained silent.

"I work for Zane Lewis." His tone was full of impatience and irritation. "We reached out to you, offering you protection. You agreed to talk to us. By the time I made it to Riverton and Evette made the call it was too late. Tamir had you. When we got a lock on your location in Dulzura I was a few hours too late, he'd moved you again."

"The rancher," I whispered. "We weren't there very long, just enough time for Tamir to push me into the bathroom and shove a towel at me. I showered, and when I was done, we left."

"We figured he bolted when the rancher started asking questions. Luckily the rancher had wildlife cameras around his property. We were able to identify Tamir Cohen as the driver and confirm you were alive."

That felt like a lifetime ago.

"Evette's really alive?"

"Yes. You can call her as soon as we're on the road."

I didn't know Evette in the sense that we were friends, or even acquaintances. I'd never actually spoken to her, though I did hear her voice when she called after I agreed to let Zane Lewis and his company, Z Corps, get me to safety. But I'd waited too long and Tamir had taken that call. Still, for some bizarre reason, I needed to talk to Evette, I needed confirmation she was alive. Even if there was no hope for me, if Evette made it and she had everything she needed to take down Abrams it would be worth my life.

Aviv had to be stopped.

"I'm not hurt. Tamir didn't touch me. He didn't even speak to me. It's been weeks and weeks of eerie silence," I admitted.

He let me go and gently turned me. I got my first look at the man who could either be my savior or my reaper. *God, I really hope he's the first.* It was dark—not pitch, but dim with the only light coming into the house from the rising sun. I couldn't make out his features but the sheer size of him freaked me out. He was bigger than Tamir, and the former IDF commando was not a small man. The man before me was also dressed in full battle gear, or at least what I thought would be battle gear—a black vest I was positive was bulletproof, gun magazines stuffed into the pouches, a handgun secured to the front, and a rifle hung from a sling strapped diagonally across his chest.

Tamir, too, had guns. He'd never pointed any of them at me, but he didn't hide the fact he had them. But seeing this man armed didn't scare me like it did when I saw Tamir's weapons. Maybe I should've been more scared seeing as I didn't know this person. And since I'd learned the last few years of my life had been one big, fat lie—at least my professional life had been—I was being stupid. Letting my guard down could mean death.

But staying locked in a house with no food and a trickle of dirty water means death, too. A long, drawn-out, painful death.

"Here." He produced a cellphone and held it out to me. When I took it he continued, "We need to get to the car before the sun comes up. Stay behind me, and if something happens, you run and get yourself safe, then you call the last number that called that phone. It's Zane's personal cellphone. If I can't get to you he'll send a team in to pick you up."

I didn't want to think about what could happen but I needed to know what he meant when he said *if I can't get to you.*

"Why wouldn't you be able to get to me?"

"I'll explain in the car. The sun's almost up we have to leave *now.*"

Waiting until we were in the car defeated the purpose of asking but his tone had taken on an edge of urgency that couldn't be ignored.

"Okay. I'll stay behind you and run if something happens."

Even though I couldn't see him clearly I didn't miss the relief in his posture. And that relief was a reminder that I wasn't safe, not even with this big man standing in front of me proclaiming to be one of the good guys.

CHAPTER 3

"Don't let go. I need to feel you behind me."

Delilah didn't grab the back of my vest or hold on to my belt loop. She shoved her fingers into the waistband of my cargos and held on as I walked around the corner of the house and scanned the area.

Still quiet.

The house where Tamir had stashed Delilah was off the beaten track. It couldn't be seen from the highway or the gravel road that switchbacked up the hillside, nor could it be seen from the dirt road that led into a valley. The landscape had gone from barren with only a few patches of shrubbery to dense greenery.

There were too many places for someone to hide. The hill couldn't be called a mountain by any stretch; however, it would give even the worst sniper the upper hand.

"Wow," Delilah whispered from behind me. "I had no idea what was out here. The bushes and vines mostly covered the windows."

The barred windows that had kept her prisoner.

"You didn't see when you drove in?"

"It was dark and Tamir turned off the headlights when we exited the highway. I couldn't see anything."

That was good to know. Tamir knew his way, so much so he didn't need his headlights to find the house.

"We're almost there," I told her.

I hadn't left the car too far away. Close enough I didn't have to walk miles back to it with a possibly immobile Delilah but far enough if Tamir was still in the house he wouldn't see my approach.

"It looks like a jungle."

The awe in her voice almost made me smile. The hillside was full of trees and thick underbrush but it didn't come close to what a jungle looked like, and thankfully none of the very large reptiles and other animals that could bite, sting, and kill were lurking in the grass or hanging from the branches above us.

There was nothing worse than being on patrol and having a snake suddenly dangling in front of you. I'd rather take an armed insurgent any day of the week and twice on Sunday than a snake suddenly appearing in front of my face with its forked tongue flicking inches from an eyeball.

I heard the distinct pounding of hoofs in the distance and came to an abrupt halt. My left hand went behind me and tugged Delilah closer and my right brought my rifle up.

"Do not move."

I let go of Delilah and brought my left hand up to the barrel of my AR and took aim at the clearing in front of me. Then I listened. Only one set, and by the rhythm, I'd guess a horse at a fast gallop.

"Reach around me and pull out the Glock." I felt Delilah shift, then she fumbled with the holster until she freed the gun. "Now keep your finger off the trigger, turn around, put your back to mine, and shoot anyone who approaches."

"Shoot them?"

"There's no safety device on a Glock," I informed her. "There is a bullet in the chamber. That means the gun is ready to fire. All you need to do is point and pull the trigger."

"Shoot them," she repeated shakily.

The pounding was getting closer and we were out of time.

"Yes, Delilah, shoot them."

"Okay."

That was even shakier, perhaps it was because her entire body was trembling against mine.

"Everything's gonna be fine."

"Someone's coming."

"And I'll take care of it. All I need is for you to watch our backs, make sure no one's sneaking up behind us."

"I don't see anyone."

"Good. Just stay calm and be ready to run if I tell you to. You have a gun and a phone. Everything's gonna be fine."

A horse came through the clearing, I zeroed in on the rider's forehead, slid my finger into the trigger well but stopped short of pulling the trigger when the man yanked on the horse's reins with one hand and put the other in the air.

"Friendly," he shouted in a heavily accented voice. "No shoot me."

What the fuck?

"Message. I have message only. He said to come, give you message."

"Slide off the horse," I commanded.

The man instantly did as I asked and raised both hands.

"No gun just message. No shoot."

"What's the message?" I asked and the man's right hand started to lower. "Nope, keep both hands where I can see them."

"Message. In pants."

"What kind of message?"

"In pants."

"Do you know Spanish?" I asked Delilah.

"No."

Neither did I and this would go a lot faster if I could communicate clearly.

"No shoot. Message in pants."

This time when the man lowered his hand I didn't stop him. He reached into his pocket and slowly pulled out a folded piece of white paper and held it up.

"Message in pants." He smiled. "No shoot."

"I'm not going to shoot you. Put the paper on the ground."

Not letting go of his horse's reins he bent slightly and let the paper float to the ground beside his feet.

"Who gave that to you?"

"The man."

"What man?"

"The man. He said to give you message. I watch all morning for you. He said to give you message and keep the workers away until you come. I do it."

17

"Tamir? Did Tamir give that to you?"

"Yes, the man."

For the love of all things holy. It was a sad day when I wished I was back in the Sandbox where I could communicate in one of the many native dialects.

"Where are the workers?"

"No come until you leave."

I felt Delilah stiffen behind me and I leaned back into her hoping contact would help calm her nerves.

"Anyone back there, Delilah?"

"Are you going to shoot him?" she whispered.

I ignored the clenching in my gut and what her question said about the kind of man she thought I was, and answered, "No."

Her body sagged against mine and I ignored that, too.

"Gracias, amigo," I said.

"De nada. Date prisa y vete. Es seguro," the man returned with a smile.

Since I had not the first clue what the hell he said I smiled back.

The man swung back up onto his horse and motioned for us to follow him.

"Come!" he called thankfully switching back to English. "Safe."

There was nothing particularly safe about our situation but standing there talking, leaving us wide open for someone else to come up on us, was the very definition of stupid.

"Delilah, you got your finger off the trigger?"

"Yeah."

"Good. Turn back around, hold on to me, and keep the barrel of the gun pointed at the ground." I felt her shift behind me and once again her fingers shoved back into my pants and she held on. "There's a piece of paper on the ground. When we get to it I need you to pick it up."

"I see it."

"Are you ready?"

"Yeah."

The woman was shaking so hard I found it doubtful she could walk.

"Delilah?"

"Yeah?"

"Take a breath. I'm not gonna let anything happen to you."

"Okay."

"You didn't take a breath. Breathe in and out slowly."

I didn't hear her inhale but I felt her exhale fan over the back of my arm.

"I'm okay," she muttered.

"You're better than okay. You're doing great."

My gaze went to the sun steady rising over the hill then to the dancing horse at the mouth of the clearing. We were officially out of time yet I stood frozen when I heard Delilah's soft laugh.

"Right, I'm doing great if *great* means my legs feel like jelly, my stomach's doing flip-flops, and I've given myself permanent heart damage."

"I won't let you fall."

"Thank you."

Maybe it was the sincerity I heard. Maybe it was the minute amount of trust she'd given me. Or maybe it was because I knew she was scared as fuck but she'd still laughed that had me holding my rifle with one hand so I could reach around and squeeze her hip.

"Let's go."

"Lead the way."

I led the way, only stopping so she could pick up the paper. The car came into view and with a wave, the man dug his heels into his horse and galloped away without a backward glance.

"Where in the world did you find this?" she asked as I helped her into the passenger seat. "The SUV graveyard?"

It was true, the old Mitsubishi Montero had seen better days. The burgundy paint showed more rust than color but it was mechanically sound.

"This here is what's called a classic," I teased.

"A classic beater," she returned, then her grin faded and her hand covered her mouth. "I'm sorry. I'm not being—"

"It's all good," I cut her off. "Swing your legs in and buckle up."

She did as I asked. I slammed the door and kept scanning the area as I rounded the hood.

I cranked the engine and smiled at her when the old Montero turned over on the first try.

"See, classic."

"What should I do with this?"

She held up the Glock, finger safely away from the trigger, and I debated my answer.

"Do you feel safer knowing you have a weapon?"

"Not really."

"Then put it in the glove box. It'll be there if you need it."

Delilah looked over at me and jolted like she was seeing me for the first time.

I knew what she saw. I was not a small man, but

compared to her tiny frame I was a giant. I was also kitted out with gear and an AR still strapped across my chest. While we were on the move and her mind was occupied she likely hadn't thought much about it, but sitting in a car with a stranger after what she'd been through wouldn't be comfortable.

"You're totally safe with me."

Delilah blinked. Her gaze lifted to meet mine and the hazel eyes I'd only ever seen in pictures flared. The photographs hadn't done them justice; actually, the photos hadn't done *her* justice, period. Even pale, way too thin, and dirty she was an extremely beautiful woman.

"Your arm's bleeding," she gasped.

I glanced down. It wasn't bleeding so much as it was red and welted with a perfect outline of her teeth. There were some tiny drops of blood pooling but for the most part, the blood had smeared and dried.

"You got a set of chompers on you, girl." I knew my attempt at humor fell flat when I heard a whimper. My gaze went back to Delilah. She was still staring at my arm, now with tears threatening to spill down her cheeks.

"Hey, look at me." I waited for her to cast her eyes up and when she did I saw how full they were—with defeat, shame, fear.

The fear I understood. The defeat I understood. The shame I did not. The shame gutted me. And for some inexplicable reason, there in that beat-up piece-of-shit Montero in the waxing light, I silently vowed to conquer that shame.

I squelched the overwhelming desire to reach over and hold her hand and instead gave her the only thing I could —words that would be meaningless until I could prove to her they weren't. "I'm sorry I scared you. I did the best I could, clearing the area around the house and inside before I went to you. But I couldn't take the chance you'd scream and wake up the valley. There's one of me and my job protecting you would become increasingly harder if an army showed up before I could get us secure. It was my fault. You did nothing wrong."

"I bit you like a wild animal."

"No, you bit me like a woman who was protecting herself. You did everything right back there. But your right hook can use some work. If you're up for it when we get back to the States, I'll show you some moves."

"Maybe if I hadn't been weakened because I haven't eaten in days I could've kicked your ass."

It was her turn to joke and my turn to scowl.

"He didn't leave you food?" Delilah leaned away from me and I did my best to soften my tone but I knew I failed when she flinched again. "And water? Did he leave you any?"

She shook her head and I couldn't stop the curse. "Motherfucker. As soon as we're back on the highway you can climb in the back and go through my pack. There are protein bars and water. But for now, I need you buckled up. Can you wait ten minutes?"

"Yes," she whispered.

Fuck. Whatever headway I'd made with her I'd lost. She was back to being terrified of me and now that I'd had a small taste of what her trust felt like my stomach revolted at the thought of her going back to thinking of me as the enemy.

CHAPTER 4

"What's your name?"

The man glanced over at me and smiled.

We'd been driving in silence for a few minutes when I finally plucked up the courage to speak. I wasn't scared *per se*; even if I knew he wasn't mad *at* me, he was still mad and a stranger.

"Myles."

"Myles," I repeated. "Thanks for getting me out of that house."

His lips twitched, curved up a little bit at the corners, but never fully formed a smile.

"I'm not joking. I really do appreciate you saving me from what I was sure was going to be my tomb."

"I know you're not joking. I also know you didn't want to come with me because you thought I was going to save you from the house only to kill you once I got you out."

I felt my face heat and I looked down at my lap.

"Boy, you don't beat around the bush do you?" I mumbled.

"Nope. Don't see a point in bullshitting or wasting time. The truth's the truth. It's always easier to just come right out and say what's on your mind."

Myles drove another couple of minutes while I studied my dirty hands. In the last few months, I'd had a handful of showers. Sometimes there would be soap for me to use, sometimes not. I hadn't shaved, used deodorant, brushed my teeth, or used conditioner since the last shower I took before Tamir had taken me.

I was filthy.

I knew I stank but since I'd become accustomed to sitting in my own nastiness I was nose-blind to it. That probably should've embarrassed me, but I wasn't. I couldn't muster up the energy or emotion. I was just happy to be alive. To be out of that house and away from Tamir.

"I need to check in," Myles broke the silence. "Do you mind making the call and putting it on speaker?"

It took me a moment to realize he was asking because he'd given me his phone.

And he'd given me a gun.

If he wanted to kill me would he have given me access to either? Especially the gun.

I hitched my leg and rolled in the seat just enough to pull his phone out of my back pocket.

"What's the number?"

"Just press the last number that called."

Zane Lewis.

I was supposed to call him if we got separated. Sudden fear swept over me and I wanted to throw the phone out the window so Myles couldn't call Zane. What was he going to do with me? Put me on a plane? Drop me off at a bus station? Leave me at a hotel? I had nothing. No money, no ID, no way to get back into the United States. Not that I wanted to go back. I had to hide. Aviv could never know Tamir didn't kill me. Or maybe Tamir already told Aviv and someone new was on their way to kill me.

"Hey, Delilah, hey. Slow down, sweetness."

"You can't call Zane!"

"Why not?"

"Where are you going to leave me?"

"Leave you?" Myles's hand shot out and he grabbed my arm.

"Hey!" I yanked my arm away and moved over. "Don't touch me, I'm gross."

His eyes came off the road and cut to me. They were slitted. His voice sounded incredulous when he asked, "You're gross?"

For some reason, his question cut me deep. And everything came crashing down. All the trauma, the relief, the uncertainty of my future. Everything churned together in my stomach until I felt like I was going to be sick.

"Yes," I hissed. "I'm disgusting. He locked me in that house with barely a trickle of water. I sweated my ass off all day and froze all night. I haven't been *clean* for months."

"What else?"

What else?

Was that not enough for him?

"He didn't give me a toothbrush either. You should get a tetanus shot before your arm gets infected."

"My arm will be fine. Anything else?"

"I stink and I'm humiliated and you want more?"

"Yes, Delilah. Right now, get everything out. Say it, yell it, scream if that's all you can do but get it out now so it doesn't fester. That fucker took you, held you against your will, didn't feed you properly, didn't let you bathe, what else did he do to you?"

"Nothing."

"Nothing?"

"He did *nothing* else to me. He didn't touch me or speak to me. He didn't even bother to threaten me or point his gun at me because he knew I was a scared idiot who wouldn't run. He took me and I was so terrified I didn't even fight."

The road straightened as we came out over a ridge. The thick greenery was thinning, and off in the distance, I could see patches of brown.

"I didn't fight him," I whispered.

"Do you know who Tamir Cohen is?"

"Yes."

"Then you know it's a good thing you didn't fight him. It's probably what kept you alive. Who knows what would've happened if you'd forced his hand. If you'd tried to run. If you made a scene one of the times he stopped he could've easily taken out anyone who attempted to help and then killed you. There're times to fight and times to be patient and wait."

That might be so, but I wasn't being patient and waiting. I'd been paralyzed with fear and did nothing.

The phone in my hand vibrated and I fumbled the device and dropped it on the floorboard.

"Shit. Sorry."

With my heart pounding—yes, from a phone vibrating —I leaned forward and picked it up and saw the name Zane on the screen. The pounding intensified and my hands shook. This was it. Zane Lewis was calling. I was going to discover just how uncertain my future was. My life was yet again in another person's control.

"It's Zane, should I answer?"

"Yeah. He'll keep calling then send a team to find us if I don't check in."

I tapped the connect icon and held the phone up between me and Myles.

"I got the package," Myles said.

"Any trouble?" A voice I assumed was Zane's boomed.

"Met a man on the way out. He knew I was going to be there and came to deliver a message."

"Who sent him?"

"Don't know, there was a language barrier. He left the message and told me he'd been instructed to keep my route clear of workers. I'm at the highway now and haven't seen another vehicle."

"What's the message?"

"Don't know. I haven't read it."

There was a stretch of silence that lasted so long I thought the call had been dropped.

"How secure are you?" Zane asked.

"You're on speaker," Myles retorted.

"We'll talk when you get to the hotel. I'm sending an address in Loma. You'll stop there and pick up your new papers. Ivy booked your hotel. I threatened to take the cost out of her paycheck, she laughed in my face. I'm sure you can expect an oceanfront suite."

"Where are we headed?"

"Mazatlán."

Zane sounded disgruntled. Myles did not, he chuckled.

"Do I need to find a doc?"

Myles's amusement died a quick death and his eyes came to me. His expression was so blank it took me by surprise. I didn't know a face could be so devoid of emotion. There wasn't a line, a crinkle, a twitch. Nothing.

I shook my head no and Myles verbalized my answer.

"Negative."

"Check in."

"Before you go," Myles started. "I need you to set up a call with Evette."

"Not gonna happen," Zane barked.

"This is a two-way street, Z."

"For now it's a one-way with a do not enter sign and you damn well know it. Watch your back."

The call ended and I was left confused.

"What does that mean?" I asked.

"Let's get you fed and to the hotel. I'll explain everything there."

The hotel.

"Will you leave me there?"

"No."

His clipped one-word answer did nothing to alleviate the fear that was bouncing around my chest.

"Will you explain to me what's going on?"

"First we're stopping to pick up new identities and cash. Then we're checking into a hotel. Zane's correct, it will be oceanfront and a suite. Likely it will be the most expensive in Mazatlán. You'll get a good meal in your belly, you'll get a shower, you'll relax, then we'll talk about

Abrams, Tamir, Evette, and what's happened over the two months you've been missing."

I pushed my question about the hotel and why he thought it would be the most expensive aside and concentrated on Abrams, Tamir, and Evette.

"Is Evette okay? Did they get to her?"

"That's a story for the hotel." Myles's response was firm, resolute, and held an edge of bitterness.

Guilt clawed at my insides. I should've found another way to expose Abrams and Dr. Ramon Gates and his disgusting experiments. I should've gone directly to the police as soon as I'd read Dr. Alejandro Arias' report. The problem was the police would've thought I was crazy. No one would believe the story I had to tell. It had all the makings of a futuristic sci-fi movie—and not a good one. The evil villain who planned to take over the world. The trusted right-hand man who kidnapped and killed for the villain. The mad scientist and pig brain experiments. Artificial Intelligence and super soldiers. And of course, there was the lowly woman who could blow the villain's plan, so she'd have to die.

Yeah, no one was going to believe me. Not Zane or Myles or the authorities.

My one hope had been Evette. She'd only found the first thread and hadn't begun to unravel the evil Aviv Abrams had planned. And if she'd figured out what Aviv wanted to do it was so outlandish, so unbelievable, there was a strong possibility even Evette would've laughed it off as the ramblings of a man who'd lost his mind. But Aviv Abrams wasn't rambling. He was experimenting, and had been for years.

If I told them what I knew, they'd think I was a whack

job and ditch me. Then I'd be as good as dead. Aviv knew what I'd found.

I knew way too much.

I knew everything.

And that knowledge was my death sentence.

CHAPTER 5

I'd done a damn good job ignoring Delilah's appearance —until now.

It had been easy to overlook her gaunt form, dirty clothes, matted and unwashed hair, pale skin, and the stench of fear that clung to her when she slept in the backseat on the way to Loma. She hadn't stirred when a man came to the car, wordlessly handed me a thick envelope, and walked away.

But now, at the hotel, I could no longer ignore it—I couldn't because Delilah couldn't. I wanted to beat the hell out of every motherfucker staring at her. *And* my boss for putting us up in a resort town. Not only that but a high-class, expensive resort town. Delilah had refused to go into the hotel with me to check in. And she was pissed as fuck at me when I refused to leave her in the car. The argument had led to me reminding her that Tamir was still on the loose and so was Aviv Abrams. I was a one-man show and the only person standing between her and death.

I didn't miss the look the front desk clerk gave her and neither did she. If it was possible, Delilah's already ghastly complexion bleached further. It had taken all of my control not to draw unwanted attention and punch the fucker in the face. By the time we made it to the elevator, Delilah was visibly shaking and my temper had flared to the surface.

I was powerless, completely and utterly unable to help Delilah in any way. I had no right to pull her close and shield her bodily from onlookers. There was nothing I could say to her that wouldn't sound contrite or patronizing.

"Fuck, 'em," I grounded out between my clenched teeth.

Delilah's torso jerked along with her shoulders and finally, her head snapped in my direction. Dirt and grime streaked her neck and lower part of her jaw up to her ear.

She looked like a hot mess.

A hot mess who was a goddamn survivor.

A hot mess who still managed to be so goddamn pretty her beauty burned through me.

"Do you hear me, Delilah? Fuck 'em all. Not a single one of those bitches giving you the side-eye in the lobby would've lasted a day. And those preppy-ass pussies would've shit their pants. You held strong. You didn't break. You are alive. So fuck them and their judgment. They don't have the first clue what you lived through."

She was staring at me unconvinced.

"You're right, they don't. But that doesn't mean I'm still not horrified."

"You know the difference between you and them?" I asked and took a step in her direction.

And as if to prove my next words true Delilah stood her ground and straightened her shoulders.

Atta girl.

"Thirty minutes from now, all that dirt will be down the drain, those clothes will be in the trash, and you'll still be *you*, brave as fuck. And those assholes downstairs will still be them—spineless, pretentious idiots."

The elevator doors slid open and Delilah braced until she saw that the hallway was clear then she relaxed and followed me out.

I let Delilah into the room that was indeed the very definition of wealth and class. Ivy Lewis enjoying poking at her husband. She was the only person who could awaken the beast and not get clawed, so she pushed and did stuff like book luxury suites that cost a thousand dollars a night. Normally I found this funny—right then, I did not.

The honeymoon suite.

No part of Delilah's reaction was amusing.

The white linen couch facing the gas fireplace seemed to have caught her attention. I didn't know if she was wondering like I was why the hell there was a fireplace in a beachfront resort, or if everything being a shade of white, cream, or ivory had caught her attention. The boring color scheme was broken up by teal green accents but not nearly enough to cut through the bland decor.

"What's wrong?"

"I'm afraid to walk any farther in."

The woman was killing me. I wasn't sure if I was pissed or if my heart was breaking.

"Shower!" My clipped demand was rude as hell and I

didn't give the first fuck that she was staring at me like I was a total dick.

Her eyes dropped to the cream carpet and her shoulders sagged.

That pissed me off, too.

"I'm—"

"Don't apologize to me. I can't say I know what's going on in your mind but I have spent weeks in the field. I know what it feels like to be covered in grime and guck and have it in places that are uncomfortable. You'll feel better after you shower. You take as long as you need. I'll order room service and we'll get some real food in you, that'll help, too."

"I don't have clean clothes."

Finally, something I could give her that might make her feel human. I rolled my pack off my shoulder and walked to the couch. Unlike Delilah, I didn't give the first fuck if my dusty pack left a mark on the fabric. I might've if the asshole checking us in hadn't curled his lip at the sight of Delilah. I might've if I hadn't caught a bellboy backing away from us. The couch could be cleaned—the memory of how those people recoiled couldn't be washed from Delilah's memory. So fuck them.

I unzipped the bag and pulled out a sundress I'd bought her while I was in Los Mochis. And as strange as it was I'd bought undergarments as well. The underwear was just that, something to wear under her clothes. And the bra was more of a tube top. I could disassemble and reassemble any weapon you put in front of me. I could do it quickly and blindfolded. What I couldn't do was guess a bra size for a woman I'd never met in person. I also pulled out the cotton shorts and t-shirt I bought and laid everything out on the couch.

"Will any of this work until we can go shopping and get you proper clothes?"

I stepped to the side so she could get a better view of the haul. When seconds ticked by and she hadn't answered I turned to look at her.

She was standing where I'd left her but now her arms were wrapped around her middle like she was holding herself together. I didn't know how long her hair was because it was in a knot on the top of her head. There might've been a rubber band in there somewhere piling it together but now there were literal knots that looked more like matted clumps. I knew from her picture her hair was dirty-blonde and at one time it brushed past her shoulders in healthy, shiny strands, but right then the strands looked more brownish than blonde. She was way too thin and her cheeks were slightly sunken in. And those greenish-brown eyes were so full of pain I wanted to carry her into the shower and help her scrub away the nightmare.

Yet with all of that she somehow still managed to look beautiful.

"You're killing me, sweetheart. Say something."

"Thank you." I shook my head but she got in there again before I could speak. "For thinking of clothes. That was thoughtful of you, Myles. And I want you to know I'm grateful—for everything you've done so far. I'll find a way to pay you back."

"The way you can pay me back is by coming over here and picking up your clothes. Then you can thank me by usin' up all the hot water in this joint. Then you can thank me by eating the food I'm gonna be force-feeding you over the next few days. You do all of that, we'll call it even."

Finally, she smiled.

My gut tightened and my heart constricted. And I knew I'd buy her a hundred more dresses to see that smile.

"Not sure if it's possible to use all the hot water in a place like this, but I'll certainly try."

I watched her walk across the cream carpet with her head held high until she reached the couch, then she bent, picked up the clothes, and straightened. She'd taken two steps before she stopped and said, "The letter's in my back pocket. You mind getting it out?" She was holding the clothes out in front of her so they didn't touch her dirty shirt. "I don't want to mess up the clean clothes."

My gaze dropped to her ass and I saw the corner of the paper peeking out of the pocket. I did my best not to linger—not my hand in her pocket or my eyes. Both tasks were hard, and only one I accomplished.

With one more smile, this one tentative but still a grin, Delilah made her way to the bedroom and closed the door. I waited, and just like I thought she would, I heard the lock turn.

Good girl.

I unfolded the crumpled paper.

KEEP HER OUT OF SIGHT AND OUT OF THE WAY. YOU WILL KNOW WHEN IT IS SAFE FOR HER TO GO HOME.

Two sentences. That was it.

The script was neat and in all capital letters. No salutation or signature, but it didn't take a genius to deduce who left the note.

Tamir Cohen.

No explanation of why he'd called Tex. No explanation of why he took her, and while he didn't treat her with kindness, he hadn't physically harmed her.

More questions than answers.

I pulled out my phone and called Zane.

"You at the hotel?"

"Yeah, and I gotta tell you, normally, I find your wife's pranks the highlight of my day. But this bullshit of putting us up in a swank hotel when I got no option but to make a woman who looks like she just crawled out of a sewer pipe and doesn't smell much better walk into the lobby and have people fucking stare and back away from her... not finding that shit fucking funny."

I heard a gasp, and I closed my eyes.

"I'm so sorry, Myles," Ivy wheezed. "I wasn't thinking about that. Shit, I didn't think at all. Is she okay?"

"Would've been nice to know I was on speaker. I could've cushioned that, brother."

"I don't need anyone cushioning anything," Ivy resorted testily. "I screwed up. I wasn't thinking about you being there by yourself. Did people really back away from her?"

I walked to the floor-to-ceiling windows that overlooked the crystal blue ocean and took a deep breath.

"Yeah. It was pretty fucked. Once I got her into the room she seemed better."

"No, she wasn't," Ivy called me out on my lie.

Damn.

"You're right, she wasn't better. But she will be after she cleans up and gets some rest."

I checked my watch and had a hard time computing

the number of hours I'd been awake—a testament to how sleep deprivation slowed your mind. Even the simplest mental math was becoming difficult.

"We're in for the rest of the day," I declared and turned away from the beautiful view. "But before I let you go, I read Tamir's message."

I rattled off the short note and heard Zane grunt.

"I fucking hate riddles. Whatever happened to good old-fashioned communication? You know, say what you mean and mean what you say. Is that a threat? What happens if we don't keep her out of the way? Is he going to kill her? Maybe write us another note? I miss the old days when assassins assassinated their targets and didn't take them on a two-month joyride. And how the hell will we know when it's safe for her to go home? Is the fucker gonna shine his bat-light and hope I see it, send a smoke signal, an email? *And* when the hell did I become the king of the castaways?"

Jesus.

I was too tired to listen to Zane rant and he could go on and on for hours.

"You're the king of something, Zane Lewis," Ivy snapped.

"If you bring home one more cat, I'm gonna be the King of the Pussies," Zane returned. "No more damn cats. I'm buying my son a dog. A big one."

"Sorry Z, that nickname's taken," Gabe put in.

"Who's there?" I asked.

"Just the three of us. We're in Zane's office," Gabe told me. "Evette's downstairs. She wanted to come in just in case there was more word on Delilah."

A few months ago, a miracle had happened. Gabe

Harris grew a heart. Or, more accurately, he found the woman who would force him to open it to the possibility of love. The poor idiot didn't stand a chance. Evette London had walked into Z Corps needing help, and before Gabe knew what hit him, she had him wrapped around her finger.

"Delilah wants to talk to her."

"Have I lost *all* control?" Zane growled.

"Did he ever *have* control?" Ivy snarked.

"The answer is no." Then Zane went on to underline his verdict. "Not until we get a handle on Tamir and the situation. I have a deal in place with Abrams ensuring Evette's safety. Now that we have Delilah in custody, Aviv will rightly assume I've broken that deal. Myles is alone in Mexico with a woman we don't know and haven't vetted. I'm not taking any chances. Delilah and Evette can bond or do whatever it is women do *after* we've neutralized Tamir and Aviv."

I didn't get a chance to question Zane about what he meant by *we have Delilah in custody* before Ivy cut in.

"I don't understand what the harm is in allowing Delilah to talk to Evette. It will help build trust."

Without missing a beat, Zane slipped back into his normal sarcastic self.

"Woman, you get I'm a smart man, yeah?"

"No, I *get* you're bossy, stubborn, and untrusting, and it's worth the repeat, *bossy*. A smart man who wasn't exasperating would understand that allowing Delilah to speak to Evette would help us. The more Delilah trusts us, the more she'll tell us about Abrams."

"Something I've learned over the years. Something I should've done way back when Leo brought Olivia into the family—keep the women separated. This is a divide-and-conquer situation. You women, you're dangerous. All of you in your own right, but together, you all are scary as fuck. Together, you all can manipulate and plot. Together, you can plan your world domination. No way in hell am I allowing Evette and Delilah to scheme to take down an Israeli defense contractor who has millions of dollars tied up in projects. Millions of dollars that Aviv Abrams doesn't want to lose. Money and contracts he'll protect by unleashing his security team, which consists of some of the best commandos in the world.

"If Evette is involved, Anaya will jump on board, and Kyle will lose his mind. Anaya gets in on the action Tatiana, Emerson, and Eva will take her back and I'll have three more men pissed as fuck. Then there's you, my wife, and I know you. You'll sink your teeth into this and rope in Violet, Olivia, Erin, and Jasmin. Once that happens, we have war. So to contain the situation before there's bloodshed, there's a moratorium on communication. Myles will get the intel we need from Delilah and Gabe will keep Evette far away from Delilah."

Zane was spot-on with his assessment. The women would rally and there'd be trouble. Especially once Jasmin Parker got involved. Jasmin was the only female Z Corps employee who was part of a squad. Long before Jasmin joined the Red Team or married Zane's brother Lincoln she and Zane had history. An ugly history that included being captured by a group of Russians and tortured. Out of that came deep respect and loyalty. Jasmin would absolutely want in on the action and once that happened, all hell would break loose.

"I won't—"

"You're right, Ivy, you won't," Zane cut his wife off.

"Don't be an asshole," Ivy warned softly.

"You know I love you. From the bottom of my soul, I love you. You get I'm trying to keep my men from going rogue. Their women get involved there will be *war*. You get caught in the middle of this I will scorch the earth. Told you once, told you thousands of times over the years my life ends without you in it. Aviv Abrams gets a wild hair up his ass and even looks at you or my son, I will burn him and everyone around him to the ground. There will be no more Abrams, but also, there will be no more Z Corps. I will call in every marker, spend every last penny I have, I will use my men to do horrific things, and you know they'll blacken their souls for me. So, please, Ivy, do me this one favor—stand down."

"Okay, Zane, I'll stand down."

At Ivy's soft and immediate acquiesce something clicked inside of me. It wasn't Ivy's swift agreement to her husband's demand. It was that Ivy knew Zane—knew him in a way that none of us would ever know him. It was instinctual and deep-rooted. Ivy was strong enough to take on a man like Zane; she knew when to push him and stand her ground, and when something was truly important to Zane when to give him what he needed.

I hadn't felt a touch of jealousy when my teammates found women and fell in love. I hadn't been envious when my friends on the Gold Team had introduced me to their wives. Actually, I hadn't given much thought to relationships in general. *If it happens, it happens* had always been my general thought about finding a wife. I wasn't opposed but I knew myself well enough to know I would never settle.

41

But right then, hearing the interaction between Zane and Ivy—their connection as strong as it was that even over the phone thousands of miles away, I could feel the love my boss had for his wife—I was envious as fuck.

That was what I wanted.

That was why I refused to settle.

It was all or nothing.

"What's your next step?" Gabe asked, pulling me back to the conversation.

"Get Delilah to trust me."

"That shouldn't be hard," he incorrectly surmised.

"It's gonna be damn near impossible," I told him. "The company she worked for is involved in some shady shit. They employed a man who snatched her and held her hostage for two months. Then I come in, scare the shit out of her, snatch her up, and now I'm essentially holding her hostage."

"That's not what you're doing," Gabe argued.

I glanced down at Delilah's teeth marks that said that was exactly what I'd done.

"Believe me, Gabe. That's how she sees it. The woman has been stripped of her power. Tamir didn't hurt her physically but he knew what he was doing treating her to two months of silence. I think that scared her worse than if he would've threatened her every day. She doesn't trust me and the little pieces she has given me aren't gonna get us what we need."

"You can work her around," my friend said confidently.

But the thing I didn't want to *work* Delilah. I wanted her to trust me because I'd earned it, not because I was bullshitting or lying to get intel.

"I need to order food before Delilah's done with her shower. I'll be in touch."

"I'll have stuff delivered to your room," Ivy rushed out before I could hang up.

"What kind of stuff?"

"Female stuff."

I wasn't going to ask. Asking would mean a ten-minute explanation about shit I didn't care to know about.

"Thanks, Ivy."

"Least I can do after my screw up. I'll get the basics and have them sent right up, but ask her if there's anything specific she needs."

"Do I look like I'm running a day spa? The basics will do," Zane grunted.

"You look like a man who needs to do as many good deeds as you can before you die so you don't end up in the bad place."

"The bad place?"

"Hell, Zane," Ivy snapped.

"Seriously? That's all it takes to—"

"I'm hanging up," I told Zane before he could go on another tirade.

"Is it too soon—"

"Yes!"

I disconnected.

I didn't need Zane to tell me to "glove up" or "use protection." Not only was I not fifteen, I had control over my body and emotions.

Famous last words.

43

CHAPTER 6

I didn't know exactly how I ended up sitting in the tub. But there I was on my ass with water raining down from the showerhead. I'd scrubbed and scrubbed until that tiny bar of hotel soap was a useless sliver. I'd used both of the bottles of shampoo and conditioner in the little basket on the counter by the sink.

I was still dirty and the washcloth lying near my toes was stained brown.

I'd been in the shower a long time. The water hadn't run cold yet but my mind had run away from me and I couldn't stop replaying the last six months of my life. If I'd done one thing differently I wouldn't be in Mexico. I wouldn't have been sitting in the tub of an expensive hotel wondering how I'd lost everything, wondering if my landlord had sold all of my belongings or thrown them out. Wondering what happened to my car. Wondering when I'd become such a workaholic that I'd lost all of my friends to the point they never called—not to ask me to dinner, not to shoot the breeze, not to call the police when I went missing.

I didn't have to wonder if my mom missed me, she was a nasty piece of work that only cared about herself and the next man she could sink her claws into. There could've been missing posters with my face on them and unless it read "REWARD" at the bottom she'd walk on by. Though her last three husbands seemed to have taken a liking to me so one of them might've called, but they'd been traded in for richer models.

One different choice.

Back in the beginning, if I hadn't looked at that stupid file, I'd be sitting at my desk right now oblivious to my boss's sick research.

And more people would die, you selfish twit.

After I'd covertly reached out to the reporter Evette London, I'd sent her everything. She'd been looking into the Timor-Leste land lease and once I saw the pictures, the horrific things Abrams had paid the rebels to do to the village, orphanage, and Peace Corps workers who were there, and found out Evette's friends were among the workers, I knew she'd expose Abrams.

Especially after what had happened to Evette's friend Kalee Solberg. She'd been left behind in that pit of dead girls.

Evette quickly became my only ally.

Or was she my scapegoat?

No! I'd carefully vetted Evette. She was a respected reporter with a reputable news organization. People would believe her even if the story was unbelievable.

There was a knock at the door and I scrambled to

stand. My foot slipped on the stupid washcloth and I landed on my hip and elbow. One leg was cocked at a weird angle and I almost kneed myself in the chin. I'd barely untwisted when Myles called out.

"You okay in there?"

"I was until you scared the shit out of me," I blurted out.

"Sorry, you've been in there a lot longer than I thought you'd be. I just wanted to make sure."

"Thought you told me to run the hotel out of hot water."

I heard his deep, rumbly chuckle through the door and my eyes drifted closed. I wasn't sure I liked the way the sound made me feel. Something else I learned beyond not trusting anyone was not to trust myself. I'd made so many mistakes it was obvious I lacked the gene that made a person make good decisions.

I probably got that from my mother.

Though, I didn't know who my father was, so he could've passed it down. But evidence suggested he had the self-preservation gene in spades. He'd fled before I was born. Too bad he hadn't waited around for Marla to pop me out before he split.

"I didn't think you had it in you to waste five days' worth of water."

I turned my head toward the door, and even though Myles couldn't see me I still gave him a dirty look.

"Are you calling me environmentally irresponsible?"

"Nope. I just wanted to make sure you hadn't turned into a prune."

He was still chuckling when I looked down at my wrinkly fingers.

"I'm getting out," I shouted.

I wasn't sure why I yelled my announcement but I felt compelled to make sure he was out of the room before I turned off the water.

Wait.

"How'd you get into the bedroom? I locked the door."

"Picked it," he told me breezily. "Hurry up, Namora food's here."

"Namora?"

"I'll tell you about her when you get out. I'll lock the door on my way out."

I waited a few moments before I stood and turned off the water. I reached out of the shower, grabbed a crisp, white towel, and brought it to my face.

Bleach.

I inhaled a second time just to breathe in the clean smell. When I pulled it away I was happy to see it was still white, unlike the washcloth. I stepped out of the tub and kept my back to the mirror. I wasn't ready to face what I looked like. I'd caught a glimpse in the lobby and it was mortifying. I dried my legs and ignored the eight weeks' worth of hair that had gone from prickly to nasty. I rushed through the rest of the drying-off process. I couldn't stop and think about why my pits now looked like a man's. I didn't bother to finger-comb my ratty hair before I wrapped it in the towel turban-style and yanked a second towel to wrap around my body. If I did stop and think about *why* I hadn't had access to a razor or *why* my hair was in knots, I would break. And I didn't have time for a full-scale freak out.

I needed to keep my shit together and plan out my next move. Be prepared if Myles gave any indication he wasn't the hero who'd rescued me but my newest captor. I had to stay sharp. Before Tamir had snatched me I was going to talk to Zane through Evette and weigh my options. He'd offered me protection—a safehouse, but how safe was this house? The only thing I knew about Z Corps was what I'd read online and as I found out the hard way the internet lied.

I opened the door and peeked out.

No Myles, and the door was shut. I dashed across the room and turned the knob.

Locked.

I found the items that Myles had purchased for me. I tore open the packaging for the underwear and froze. I wasn't sure what I was expecting but it certainly wasn't what I was holding. Hell, I didn't even know *what* I was holding. They looked like something that would be worn in the 1940s. They were more than full-bottom briefs and they were pale blue and shiny. Yes, the underwear was shiny. I didn't know there was such a thing as shiny underwear. And—lucky me!—there were three pairs. I turned them around and nearly busted a gut. The laughter that pelted out of my mouth was involuntary but once it started, I couldn't contain it. The center seam was ruched and if that little detail wasn't enough, from the hip to the seam on both sides there were strips made of teeny-tiny lace. Yes, there were ruffles to complete the look.

I slipped them on and pulled the waistband up…and up…and up farther until the elastic settled well above my belly button.

Awesome! High-waisted, shiny, booty-ruffled, ruch-gathered-in-my-asscrack panties.

They covered so much I didn't need to wear shorts—though I would of course. I rummaged through the rest of the clothes and found a tube top that I was positive Myles had planned on me using as a bra. As grateful as I was he hadn't attempted to guess my size, I felt a twinge of disappointment he hadn't found one of those pointy, bullet bras to go with my shiny panties.

I opted to wear the t-shirt and cotton shorts. Both were too big. I had to roll the waistband of the shorts to keep them up, which meant the top five inches of the panties were exposed. But the t-shirt hid what the shorts didn't and landed mid-thigh. I left my hair wrapped and headed for the door.

But before I could open it I heard Myles talking. Someone else was out there. I could hear two male voices. One belonged to Myles, one did not.

My heart rate quickened and despite the cool air in the room, my body went hot. I could feel the sweat beading on my forehead. I looked around the room for a weapon but my options were limited—as in, nonexistent. The TV was too big for me to pick up, the lamps were mounted on the wall, three pens sat on the dresser but that was it. I could climb out onto the balcony but then what? We were on the top floor, I couldn't jump—or I could but I just wouldn't make it. I was still scanning the room in the hopes something would magically appear when I heard Myles's deep voice boom.

"For your trouble."

There was a moment of silence, then the other man spoke, "Thank you, Mr. Barron."

Perfect English.

That was weird.

Scary weird.

I heard a door close, then nothing.

Did Myles leave? Was this new man out there to take me?

What just happened?

There was a knock on the bedroom door, and I felt the scream bubbling up and barely covered my mouth before it slipped out, my hand quelling the sound to a muffled groan. I couldn't move. Just like when I found Tamir in my hotel room back in California. I was paralyzed with indecision and fear. A smart woman would do *something*. But like a deer caught in headlights, I froze. Stupid-*stupid* me.

"Delilah?"

That was Myles.

I didn't answer. I couldn't answer. What if the other man was still out there waiting to take me? What if Myles had invited the other man in and the door I heard close was *behind* the man. What if…

"Everything alright in there?"

He sounded concerned.

Don't trust him.

"Babe, you got two seconds to answer me, then I'm opening the door."

Now he sounded worried.

I still couldn't trust him, couldn't trust his alarmed tone.

"Don't come in here."

"Okay, I won't. What's going on?"

God, why did he sound like he actually cared?

"I...um..." I stared at the door, praying a lie would come to mind.

"No one's here, Delilah. Did you hear the door? Is that what freaked you out?"

Great, now I could add perceptive to the mental list I was keeping about all things Myles. The top of that list was devastatingly handsome. Something I was actively trying not to think about, however, he was so hot that even being scared out of my head I couldn't miss it. I wanted to ignore it, as a matter of fact, I wished he looked like an ogre instead of a freaking movie star but that certainly wasn't the case. He was also strong and tall and had broad shoulders and great forearms, and his biceps stretched the material of his t-shirt.

"Delilah?" he called again.

"Yes, I heard you talking to someone."

He muttered a few curse words and I wasn't sure if that was good or bad. Was he mad I'd spoiled his plan? Were they going to ambush me when I went out into the living area?

"Ivy sent over some stuff for you. I haven't gone through the bag but I see a hairbrush, toothpaste." There was rustling on the other side of the door. "Bottles of hair shit, deodorant, a toothbrush—"

He had me at toothbrush.

"Who's Ivy?'

"Ivy Lewis, Zane's wife."

That was strange. Why would a woman I didn't know bother sending hygiene products?

"Why would she send me stuff?"

"Why?"

"Yes, why? She doesn't know me."

"Because she knew you needed them. Because she's a nice person. Because she felt like shit for booking us into this swank hotel and not thinking about the state you'd be in when I found you. Luckily you were uninjured but she should've known better. Or alternately, when we got here I should've called the office and had them find someplace else. I didn't and I apologize. It was a shit thing to do, making you do something you were uncomfortable doing."

My hand was on the knob, all I needed to do was twist the lock and open the door. I wanted to. He sounded sincere, he sounded like he cared that I'd been horrified at the people staring at me. And I really wanted the toothbrush.

Was I really going to risk my safety for clean teeth?

Yes! Yes, I was.

I slowly opened the door. Myles took two giant steps back and held out a white plastic bag that wasn't huge but it wasn't small. The hotel's name and logo were stamped on the front and it looked like it was stuffed full.

My gaze lifted and our eyes locked. His were intense but gentle. I wasn't sure what mine looked like but my guess—and it'd be a good one—that mine looked startled because I was.

My breath started coming out fast. I wanted to shrink away and break the connection but I couldn't stop staring.

"Tell me what you need," he invited.

"What?"

"I don't want you to be scared of me. What do you need me to do, Delilah?"

"I don't know."

As soon as the truth came out of my mouth I wished I could pull it back in.

"I'll set this stuff on the table and move across the room. Will that help?"

"What?"

"Babe, you're standing in the doorway looking at me like I scare the shit outta you. I get why, but I don't like it. I'll give you what you need but you gotta tell me what that is."

I hadn't been scared, I'd been enthralled by the way his light brown eyes had softened when he saw me. *Better that he thinks I'm terrified of him than to know the truth.*

"I was just startled when I heard the other voice. I didn't know what was happening out here."

The muscle in Myles's cheek jumped and I wondered if he knew I'd been worried that he'd left me—or worse, had allowed someone into the room to hurt me. The gentleness in his gaze disappeared and not just because he turned slightly to drop to the bag on the table which meant he'd broken our connection. It happened as soon as I'd admitted I'd been startled. His soft and giving demeanor turned hard. Almost like he was disappointed in me, something about that made my heart clench.

Not only couldn't I think about why his reaction affected me so much, but I also refused to contemplate why my belly bottomed out.

So what, he knew I didn't trust him? I *shouldn't* trust him and he shouldn't trust me.

Myles stepped away from the table and I took a few strides into the room, just far enough to reach the bag, and picked it up.

"Thanks," I muttered and dashed back into the room.

I dumped the contents on the bed and rummaged through the items until I found the toothbrush and paste. Then I sprinted to the bathroom and brushed my teeth. I rinsed, spit, and started over.

It took three washings.

And I never once glanced into the mirror.

I wasn't ready to see what I'd find.

CHAPTER 7

I had no reason to be pissed, yet I was fuming.

Not only did Delilah not trust me she thought I was some sort of piece of shit that would harm her. She didn't say it but she couldn't hide it. The woman actually thought I'd allow someone into our room who would cause her harm. I'd bet my savings she stood in that fucking bedroom while I was tipping the delivery kid thinking I was setting her up to be taken again.

Gabe was wrong, there was no scenario where Delilah trusted me. There was nothing I'd be able to say to her to prove I was on her side. That I was there to protect her and not hurt her.

My attention went from the window to the bedroom door as Delilah walked out. In her haste, she hadn't shut the door but I knew better than to think that was anything more than an oversight on her part.

"Feel better?" I asked.

"So much better."

She sounded like she meant that.

"Good. Hungry?"

"Yes. But before we eat, may I ask you a favor?"

I wanted to tell her she could ask me for anything and I'd give it to her as long as she promised never to look at me with her haunted eyes again but instead with one of her pretty smiles.

But I didn't say that. Instead, I invited, "Ask away."

"I tried to get out all the knots," she started sheepishly. "But I couldn't get the back. Would you be willing to help me?"

"You want me to brush your hair for you?"

I glanced at the towel on her head and she flinched. Then she dropped her gaze to the floor. "I know it's weird. I'm sorry. I shouldn't have asked."

Killing. Me.

"Will you please look at me?"

Slowly, so damn slowly, her eyes lifted.

"I'll brush your hair. But Delilah, I don't know how much more of this I can take."

"More of what?"

"You looking at me like you're preparing for me to strike. I'm not gonna hurt you. I'm not gonna leave you. I'm not gonna turn you over to Aviv or Tamir or any-*fucking*-one. I'm here to protect you. And the fuck of it is, I understand you got no reason to trust me, but I'm asking you to tell me what I need to do to start working towards that."

"Why do you trust *me*?"

"Come again?"

"You gave me a gun. I could've shot you in the back and run off." I felt my lips curve up into a smile, luckily I had the wherewithal to quell my laugh. "Why are you smiling?"

"Babe, you were shaking so hard it was doubtful you could've held the gun steady enough to aim."

"So why'd you give it to me?"

"It was just you and me out there in an uncertain situation with someone coming up on us. I needed to know that if something happened to me you could protect yourself."

I didn't miss the tick in her jaw or the slumping of her shoulders.

"Like you said, I was shaking so bad the gun would've been useless."

"I reckon if I was lying there bleeding out or dead you'd find the strength to rally. And you had a phone," I reminded her.

"And you would've been wrong. I'm not that kind of woman."

What the hell did that mean?

"You aren't that kind of woman?"

"No, Myles. In the face of danger, I freeze. I'm not strong or brave. I don't fight—"

"Woman I got your teeth marks scarred on my arm that proves otherwise." Her gaze darted to the bandage on my forearm but I didn't allow her to remark before I continued. "And if you're talking about Tamir we already went over that. Cohen could've killed you a hundred different ways, some painful, some instant. The mere fact you're standing in this room is proof you did the right thing. I think he was struggling with what he was going to do with you. And if you'd fought him, you would've made the decision easy. He would've had no choice but to kill you. But you staying quiet and compliant gave him the opportunity to stash you somewhere he thought you'd be safe."

"Why do you think that?"

"You wanna sit on the floor in front of the couch or in a chair while I brush your hair?"

She blinked at my abrupt change of topic then looked at the chairs situated around the kitchenette table.

"I better sit in a chair. My hair's pretty long. I don't think you can brush it if I'm sitting on the floor."

The picture I had of her was from Abrams's website and looked to be a few years old. In it, her hair was pushed behind her shoulders so I couldn't tell its length. And for some crazy reason, I was dying to see how long it was. And even crazier, I wanted to run my fingers through it.

"Tell me something," I started as I walked across the living space. "Why don't you have any social media accounts?"

"Because I work in IT and I know how easy it is to get all sorts of personal information about someone. So why would I make it easier on some sicko who's trolling for his next victim?"

Smart.

After all, she was correct. With a few keystrokes, Garrett, our in-house intel specialist, could find anything about anyone.

"What'd you guys dig up on me?" she asked.

I pulled out the chair and gestured for her to take a seat, but she turned the chair around and straddled it.

"Trust me, it's long," she murmured.

Trust.

58

There was that damn word.

Delilah handed me the bright pink brush and tipped her head forward to unwrap the towel. When she flipped her hair back I was shocked when the tangled ends reached down to the chair cushion.

"Holy shit."

"Told you. That's what happens when you're a workaholic and too lazy to style your hair."

"You've lost me," I returned, still staring at her hair wondering how the hell I was going to tackle the mess in front of me.

"I work a lot so I don't take the time to get my hair cut. And besides, short hair means you have to style it and I'm far too lazy for that."

There was something in her tone that told me she wasn't telling me the whole truth but I didn't call her out on it. Instead, I focused on the task at hand.

"Maybe now's the time I should tell you I've never brushed a woman's hair."

"Never?"

"Never," I confirmed.

"You start at the bottom…"

It took her a few minutes to explain how to hold her hair and brush below my fist so I didn't yank the strands and hurt her. She also explained since she had thick hair I needed to do it in sections. By the time she was done, I was fairly confident I could accomplish my mission.

With a fist full of Delilah's hair and the brush in my other hand I asked, "Does the name Garrett ring a bell?"

"Yeah. He sent me an email. Is that his real name?"

"It is. He's our intel guy." I ran the bristles through her hair and when she didn't make a sound or move, I continued to brush and answered her earlier question. "When Evette came to us asking for protection, your name came up immediately and Garrett started digging. I have a complete file on your life. Education, employment history, credit report, current and previous addresses starting from childhood, your family, your friends, anything he could find. And you should know, Garrett's thorough."

I missed it at first, the stillness in the air, the lull in her breathing—it wasn't a tranquil calm, it was turbulent. But then it would be, I'd just admitted Garrett had combed over her personal life. She'd have no way of knowing how deep he dug but I warned her he was thorough.

Delilah didn't have any ghosts in her closet but her family was fucked. Especially her mother—that bitch had bones rattling bones. The woman was a man-eater and that was putting it nicely.

"Thank you for being honest with me."

Her whispered gratitude felt like a dagger to the gut. I should've let the topic end there but she'd thanked me for being honest so I had to come clean about everything.

"Before you sent the information on the guy who'd been attempting to end Evette and we figured out you were in California we went to your mother's house and had a chat with her."

"Where's she living now?" Delilah asked with a hint of sadness in her tone.

She didn't want to care but she did.

"North Carolina."

"So not too far from where I live...or, lived. I don't think I actually have a home anymore."

I had no idea what became of her apartment. When

my teammate Kevin and I went to Delilah's apartment in Virginia it had been ransacked and there wasn't much left that was salvageable but I still made a mental note to ask Zane what her landlord did with her belongings.

"She said she hadn't seen or heard from you in a few years."

"Sure, if a "few" means five. Did she tell you why?"

"No, Delilah, and we didn't ask. Garrett ran her financials and he didn't find any large sums of cash being taken out of her accounts or her husband's and nothing on their credit cards to suggest they were helping you so we left it at that."

"You keep saying *we*. You weren't alone?"

"No. I had Kevin with me, he's a member of my team. Good friend, too. He was with me until two weeks ago. Actually, once we had confirmation Tamir had you, Zane sent the Red Team and Garrett for backup."

"Red Team?"

I continued to brush. The bottom three or four inches were tangle-free but just below where her bra strap would be, there was heavy matting. Big clumps of hair were knotted tightly and I was having to carefully pick it apart.

"Z Corps is structured into Teams. Red, Gold, Blue. Each team has a specific skill set."

"What team are you on?"

"Blue."

I snagged a few strands of hair in the brush bristles and Delilah jerked her head to the side.

"Shit, sorry," I murmured.

"How bad is it?"

I wasn't sure how to answer. This felt like one of those trick questions where a woman asked if her ass looked big in a pair of jeans and no matter the man's answer he was fucked.

I felt compelled to lie.

I didn't, I evaded.

"I'm getting the tangles out."

She fell silent for a few moments and I worked on her hair, marveling at the thickness. And the longer the silence stretched the more my mind wandered until all I could think about was how much I wished my hands were fisting her hair for other reasons. Pleasurable reasons.

"Tell me about your team."

Thankful for the distraction, I launched in.

"Owen, Gabe, Kevin, and Cooper. Before Owen came to work for Zane he was in the Navy. Good guy, solid. He's engaged to Natalie. The woman is crazy-brave. She grew up a Mob Princess, hated the life, wanted no part of it, and when her uncle got jittery she was gonna go to the feds he sold her into a human trafficking ring. We found her while we were on an op. She had no place to go so Owen took her in and they've been together since. Kevin was in the Navy, too. So was Gabe, actually. Kevin's the funniest out of all of us, but only after you get to know him and his sense of humor. The guy's got no filter so either you get him and you think he's hilarious or you hate him. Like him or hate him he'd never turn his back on anyone. The guy is giving to a fault. Cooper is the newest member of the team and his brother Jaxon is on the Red Team. Coop used to live in California. He was LAPD SWAT. I'm not sure exactly what happened, just that a takedown went bad and he quit."

"And Gabe?"

Of course she'd pick up on me purposefully leaving him out.

"Gabe's complicated. Or I should say his history is complicated. He and his mom were homeless for a time. He had a lot of issues surrounding that to work out. For a long time, I didn't think he'd ever move past them. Thankfully he has. If Kevin's the most giving of his time, Gabe's secretly the most giving with his money. He gives a shit ton to homeless shelters and various programs for men and women trying to get on their feet, and food pantries. He thinks we don't know and we let him have that because none of us want him to be uncomfortable about it. He also thinks we don't know he volunteers at shelters."

"What about you?"

Normally I wasn't a fan of talking about myself but I'd tell her anything she wanted to know if that meant I didn't have to answer anything else about Gabe.

"I grew up in Colorado. Joined the Army straight out of high school. Did my time and when it was time to get out I went to work for Zane."

"Why was it time to get out?"

Fuck.

My gaze dropped to my arm and my eyes roamed over my tattoo there. The reminder that was inked into my flesh to never forget. And not a day went by where I didn't remember my fuck-up and the man who lost his life because of it. Bad intel had started the clusterfuck of a mission but it was me who missed the warnings.

"I became ineffective."

"I don't believe you but I can hear it in your voice that

you don't want to talk about it so we won't. Is Owen the only one who's in a relationship?"

Jesus.

I considered telling her about Jeremy and why I left the Army. That story would gut me. But there was no telling how she'd react when I told her about Gabe and Evette. Or more to the point what had happened to them when Abrams's competitor, BZ System, caught up with them and tortured Gabe in front of Evette to get information on Delilah's whereabouts. That was ultimately the conversation I did *not* want to have with her.

"Gabe is with Evette London."

"He is?" she breathed.

So far, so good.

"They got together shortly after she arrived in Maryland, and by that I mean they were giving each other lovey-eyes before Kevin and I left to find you. Which was about fifteen minutes after she gave us the information she had on Abrams. I haven't been back to Maryland since so I can't say I know Evette, but from what I hear Gabe's madly in love. Which is good seeing as he's asked her to marry him."

Delilah's shoulders snapped back and we lapsed into an uncomfortable silence. I felt like this was another one of those tricky situations, only this time I was afraid Delilah was a ticking timebomb—and one more wrong word and she'd explode.

"Do you live in Maryland?"

"Yeah."

"And you haven't been home since you started looking for me?"

I stopped brushing and waited for her to continue.

When she didn't I reminded her, "Can't look for you if I'm sitting on my ass in Maryland."

Delilah hunched forward and whispered, "You know about my life."

Jesus fuck. The minefield was getting harder and harder to navigate.

"I do."

"So you'd know, since there's no father listed on my birth certificate, I never had one. He didn't even stick around to give me his last name. And since then my mom's moved from man to man. She dragged me along but it was like I wasn't there. She gave me her maiden name but since then she's been married so many times, had so many different last names I've lost count. But not me. I've always just been Delilah Watts, Venessa's forgotten daughter."

I had no clue what any of that had to do with me living in Maryland or being on the road looking for her. What I did know was I hated the sadness in her voice. And she wasn't exaggerating—her mother had been married twelve times. All of them ending in divorce, ten of them ending in healthy settlements. This was because Venessa Hudson exclusively married rich men who simply threw money at her to make her go away. Which she did, then promptly went back on the hunt and just as promptly found another sucker to sink her claws into.

"Thank you." I could barely hear her soft words.

"Not sure why you're thanking me."

"No one has ever looked for me and not because I've never been missing. They've just never looked. I've never mattered to anyone. So, thank you for looking even if it was your job."

The fuck of it was, it hadn't been me who'd stepped on one of those mines that littered our path, it was Delilah who blew the bitch sky high. I felt my body string tight, bracing far too late, thus I had no way to defend the pain —her pain—as it sliced through me. No child should ever feel forgotten.

"Since we're being honest, you should know Evette London was the client, not you. When she came to us, she thought those emails and pictures you sent were threats, not you passing her intel. Initially, Kevin and I were sent to apprehend you. It took some time for us to realize your role, then realize you were in trouble. You should also know once Evette was safe and she had the opportunity to look at everything with clear eyes, she became your champion. She figured out you were helping her and she was worried about you. The rest of us were on the fence. You were sloppy when you were communicating with Evette. We couldn't be sure if it was a setup, if someone was using you as the fall guy, or if you were on the up-and-up and were trying to bring down Abrams."

I was glad Delilah was facing away from me. It was easier to admit uncomfortable truths when you weren't looking the other person in the eye.

It was also a damn good thing I couldn't see the hurt on her face when the sound of it in her voice cut me to the quick.

"You thought I was trying to harm Evette?"

"Yes."

"Do you still think that?"

"No. If I did I wouldn't've continued to look for you even though Zane pulled the rest of the team back to Maryland. Two weeks ago we ran out of leads. He wanted everyone back to the office to regroup. They went but I stayed."

"Why?"

"Because there was no way in hell I was going to fail you."

I heard her swift inhale and that hurt like a sono-fabitch.

What I didn't tell Delilah was that I knew the sour taste of failure and I was never going to choke on it again. I would never blindly obey another order. Unlike the Army, Zane didn't argue with instinct, he allowed his men to follow their intuition. He might've bitched about it but ultimately he'd given me the latitude to follow my gut. He believed me when I told him I knew Delilah was close. He hadn't scoffed when I explained I could feel her near.

And that was the weird part—every time I'd gotten close to a location where she'd been held I could sense her. I don't know how or why but I couldn't deny there was a connection.

I could just feel her.

CHAPTER 8

Silent tears wetted my cheeks. A useless talent I learned at a young age—I couldn't control the emotion from leaking from my eyelids but I could control the noises I made. I could quietly release the pent-up hurt and not move a muscle while doing it. My mother liked me quiet, her husbands didn't mind me around as long as I wasn't any trouble. So I never caused trouble, I rarely spoke, and I learned to cry silently.

My problem was I didn't know the source of the pain. I didn't know if I was hurt because Evette thought I was behind the murder attempts, that Myles had thought I was capable of such horrible deeds, that I'd screwed up and didn't know someone at Abrams was watching me. Or if the agony burning through me was from the knowledge that Myles hadn't given up. He'd continued to look for me after he'd run out of leads, that he hadn't been home in a really long time because he didn't want to fail me—a stranger. Yet, my own mother had no clue I'd gone missing, nor did it sound like she cared when Myles spoke to her.

"Delilah?"

God, I like hearing him say my name.

"It was never my intention to hurt Evette," I told him. "And I wasn't being sloppy. At the time I didn't know the program I'd installed to mask my IP and email server had been disabled. I didn't know I was being watched."

"When did you figure it out?"

"When Garrett replied to an email I'd sent Evette. I had a no-reply mailbox set up, but his email showed up in my work inbox. I opened the raw source header and saw that the original email I sent to Evette had gone through Abrams's servers —which it shouldn't've. I checked the rest of the messages and found that all of them had. So, I guess I had been sloppy in a way because I wasn't diligent in checking my machine. If I had been I would've found the software someone installed. Whoever did it was good; they buried it deep and I had no clue everything I was doing was being logged."

"Why didn't you just come straight out and tell Evette what was going on?"

Such a simple question with a complicated answer. One that would make me sound a little nuts. A question that would mean I'd have to go explain what Abrams was really doing and that was not a rabbit hole I was ready to go down.

"How are those knots coming?"

Myles had stopped brushing but I was sure he was nowhere near done.

I heard his disappointed sigh, then I felt him lift my hair off my back. I ignored the tingles his hands in my hair caused and readied myself to justify the change in subject.

But Myles let me off the hook.

"I'll give you that, Delilah. I get why you're holding your cards close but you gotta know I can't help you if you don't let me."

"I'm not sure I want anyone's help," I admitted.

"Seems like you did when you reached out to Evette."

"And look where that got her? The only reason she's still alive is because Aviv outsourced the job to some dumbwit and didn't send one of his commandos. If he had, she'd be dead and that would be on me. I have enough guilt, I think I'm better off on my own so no one else gets hurt."

"No one else but you?"

"Correct."

"Right," he muttered.

I didn't have to be facing him to know he was angry, his tone clearly conveyed his irritation. I ignored that, too. I was becoming quite skilled at overlooking and rejecting behaviors I didn't want to acknowledge.

Another useless talent.

"I hesitate to tell you this but I don't think these knots are going to come out."

"Damn."

"I can keep trying," he said gently. "But there are two big clumps that look like they've been dreadlocked."

"Can you cut it?"

"Cut what?"

Despite my shitty thoughts and the dire state of my hair, I found myself smiling at his high-pitched tone.

"My hair."

"You want me to cut your hair?"

I felt a hysterical giggle bubbling. The lunacy of my situation hit me all at once. I was in a hotel room with a perfect stranger who had purchased me shiny, ruffle-butt, high-waisted panties—oh, and we couldn't forget the ruching that was right then bunched up in my butt crack. They were so ugly I'd actually considered pulling down my shorts to show him the hideous undies he'd bought. I didn't know this man yet he'd spent months looking for me, rescued me, and had spent the last near hour brushing my hair. A few hours ago he'd easily held a man a gunpoint, yet asking him to cut my hair made his voice crack like he was going through puberty.

"Yes, Myles, I'd like for you to cut my hair. Right above where the knots are."

"I can't cut your hair."

"Do you not know how to use scissors?"

"Don't be crazy. We'll make an appointment with a barber."

I lost the battle with the laughter and it poured out of me. My shoulders shook with it. My body rocked with it. There was no reason for me to laugh but once the valve opened I couldn't close it. It was like thirty-five years of pent-up frustration and hurt were flowing out of me.

It made no sense, it was totally illogical, it was absolutely ridiculous. But it happened. And once it started I couldn't stop it. All my life I'd had shitty luck. It started when I was born to a shitty mother, and escalated from there. I'd never bothered wishing for anything because I knew I'd never get it. I didn't bother asking for help because I knew I'd never get that, either. And most importantly I learned people were exchangeable so I never bother forming bonds. None of that was funny, yet I was laughing my ass off. It wasn't funny my hair was going to be cut off but I was laughing. My life sucked and that *really* wasn't funny, but I was laughing.

"A barber?" I stammered. "You don't spend a lot of time with women do you?"

"Guess not."

There wasn't a hint of humor in Myles's retort. I craned my neck and glanced over my shoulder. I regretted it instantly. I should've minded my own business and kept my eyes forward but for some insane reason, I wanted to tell him it was okay to laugh with me.

It was obvious he didn't find anything funny about me cackling; not only that but he looked lost in thought—deep thought. But when his eyes met mine they changed from thoughtful to pensive. Technically there was only a vague distinction between the two looks but the nuance was clearly there.

"What's the matter?"

"I was just thinking, three times I've heard you laugh, never *seen* you do it, but each time it felt good knowing you were doing it."

What in the world did that mean?

I wasn't brave enough to ask.

I wasn't brave—period.

So, I blurted out, "You bought me shiny ruffle-butt panties."

Myles did a slow blink. I watched him do it—the whole time, I never took my eyes off his. It was amazing to watch because when his lids opened his eyes were dancing.

"Say what?"

"You bought me underwear," I reminded him.

"Yeah."

"They're powder blue and the waistband comes up higher than my belly button. They're like old-fashioned briefs only higher. And they have tiny strips of lace across the butt. That's what I was laughing at in the bedroom. I'm grateful for clean undies but these bad boys are…well they…I don't know what they are but if I knew you better and we were friends I'd drop trou and show you."

That earned me another slow blink, which I again watched with extreme fascination because now his full lips had curved up into a grin. And I liked that he was smiling at me.

"And just now I was thinking about how horrified you sounded when I asked you to cut my hair. Apparently, you can handle a gun just fine but you have serious issues wielding scissors because your voice cracked."

His smile waned and for some reason, I felt like I lost something dear to me.

"It's just hair, Myles."

"No, baby, it's your hair. *Yours!* And you shouldn't have to fucking cut it."

That came out rough and jagged, mean and angry—not *at* me but on my behalf.

Whoa, Nelly.

And calling me Baby? What was up with that?

"I agree with you. I shouldn't and it sucks that I have to. But you know what would suck more? Having to feel all that hair matted and remembering how those mats got there. I'd rather you just cut it and move on."

Without a word, Myles turned and moved across the room to his backpack and unzipped it. While he was

73

digging through his kit, his shirt lifted, exposing the holster at his hip. I wasn't a fan of guns, never had been, and I really wasn't a fan when Tamir had me and I knew he could turn his on me at any time. But seeing Myles carry one put me at ease. With him it meant protection.

Myles straightened and strode back into the kitchen. He set the smallest pair of scissors I'd ever seen down on the table.

"These are your choices," he started. "Those." He pointed to scissors. "Or this." His hand went into his pocket and in one smooth motion, he pulled a knife out and flicked it open.

I took in the long steel blade, then the tiny scissors, and it was a no-brainer.

"The knife."

"You're sure?"

"Of course I'm sure. It would take a year if you used those tiny—"

"No, babe, you sure you want me to cut it? We can go out tomorrow and find a... haircutter woman for you."

"A haircutter woman," I repeated with a smile.

Myles shrugged and returned my smile. It wasn't real, it didn't reach his eyes, but it was better than seeing him scowl so I'd take it.

"Yeah, I'm positive." To underline my statement I twisted so I was looking out the window and my back was again to Myles. "Are you sure that knife is sharp enough?"

Tingles exploded on my scalp when Myles gathered my hair. I shoved that aside along with the pleasant quivers that accompanied the tingles by reminding myself my life was in shambles, I was marked for death, and Myles was not there to play hide the sausage.

I bit back my laughter, knowing if it became audible Myles would ask what was funny and I'd have to scramble to find a lie to cover up my immature sense of humor.

Myles didn't answer verbally. His fist tightened in my hair, and then the pressure was gone. I didn't even hear it; just like that in a flash, he was done.

His soft question took me by surprise. "Do you wanna see it?"

"No."

I felt rather than saw his presence slip away and I sat there with my head bowed.

It was just hair. It would grow back. I wasn't particularly attached to my long hair but damn it still stung. It stung because it wasn't my choice, the knots had to be cut out, either by Myles or a stylist, or me. Weirdly, I was happy it was Myles.

I hadn't recovered when I felt him come back, then I felt both of his hands on my shoulders before he commanded, "Lift your head."

I obeyed and he immediately went back to brushing while I stared at the ocean through the bank of windows in front of me.

"Who's Namora?" I asked.

"Right, Namora the sub-mariner. She's an old-school Marvel superhero. A mutant/human hybrid—super-human strength and swimming. She also has wings on her ankles so she can fly. Everyone thought she was dead but she was forced into hibernation. She's a total badass and because of that she was actually cloned."

I felt my skin start to crawl.

"Why would you call me Namora?"

"Because she's more badass than Aquawoman and you

were taking a really long time in the shower. It was the best nickname I could come up with on the spot. You know, water…aqua…sub-mariner."

Myles fell silent and I was too busy keeping my heart rate under control to fill the silence. No one in my life had ever attempted to give me a nickname, not even a shortening of my name. Nothing. Not even in elementary school when kids were awful did a bully or mean girl turn my way and call me a name. I was just there in the background cruising along, unnoticed.

"It was a stupid—"

"Please don't take it back," I interrupted.

There was a weighty pause then a soft, "Hungry?"

I smiled at the window. Myles was being cool, not asking questions and taking us from uncomfortable to normal.

"Actually, I'm starving."

"You mean those cardboard snacks I gave you didn't fill you up?"

Now he was being cooler and joking.

"You strike me as a man who knows this, but at the time those bars tasted like heaven."

"When I was out in the field at some point, normally around day five or six, the tuna MREs started to taste good. By two weeks in, no one bitched about the chicken in mystery sauce."

"Yeah, I don't know about that. If you would've offered me freeze-dried chicken that came back to life with water, I would've been grateful but I would've turned my nose up at it."

Myles stopped brushing my hair and said, "That's why we didn't eat those until we had no other choice. They're nasty as fuck. Lucky for you there's no chicken on today's menu."

That had me wondering what *was* on the menu, as well as a whole host of other questions about his time in the Army.

One of those plates with a silver lid over it appeared on the table, then the lid came off and there was a huge bowl of fresh fruit—strawberries, cantaloupe, grapes, and blueberries.

"I wasn't sure what you liked," Myles grumbled as if he didn't like not knowing my preferences.

"I'm not picky," I said but quickly amended my answer, "As long as it doesn't come in a ready-to-eat pouch."

"Good to know."

He set down more food, this one a plate of pasta. The delicious aroma of garlic and basil wafted through the air and I groaned my appreciation.

"Wow. That smells so good."

Next up, a turkey sandwich with rice.

"No fries?" I feigned outrage.

"Be a few days before your stomach will be able to handle the grease."

"Right," I muttered.

"Hey, in a coupla days I'll take you anywhere you wanna go and you can load up on all the grease and sweets you want. Promise."

That meant he'd still be around in a couple of days.

"Do I get a burger with my grease?"

"Yep."

"And a hot fudge sundae with nuts and two cherries?"

"I'll sport for three if it'll make you happy. Now dig in."

Myles placed a silverware roll in front of me and took

the seat across from me. When his gaze lifted he snorted a laugh.

"You gonna eat sitting backwards in the chair?"

"Would it offend you if I did?"

"No."

I might've looked ill-mannered but I was comfortable.

"How are we eating this? Family-style or eating off the same plate?"

"However you want."

I unrolled my utensils, picked up my fork, and stabbed a piece of strawberry.

"Works for me." Myles laughed and followed suit.

Five minutes later I'd eaten five juicy, best-tasting-ever strawberries, three bites of a turkey sandwich, and I was full.

"This sucks. I want to keep eating but my stomach feels like it's going to explode."

"Best not to push it and make yourself sick. You'll be hungry again in ten minutes and if you're not, we have a mini-fridge," Myles said after he chewed a bite of pasta.

"Don't eat all of that. I didn't get to try it."

"It's gross, you won't like it." He grinned and shoveled another bite in his mouth.

"I think that fruit's spoiled. You better not try any," I played along.

"Thought it smelled rotten."

Myles's smile split his face and I was momentarily stunned by how handsome he was.

Damn.

"So, your last name is Barron, huh?"

"Nope. Simms."

"I thought the guy at the door called you Mr. Barron."

"He did. That's the name we're checked in under. You were sleeping in the backseat when I stopped to pick up our new identities."

Holy shit. I couldn't believe I slept through that. Actually, I shouldn't have slept at all; it was dangerous and stupid.

Myles's eyes narrowed but he didn't call me on my thoughts.

"Wanna know your name?" he inquired.

"Sure."

"Irene Flora Barron."

"Are you joking?"

"Nope. And I'm Cornelis Archer Barron."

He looked perfectly serious. Then it struck me he was telling the truth. Our fake identities were Cornelis and Irene Barron. And since we shared a last name that meant we were fake married.

I was fake married.

My body started rocking and I started sputtering until I busted out laughing. This went on a long time until I realized Myles was smiling but obviously didn't find the same humor in the situation as I did.

"Better than I thought."

"What is?"

"Watching you laugh."

I sucked in a breath and officially could no longer overlook the chills his voice created.

CHAPTER 9

The shrill ring of my phone woke me. I rolled and tagged it off the coffee table and was immediately irritated when I saw the time.

"You realize it's five in the morning, right?" I snapped.

"Am I interrupting something?" Zane asked.

"Yeah, sleep."

"It's been two days."

He was correct. It had been two days since I'd pulled Delilah out of the house Tamir had left her in. But it hadn't been two days since I'd last spoken with Zane—it had been less than twelve hours.

"And?"

"You need to push her."

"No."

"Don't make me have Ivy email you the new hand-book. It clearly states I'm in charge of all women until the mating ritual is complete. At such time, the male takes over all financial responsibly and then and only then may he start to make decisions on her behalf."

"I hope to fuck you're joking and you didn't ask your wife to actually type that up."

"Do I strike you as stupid? I had Garrett make the changes. I enjoy my testicles hanging where God put them and not on my mantel where my wife would likely display them."

"First, you don't have a mantel in your penthouse. Secondly, I'm gonna cut off the whole kit and caboodle— that's cock *and* balls—unless there's a point to this call."

"Testy." Zane chuckled.

"I made myself clear last night when we spoke. I'm not pumping her for information. The woman's been through enough. She'll tell you what she knows when she's ready or she won't. Cohen's obviously got something planned. We let that play out then we move accordingly."

"Your little vacation in Mexico's taking up the Prophylactic Fund. You run it dry there'll be nothing left when Kevin's and Cooper's turn rolls around."

Sarcastic bastard.

"You know this is much more fun when I'm sitting on the sidelines listening to you give the other guys shit."

"I'll bet it is. Though, it's always fun for me."

"Right. Even though it's technically Abrams's money funding our stay in Mexico. Just so you stop bitching, send me a bill and I'll pay for it personally."

"So you've mated—"

"Seriously. The sun's not even up and you're pissing me off."

"You know what would cure that?"

"Me hanging up on you?"

"No, you talking to Delilah."

I'd been doing nothing but talking to Delilah over the

last forty-eight hours. She'd told me about her mother's first ten husbands, and I told her about the last two she hadn't met. During that conversation, she seemed particularly detached. It was as if Delilah were telling me about someone else's life. I'd told her about growing up in Colorado, my parents, and that I was an only child. We'd touched on my military service but she seemed to sense when she was skirting a line, and she'd artfully change the topic. She was easy to talk to, easy to listen to, easy on the eyes, just plain easy. And that was becoming worrisome seeing as it had taken about twenty-four hours before her smiles came fast. The more relaxed she became, the more she let her guard down and I figured I was close to the real her. So, we'd shared meals, we'd laughed, we'd watched horrible reality TV (her idea), and we'd talked a lot.

Just not about what Zane wanted me to talk to her about.

"You know I got nothing but love for you so I say this with respect, back the fuck off. She's been through enough and I'm not just talking about Abrams and Tamir. Though she gave years of her life to that job and just to say, their employee loyalty program sucks ass if what you get is kidnapped and left for dead. She needs time to heal from that and she's gonna get it. You don't like it, bill me for our stay and put me on unpaid leave."

"What kind of asshole do you take me for?" Zane's tone had taken on a hard edge. "I want you to talk to her so we can fuckin' end this for her, for Evette, for Gabe. Waiting for Tamir to make his play leaves you vulnerable. Either you talk to her, I send a team down there to watch your back, or you bring her back to the States. We have options; Abe already gave us the go-ahead to use his cabin. We have Fish or Rhode in Idaho—either of their places would work. Texas is an option, Ghost and his team are always in to help. Or we can send her to The Refuge; that retreat out in New Mexico. Chaos runs a tight operation and she'd be safe there."

Fuck, he had a point. This had to end. Christopher "Abe" Powers was a former SEAL, his cabin had a top-of-the-line security system—courtesy of Zane after Olivia and Leo's mishap while staying there years ago. I knew Keane "Ghost" Bryson and his Delta team from my time in the Army. They were all good, solid men, they'd take good care of Delilah. I didn't personally know anyone who worked at The Refuge, but I'd heard about the man Chaos and his compound in New Mexico. Zane trusted him so that was enough for me.

During Evette's ordeal, Zane made an arrangement with Aviv Abrams—Evette was off-limits. Zane had also squeezed Aviv for half a million dollars for what Zane had declared was reimbursement for endangering Gabe and Evette's lives. But that deal didn't extend to Delilah. As a matter of fact, Zane had agreed Delilah was none of his concern and Z Corps wouldn't interfere in whatever Aviv had planned for her. Zane never had any intentions of honoring his part of the deal. Which meant Evette and Delilah were still in danger.

"I'll ask her which she prefers."

"Myles—"

"I told you I'll ask her and I will. I warned you she didn't trust me and she still doesn't. But whatever headway I've made to get her to a place where she feels minutely safe isn't gonna be torn down by me pushing her to talk to me."

There was a few moments of silence and then a miracle to top all miracles happened. Zane Lewis gave in.

"Whatever you feel is best, I got your back."

I blinked into the darkness and momentarily wondered if I was hallucinating. Then he opened his mouth and in true Zane fashion got in the last word.

"Don't be a fool and forget to cover your tool."

Immature bastard.

Zane disconnected and I tossed my phone on the table before I leaned back into the couch.

"Jesus," I muttered.

"That bad?"

My head turned toward the bedroom door. Delilah was standing there leaning against the wall, her arms crossed in front of her, her clothes rumpled from sleep, looking absolutely adorable. Maybe a safehouse was the way to go. I was getting too close, way too fucking close.

"Sorry I woke you."

"You didn't, Zane did. That's who you were talking to, right?"

"Yeah. It's seven back in Maryland so he decided to spread his sunshine all the way down here in Mexico."

She didn't miss my sarcasm and replied with the same, "Well, that was nice of him."

"He's *nice* like that."

The mockery left her voice when she asked, "But you like him?"

"If by like you mean I trust him with my life and I'd lay down mine for his, then yes. If you mean like as in most of the time I want to shove a sock in his mouth to make him stop speaking then yes again."

"What does he want you to ask me?"

"Go back to bed, baby. We'll talk later."

Delilah didn't go back to bed. She walked farther into the living area and didn't stop until she was at the couch. Then she unceremoniously plopped herself next to me.

"I'm wide awake. And besides, if you think I can go back to sleep knowing you're out here brooding, you're crazy."

"I'm not brooding," I denied.

Delilah bumped her shoulder against mine and asked, "Then what do you call sitting in the dark scowling?"

"Thinking."

Her soft, husky laugh filled the room. I was powerless to stop my pulse from picking up. Totally incapable of stopping the arousal that coursed through my veins.

Just from a laugh, a smile, a soft look.

The more relaxed Delilah became around me the more she opened up. The more comfortable she became the more she nudged, touched, brushed by me, and right then she was sitting damn close.

"Tell me what you're thinking about?"

What I was thinking was the sooner this ended the sooner Delilah would be safe, and once she was free and clear of Abrams I could make my move. And since it had only been two days and it was becoming increasingly harder by the hour to keep my hands to myself, I needed to stash her somewhere so I could get on the hunt.

"Zane wants me to talk to you about getting you to a safehouse."

Delilah shifted next to me and pulled her heels up to

the edge of the couch, then wrapped her arms around her shins.

Balled up in an effort to protect herself.

"You want to get rid of me," she whispered.

"Fuck no!"

Without thought, my hand went to the side of her neck and my thumb stroked the underside of her jaw, something I'd been wanting to do for days. Each time she'd turned one of her brilliant smiles in my direction I wanted to hold her just like this. I wanted to know if her skin was as soft as it looked and the only parts of her body I'd allow myself to think about were her neck, the line of her jaw, the shell of her ear, her cheeks, her lips. Thinking about all the places below her shoulders I'd like to explore would be too dangerous.

"I want you safe. I want you someplace where I know no one can get to you. Zane offered to send some men down to watch over us but, baby, they just spent weeks away from their families for me—knowing I wasn't going to give up finding you, they stayed. I can't ask them to do it again not knowing how long this is going to take."

"How did you find me?"

"Tamir contacted a man called Tex and told him your location. Before that, Tamir was leaving us breadcrumbs. Sometimes he'd make sure his face was visible on a camera, or he'd use his credit card, he'd send an email, things he knew we'd be tracking and would easily give away his location. But that stopped when you left Los Mochis. It was radio silence until he called Tex. Tamir gave Tex a warning to keep you off radar as long as possible. The note he left said the same thing, to keep you hidden and we'd know when it was safe for you to go home. Tamir obviously has something planned and I don't want you getting caught up in whatever he's doing but we can't hide in this hotel indefinitely. And Zane has a point, you and Evette are still swinging until Abrams is brought down."

Even in the dim light, I could see Delilah's eyes widen. "I thought you said Evette was okay."

"I told you she's alive, she's happy, and she's protected. But the deal Zane made with Aviv only keeps Evette safe if we don't interfere with his business. We've interfered in a big way by taking you—"

I got no more out before Delilah was struggling to pull away.

"Let me go, Myles."

"No."

"You have to."

"No."

And to underline my denial I dug my fingers into the back of her neck and pulled her closer while at the same time I leaned in, bringing us face-to-face.

"Myles."

"Listen to me carefully, Delilah. There is no scenario where I let you go. There's nothing you can say or do that's going to change my mind about this. We stay here and wait this out or I take you to a safehouse. If you choose the safehouse, I'll take you there, but I won't be letting you go."

"Why?"

"Why won't I let you go?"

"You should let me go. Aviv won't stop until he kills me. I don't know why Tamir didn't do it, but Aviv's not going to be happy. He'll send someone else or come after me and do it himself. He can't let me live. You need to leave me here and forget you found me. Forget you know me. If not for your safety then for Evette's. I never should've dragged her into this mess. It was selfish and mean and now she's still in danger because of me."

I had my suspicions why Tamir didn't kill Delilah, but they were just that—suspicions. Though they were good ones considering the Cohens were known in Israel, respected, a family that was bound by honor and service. It was a stark contradiction to the Tamir Cohen who worked for Aviv Abrams. It was true; war changed a man, daily doses of death and destruction changed your DNA —sometimes for the worse. But something felt way off. If Tamir had turned he would've slit Delilah's throat and left her dead body in Riverton. He wouldn't have batted an eye taking her life. If he'd turned he wouldn't have shown even the sliver of decency he'd shown Delilah. He would've tortured her endlessly until she told him what she knew then killed her. Not to mention if the man didn't want me to find Delilah he wouldn't have on two separate occasions tipped his face toward a camera on the street and do it for a good long while making sure facial rec would ping.

"Evette's safe, my team's watching out for her. Another reason I don't want Zane shuffling men. Red Team was deployed because Gold Team has a case they're working on and my team's tied up with Evette. Zane needs all the men working on shit that pays our salaries."

Delilah stiffened and I knew I fucked up.

"That's not what I meant."

Before I could get any more out Delilah interrupted, "I

88

heard you tell Zane to bill you for the room and put you on unpaid leave."

"Listen to me." I raised my other hand and captured her face, guaranteeing I had her attention. The problem was, that meant I had her attention, *all of it*—all of *her*—so close. And when she sucked in a breath it felt like she pulled it from my lungs.

"*Myles.*"

A whisper of a sound.

The breaking of my resolve.

Fucking hell.

"I'm not leaving you unprotected. I will keep you safe and I need you to believe in that."

"Okay."

Christ. That was too easy.

"Okay?"

"I believe you. But I want you to tell me what you're hiding from me."

Yep. Too easy.

"Delilah—"

"You told me you didn't waste time on bullshit, that the truth was the truth. You asked me to believe in you, now I'm asking you for the truth."

Goddamn sneak attack.

Then I made a decision, one that arguably was stupid as hell but the smartest thing I'd ever done. I let go of her and stood. Once I was on my feet I pulled Delilah out of her protective ball and forced her to her feet, then I made her follow me into the bedroom.

"What are you doing?"

"Telling you the truth."

"And we need to be in the bedroom for this to happen?"

"Yep. Climb up."

Delilah did as I asked and I followed her onto the mattress. Since I was making questionable choices I continued down that path and arranged our positions so her head was resting on my chest and her arm was over my stomach.

"Myles—"

"Brace, baby." I heard her inhale and launched in. "Gabe and Evette were kidnapped. Not by Abrams, by two men who work BZ Systems. Evette was unharmed. Gabe took a beating that left him in a coma. The men BZ sent, Jacko Yaffe and Mario Newman, were arrested and made false confessions. The police bought their kidnap for ransom story and we allowed that stand even though we knew Bryan Zaslow sent those men because he's looking for you."

"Me?"

"Yes. Gabe and Evette were interrogated about your whereabouts. That's the only info they were after."

Delilah's body went solid and I tightened my arm around her.

"What happened to Gabe and Evette isn't your fault."

"I don't know how you can say that when they were interrogated about me."

"I can say that because you didn't kidnap them. You didn't beat the fuck out of Gabe and scare the shit out of Evette. I know you didn't because you were already with Tamir living your own nightmare. This is on Bryan Zaslow and Aviv Abrams and whatever fucked-up war they've got going on between them."

"BZ is Abrams's direct competitor," Delilah told me.

"Know that, baby."

"Abrams has been awarded the last five big defense contracts, winning them over BZ Systems."

"Know that, too."

"One of them was the new Cognitive Radar program that would put Abrams worlds ahead of BZ. So far ahead BZ might not ever be able to catch up. But there was a hold-up on production due to a silicon shortage. That was why Abrams wanted to lease land in Timor-Leste, in the village where Evette's friends were working with the Peace Corps. The Prime Minister was on board with the lease deal and was ready to kick the Peace Corps workers out of the country. The villagers would have no choice but to pack up and move. There was an orphanage in the area, too. The Prime Minister suggested the kids all be moved to locations in the city. But the President stepped in and blocked the deal. That's when Aviv sent Tamir to Timor-Leste. A few weeks after Tamir returned, the village, orphans, and Peace Corps were no longer an issue because the rebels attacked."

Jesus fucking shit.

"Abrams was trying to get deals in El Salvador and Croatia," I reminded her even though she was the one who'd sent that information to Evette.

"Aviv didn't want land in El Salvador. He wanted a scientist who lived there."

I thought back over the intel that Tex had dug up and came up with the dead scientist's name. "Alejandro Arias. He found a new way to engineer brain cells by reprogramming skin cells to become stem cells."

"Aviv wanted Alejandro Arias and Dr. Ramon Gates to

91

work together on an AI project. He called the men his Dream Team. Aviv spent a fortune on a facility in Croatia."

"Delilah, how do you know all of this?"

She was quiet for a long time. Long enough for my frustration to mount. I promised myself I wouldn't push her for answers. But I couldn't deny it was disappointing she didn't trust me.

"I don't want you to think I'm crazy," she whispered.

"Why would I think you're crazy?"

"Because it is *crazy*. What Aviv's been doing, what he's planning, it's totally insane and I'm afraid you won't believe me, that's how crazy it is." After she said that, she burrowed her face into my chest and finished on a mumble, "I want you to believe me but the story's so unbelievable I won't blame you if you didn't."

It was then I took my idiocy to a whole new level and let my hand travel up her arm until I encountered her hair. Then I let myself do something I'd been dying to do since I first brushed it—I ran my fingers through her much-shorter, much-softer, tangle-free hair.

Thick and soft.

The kind of hair a man wanted draped across his bare chest, the kind he wanted to see splayed over the pillow next to his, the kind that a man fantasied about across his lap while he watched his cock disappear between her lips.

"I will believe whatever you tell me."

"Promise?"

"You have my word."

Delilah gave me her weight and relaxed.

"I think Aviv's experimenting on soldiers' brains."

There was no way I heard that correctly.

"Say again?"

"And I think he's been doing it—or has been involved with people who have been doing it—since he was in the IDF."

Jesus Christ.

CHAPTER 10

Holy freak, I did it. I said it out loud.

"I'm gonna need you to explain what that means."

"Promise me one more thing?" I asked.

"Alright."

"I need you to promise me I can trust you."

Suddenly I was no longer pressed to Myles's chest, I was rolled to my side and Myles was up on his elbow looking down at me.

Square in the eyes.

His other hand came up and it went to my jaw. It slid up until his fingers glided into my hair and his thumb grazed my temple.

Oh boy.

Warmth gathered in my belly and spread until flashes of heat shafted through my body. Something I'd never felt before—a cross between arousal and excitement. Or perhaps arousal was simply exciting, and since I'd never truly felt it before I wouldn't know how exciting it was. The electricity that sparked every nerve ending to life.

The anticipation that pebbled my nipples. The thrill of desire that pooled between my legs.

He didn't unlock his eyes from mine when he promised, "I swear you can trust me."

My chest heaved in a hopeless attempt to draw in oxygen. My heart hammered in my chest as it filled with a deep yearning. My legs shifted and I squeezed my thighs together to quell the ache.

"Baby, you can trust me," he repeated.

No words would form so I nodded.

Myles's face started to get blurry and I took more of his weight as he leaned closer.

"Breathe, Delilah."

I didn't breathe, I couldn't.

"Breathe, baby."

That did it. The air whooshed out of my lungs. However, the shock of Myles's lips brushing against mine left me once again deprived of oxygen.

"I'm gonna kiss you."

I felt those rumbled words vibrate on my lips, then they shot straight between my legs, and the throbbing that had started intensified.

Thankfully, Myles didn't require a response; he just did what he said he was going to do—he kissed me.

That electrical charge of arousal skyrocketed when the tip of Myles's tongue did a slow glide over my bottom lip. On instinct, my mouth opened and my tongue followed his along my lip, tasting him there. I couldn't contain my moan.

"More?" he asked against my mouth.

Again, I nodded.

His fingers in my hair pressed in and my scalp started

to tingle, along with my breasts, and my nipples. My sex didn't tingle—it contracted.

"You sure?"

"Yes," I pushed out.

After that, he stopped talking and started taking. The first thing he took was my ability to think. My hands that had been lamely fisting the sheets at my side moved. As if they had a mind of their own—one went to the nape of his neck and the other cupped his firm ass. I felt the muscles under my palm constrict to accompany that goodness as he deepened the kiss.

Which brings me to the second thing he took—my inhibitions. They completely faded away. My hips lifted, intent on contact to relieve the building need, and at the same time, my fingers dug into his behind, urging him closer. Myles shifted so he was on top of me, my legs instantly opening to give him room, and ground his erection against my center.

The third thing he took was his time. There was no urgency as his tongue danced with mine; he was showing me what he liked—teaching me but at the same time learning. Each time he rocked his hips while his tongue stroked mine, I moaned so he'd do it again. When I arched into him and rolled my hips he growled so I kept doing it.

Being kissed by Myles, being surrounded by his scent, feeling his heavy weight on me, his hand in my hair—all of it was out of this world. So good I was lost in him and sinking deeper.

I was ready for more when the unthinkable happened —his phone rang.

Myles's big body went solid and he abruptly and unfortunately broke the kiss.

"Fuck," he grunted.

He pulled back slightly and said, "I gotta take that."

"Okay," I replied through my haze.

"You hafta know, no way in hell I'd answer unless I had to."

"Okay," I repeated.

Really there was nothing else to say and if there were, I didn't have it in me to formulate an intelligent thought.

"Christ, you're pretty."

His hand came out of my hair and the tips of his fingers trailed down the side of my face. His touch was feather-soft and reverent. When he was done with that he planted his hand on the bed next to my head and pushed up.

The phone was still ringing but he made no move to leave me. His eyes were scanning my face and once he was done his gaze came to mine. In the last few minutes, Myles had taken a lot, but on his knees staring down at me I learned he wasn't done.

"Sweetest kiss I've ever had, bar none."

And with that, he left the bed, taking my heart with him.

I felt a smile tipping my lips but before my smile could fully form I heard Myles's angry growl.

"What the fuck?"

I scrambled off the bed and made it into the living area as he said, "You're fucking kidding me?"

His eyes sliced to mine and I saw him heave a breath, then another, until some of the anger cleared his expression. "Right. How's Violet?" There was a pause then a muttered, "I bet he is. Owen told me he was looking into it and found information on Bronson Williams. Did

97

Garrett find anything else?" A shorter pause. "Okay. When you're done with that, we need to brief and Tex should be on the line."

As I watched Myles listen to whoever was speaking on the other end it hit me; he wasn't hiding his expression or the conversation. I'd seen Myles blank his emotions—he could mask them so completely it was a little scary—but since we'd gotten to the hotel he'd done what he could to put me at ease. We'd talked about a lot of stuff but until a little bit ago he hadn't asked me about Aviv Abrams, what I knew, how I knew, or why I ran. He'd told me a little bit about Evette, and he'd admitted they—and that included him—thought I'd been threatening Evette instead of trying to help her. He could've lied about that or not told me at all, but he'd been honest.

"Yeah, we'll be here."

Myles pulled the phone away from his ear and with his gaze still on mine, he took more. By the time he was done proving he trusted me, any vestiges of apprehension melted away.

"That was Zane. A while back when me and my team were in Idaho some shit went down in Maryland. There was a pipe bomb detonated in the parking garage of Z Corps."

"Was anyone hurt?"

"No. Actually, there was no damage. That stunt pissed off Zane but the real concern was two of our guys had their houses hit. Not with pipe bombs, but they had rocks thrown through their windows if you can believe that shit. Leo, he's with the Red Team, caught the guy—a twenty-year-old kid. No priors, no past trouble. The kid said he was jacking around, apologized, and paid a fine and restitution. The thing is all three of these happened at the same time. Unfortunately, Thad, he's with Gold Team, didn't see the guy who did his house, and his security cameras didn't catch the person. The cameras in the garage at the office caught the pipe bomber but he was wearing a mask. Zane takes threats seriously when he believes they're credible, and he gets a lot of threats. So when he receives a letter saying *the stones you throw will one day come back to you* he throws that shit in a drawer and doesn't pay it any mind."

"But when actual stones get thrown at his employees he starts paying attention," I surmised.

"Exactly."

"And did something else happen?"

"One of the guys on Red Team, Jaxon, is married to a woman named Violet. Yesterday, Vi was at the mall. When she came out, her window was broken and there was a rock on the driver's seat."

"Holy crap. But she's okay, right?"

"Yeah, Violet's fine but Jaxon's pissed the fuck off. His brother, Cooper, is on my team and Coop's on a tear, too. So Zane's got his hands full at the moment. He's gonna call back in an hour so we can talk to him about what you told me about Aviv."

Unpleasantness surged through me. I didn't want to talk to the unknown Zane Lewis who called first thing in the morning and annoyed Myles.

"Trust me, baby, everything's gonna be fine."

I called up the strength to ask what was really bothering me, "What if he doesn't believe me?"

"There is nothing you can tell Zane that would shock him. He'll believe you."

"What if—"

"Trust. *Me*."

This seemed important to Myles, that I answer with an affirmative. But it was just as important to me that Zane, Evette, and Myles didn't think I was totally off my rocker when I told them what I'd found. I trusted Myles because so far he believed me, but I wasn't so sure anyone else would, and that was what I was struggling with.

"Baby, I wouldn't set you up to get burned."

The sun had yet to rise but there was a soft glow coming from the kitchen area, enough for me to see the fierceness on Myles's face. He'd promised to protect me, and I figured that meant emotionally as well.

"I trust you."

When Myles didn't speak I filled the silence. "I'm gonna go shower before Zane calls."

I watched Myles bite back a smile but I heard the humor in his voice when he said, "The first of five."

He was teasing me.

"Yesterday I only took three," I reminded him.

"Baby, I had to call down and get you more shampoo."

He'd also bought me more conditioner and soap and he'd done it without complaint. My incessant need to shower was a tad ridiculous but I didn't care. If I was still bathing three times a day a month from now I'd worry about it then. But for now, I was going to show myself some kindness and shower as many times a day I needed to until I finally felt clean.

"That reminds me, you don't happen to have any lotion in your bag, do you?"

"No. But I'll call housekeeping and ask them to drop

off some…" Myles trailed off and shook his head. "Never mind, I'll have some delivered."

"The hotel stuff is fine," I begrudgingly told him.

"I didn't miss the nose scrunch when I said I'd call housekeeping."

"It's just the hotel stuff smells like coconut and I hate that smell."

"Noted."

Now I felt bad.

"It's okay. The hotel stuff is fine. I shouldn't be complaining."

Myles moved across the small space and didn't stop until one of his hands went to the side of my neck and the other went to my hip.

"It's okay for you not to like something and it's okay for you to voice that dislike. Further, it's okay for you to complain. It's also okay for you to ask for what you want. What's not okay is each time you ask for something you need, it's followed by looking like you're preparing to get kicked in the gut."

He was wrong. It was never okay for me to voice my dislikes and it certainly was never okay for me to complain. I was to take what I was given with a smile. And I learned never to ask for more.

"Right now you've got that look again, only worse because now it looks like I delivered that kick."

Shit.

Myles's hand on my hip squeezed and he gave me a small smile. "I hope you know when you're ready to explain why you don't think you deserve to get what you want I'm here to listen."

Double shit, he was giving me an out. He was being

cool about it by not asking straight out but he was still asking and he deserved an answer. If for no other reason than for him to know he hadn't done or said something that upset me.

"My mom had a lot of husbands." *Understatement of the century.* "But the ones she married weren't the only ones around. She used to tell me that men didn't like sniveling children so I was never to cry or complain. When I got older she told me that men didn't like demanding girls and told me to be happy with what I was given. She'd also remind me that men didn't like baggage, which is what I was to her, so she demanded I stay quiet and unseen as much as possible. So that was what I did, I stayed in the background and never asked or complained or got in the way."

Myles tightened his grip on my hip after I said the word sniveling and by the time I got to the baggage part that grip became painful.

A beautiful pain. Something I'd never felt before *in my life*. A pain that was caused because he was angry on my behalf. Oh, yes, it was beautiful, so I didn't tell him his fingers digging in hurt. I savored the feel. Not only that, his eyes had become like laser beams and I knew that was for me, too.

"Your mother called you baggage?"

Oh, yeah, he was pissed on my behalf.

"Yep."

"Yep?"

"I'm not sure what you want me to say. The answer is yes, she told me I was baggage. And I don't think she meant the five-piece Samsonite luggage set. I think she was more calling me the Bargain Warehouse special."

Myles's lips pressed into two thin white lines and I knew my joke fell flat.

"I can joke about it because it happened a long time ago."

"No, baby, you joke about it so it doesn't hurt."

Damn, he was right.

I felt an unpleasant flutter in my stomach, the one I got when I thought about my mom. While I was experiencing that, wanting to push it aside and never think about her again, Myles leaned in and got close.

"Your mother lied to you." Myles's harsh words hit me like a slap across the face. "She fucking lied. You know what men don't like? Greedy, grasping, money-hungry bitches. You know what else men don't like? Bitches who treat their daughters like shit. You know what that says to a man? When he gets around to making babies with her, she's gonna treat his daughter like that. And no man who's a real man would put up with that shit for two goddamn seconds. Children are not baggage, they're a fucking gift you cherish. There's a reason none of those men hung around long. There's a reason none of them got around to making babies with her and it wasn't just because they knew she was a money-hungry bitch. I'd bet it wasn't until after she had them tied to her that they saw how she was with you. Men are not stupid, baby. We pick up on a lot of shit and something every one of that bitch's husbands would've picked up on was that you were not acting like a happy child. A happy, comfortable, well-loved child asks for things she wants, she complains, she cries, she throws tantrums, and she talks back. Kids do that shit. Happy kids who know they are loved don't hide away and never speak. My guess is they stomached that shit for as long as they could before they cut her loose."

By the time Myles was done I was breathing heavily. He was right about all of it. My mom had caught a few good ones who'd stayed longer than the rest. Husband number two tried to be a dad to me, something my mom hated because it meant she had less of his attention. And husband number five was nice to me. He'd tried to get me to come out of my shell and took me places. My mom really hated that, anytime I'd come home from being out with Harold she'd give me the death glare and I'd slink away into my room.

Myles was also correct in that she never allowed them to see the real her until after the wedding. Which meant while she was on the prowl and I was first introduced to a man she was sweet as she could be to me and I ate that shit up. I used to want my mom's love and attention. I'd stupidly get my hopes up and think she really did love me. I'd get excited and think I was going to keep getting her attention, but I never did. She'd get married and everything would go back to normal—I was to shut my mouth and go away.

"You're right," I told him but didn't elaborate.

Myles took me in and I pretended I didn't see the look of disappointment that flashed in his eyes when he brought us full circle.

"What kind of lotion would you like?"

The part of me that had been taught never to be a nuisance screamed for me to take the hotel lotion and be happy. The other part of me, the tiny sliver that begged to come out and get any scraps I could get fought hard to break free.

Just ask.

Be brave.

I sucked in a breath, Myles's clean, fresh scent filled my nostrils and I went for it.

"I would appreciate it if you'd have something delivered that didn't smell of coconuts. Actually, I don't like anything that smells like food."

"Food?" Myles asked with a smile.

"Like pumpkin, apple pie, oranges, peaches. Things like that. Though, I do like the smell of vanilla. I'm not sure if that's a food but just in case it falls into the edible category you can slide vanilla over to the like column."

Myles ratcheted up his smile a few notches and it was damn near blinding.

"Right. So you like flowery smells…and vanilla."

"Yes."

"Got it. I'll order some lotion. Anything else?"

I thought about all the stuff that Ivy had sent over. Except for the shampoo, conditioner, and soap she'd sent more than enough. And really, the shampoo and conditioner would've lasted if I hadn't used half the bottles after Myles had cut my hair to get the rest of the dirt and grime off my scalp.

Then I thought about the way Myles was smiling at me and I knew in a real way that if I asked for something he'd give it to me. I didn't need to guard myself against disappointment. I didn't need to protect myself from the pain that would cause. Myles was not Venessa.

"A pack of cinnamon-flavored gum, a Snickers bar, and a bag of salt and vinegar chips wouldn't go unappreciated. And maybe waffles for breakfast this morning."

"You got it, Delilah."

He dipped his chin and kissed me. Closed-mouthed at first until I opened and touched my tongue to his lips, then he swept his in and took over. Two seconds later he took *way* over—tilted his head and deepened the kiss. It was fantastic. Almost as good as the first kiss he gave me and the only reason the first won out was because during the first one my hand had been on his ass and his erection had been between my legs.

Myles broke the kiss, rested his head on my forehead, and in a low husky voice he commanded, "Go take your shower."

I did not move. I was rooted in place. A clash of emotions held me hostage. It was stupid really that asking for something as silly as gum and Myles readily agreeing to get it for me would stir this kind of emotional response —or any response at all.

"Delilah?" he called and lifted his forehead off mine.

"Thank you."

"You're breaking my heart."

"And you're putting mine back together."

Holy sweet mother of God, did I say that out loud?

"Um…"

"No take-backs," he growled. "You said it, straight up open, now it's mine and I'm not giving it back. I own that, Delilah. And just to give you something in return you should know I'd rip my heart out of my chest and give it to you if it meant erasing every lie she ever told you."

I buckled under the sincerity of his stare and dropped my head to his chest.

Pain rippled through me, chased by fear.

"What's happening?"

MYLES (SPECIAL FORCES: OPERATION ALPHA)

Myles answered with a command. "Wrap your arms around me."

I did as he asked and his arms slid around me.

"How does this feel?"

I said the first thing that popped into my mind. "Safe."

"You'll always be safe with me. What else?"

"It feels good."

"Yeah, it does. It feels damn good. How does it feel when I kiss you?"

Nipple-tingling, pantie-wetting, astronomically out-of-this-world good.

But I wasn't going to admit that so I settled on, "Fantastic." Then I quickly added. "Mind-stealing, exciting, perfect, and awesome."

"You wanna know what I feel when I kiss you?"

I totally wanted to know but at the same time, I didn't want to know in case he didn't feel the same.

"Yes."

"How straight can you handle it?"

"Um...I don't understand your question."

Myles gave me a squeeze then explained, "I'll tell you honest but if you need me to check that and give you gentle, I can. Or I can be me and say it straight. Either way, you'll get the truth, it's just that one way I won't hold back."

I didn't want Myles to hold anything back. He'd let me be who I was and had a mind to earning my trust so I didn't want him to be anything but him.

"I can handle straight," I told him.

He didn't make me wait.

He gave me straight.

"No lie—baby, you can fuckin' kiss. Told you already

107

and I wasn't blowing smoke—best kiss I've ever had. So it will come as no surprise when I agree it was fantastic. But it was more than that; it was fantastic in a way that it's a good thing Zane interrupted before I got down to the business of seeing what other kinds of sexy noises you can make while I'm giving you more than just my tongue."

At this juncture, I was so totally speechless I couldn't remind him he *was* giving me more than just his tongue. I had his erection grinding into me and my hand on his phenomenal ass.

"Thinking on it," he continued, "it was better than fantastic and not just because you're seriously fuckin' good with your mouth. Saying that, I'm looking forward to discovering other ways you're good with it. But it was better than fantastic because it felt *right*."

Other ways I was good with my mouth?

Yikes!

"It felt right?"

"Absolutely. All of it. And not just today. Ever since I first walked into that run-down crappy house and found you. Since you fought me and sank your teeth into my arm. Since you took my back in the desert and I knew you were scared as fuck, legs shaking, breathing heavy but you did it anyway. Since we were in the car and you had your guard up, didn't want to trust me, were probably listing in your head all the reasons why you'd never trust anyone again. Yet you climbed into the backseat, rummaged through my pack until you found something to eat, then you slept."

Realization filled his gaze. "I think you understand I want you to trust me. But thinking back, I had it not even a half-hour after I met you. Yeah, I know I did, or there was no way in fuck you would've fallen asleep with me if you didn't know somewhere deep down that you could trust me." Myles paused and his hands traveled up my spine until one stopped at the back of my neck. The other continued over my shoulder until it found my chin and tilted my head back. Once he had my eyes, he went on. "Don't know what's happening. What I know is you're safe with me, you can trust me, we're gonna get you out of this mess and home. I also know whatever it is it feels good and right."

It was rather annoying that Myles was so observant.

"Does that answer your question?" he murmured.

Nope, not even a little bit.

I was more confused, a whole lot turned on, and mystified how we'd gotten to this place. Now having shared two incredible kisses, this after we'd spent only two days together, during a time that was troubling —*understatement*—and dangerous—*again, understatement*— I was unclear how I ended up in Myles's arms. Moreover, I agreed with his assessment—not the part where I was good with my mouth—but the part about it feeling right.

And that scared me for a variety of reasons, the top of that list being that I'd learned never to want anything and I wanted more of Myles. Down from that, I was worried about what my future held, and I had to guard against heartache.

"Totally," I answered.

Myles smiled. Being so close to that smile, I found it hard to modulate my breathing. He was just so damn handsome and when his face lost the wariness he was beautiful. Which brought me to another reason to be scared. It was my experience that good-looking men didn't bother with average when they could get women who were just as good-looking as them. And I was average.

"You're a shit liar, babe. But we're running out of time before Zane calls back and I got a call to make to get you gum, candy, and lotion." He paused then he added, "and your chips."

I didn't bother denying he caught me telling a fib. That would only delay my shower and likely lead us into another conversation that would turn me on or alternately scare me more than I already was.

"It's good you didn't forget the chips," I teased him. "I think I remember you promising me a greasy meal, and since you've yet to provide that, chips will have to suffice."

Myles's smile broadened. Then he ran his fingers over the hinge of my jaw and finished with his thumb gliding along my bottom lip.

"Take your shower, Delilah," he ordered.

I decided, mostly for my mental health but also because Myles's voice had turned devilishly rumbly, to follow his demand.

I pulled out of his arms and made my way back into the bedroom. I hesitated at the door then made a decision and left it open. I gathered my clothes, the same dress I'd worn yesterday, and went into the bathroom, closing the door behind me. It was then I made another decision and left it unlocked

CHAPTER 11

The time had come.

It was two days overdue and shit needed to get settled. But seeing Delilah standing in front of the tall bank of windows staring out at the ocean with her back to me, giving me an unobstructed view of the butchered job I'd done cutting her hair, I wanted to put her into the old Mitsubishi parked in the lot downstairs and disappear with her. At least until Zane figured out what to do with Abrams and BZ Systems. I had to give her credit; the woman was fighting to hide the tremble but she was shit at it. The sight served as a reminder she was well-aware her life was still in danger.

But it was the choppy, uneven strands that held my attention. The physical reminder of what Tamir had done. She'd said it would grow back, which was true enough, but it still pissed me right the fuck off her only option had been to chop the knots out of her hair.

The phone rang. Delilah jumped, and I gritted my teeth.

"Delilah?"

"Answer it."

"Look at me."

She didn't move, the phone kept ringing, and my molars clenched.

"Please just answer it."

"Not until you look at me."

Slowly she turned. The phone stopped ringing and I unlocked my jaw only to have the muscle in my cheek tick.

Blatant fear stark in her eyes. The same wild look she gave me when I first found her.

"We're not doing this," I said as my phone started ringing again.

"What?"

"You need more time. A few days at least. Maybe more."

"What?"

"I promised you I'd keep you safe. All of you safe, that includes what's going on in your head. You need more time to sort out what happened."

Delilah glanced around the room, her gaze landing on the cluttered coffee table—an empty chip bag and candy wrapper, and next to those there were two more full bags and three extra candy bars. As soon as they'd been delivered she'd wasted no time happily tearing into both. She did this gleefully, smiling and moaning with each bite. Now she was looking at the detritus in a way that made me uneasy.

"I trust you to keep me safe," she said to the table. "Please, trust me, Myles, when I tell you I need you to answer the phone so I can get this over with."

Her gaze came back to me and her eyes were pleading. She wanted this done.

Fuck.

I lifted my hand, glanced at my phone, and took the call.

"You're on speaker."

"Everything good?" Zane's concerned voice boomed.

"Yeah. Who's with you?"

"Garrett, and Tex is on the line."

John "Tex" Keegan—the man with all the answers.

It was a damn good thing the former SEAL was on our side.

"Tex, I appreciate you making the time and jumping on the call."

"Always have time," Tex grunted.

That was a lie. Tex was always busy.

"Whatcha got for us?" Garrett joined the conversation.

"Delilah's confirmed what we knew about the lease deal in Timor-Leste. Abrams wanted to mine the land for silicon. But something we didn't know while the Prime Minister and the President were going back and forth, Aviv sent Tamir to Timor-Leste."

"Did Tamir take the pictures Delilah sent to Evette?"

"The one I sent of the village, yes," Delilah answered. "But not the…the um…not the one of Kalee in the…" Delilah trailed off and winced.

The pictures in question were of Kyle's wife Anaya, Kalee Solberg, and Piper Morgan. The pictures were taken right before the rebels had attacked the village. The second image was of Kalee's prone body in a mass grave on top of the murdered young girls from the orphanage.

"Was Tamir there during the attack?" Tex asked.

The man's voice was even, his tone neutral, but I knew he was anything but calm. Tex was close friends with Beckett "Ace" Morgan who was married to Piper. Their three children had been in the orphanage before the rebels had attacked. Piper saved their lives and later Ace and Piper adopted the girls. Tex played an important role in getting the girls to the States. And Forest "Phantom" Dalton was also a good friend of Tex's. Phantom had risked his life and naval career to save Kalee.

Kalee was at the center of Z Corps' involvement. Anaya and Evette were friends with Piper and Kalee. That friendship was what had led Evette down a dark path of vengeance that had almost gotten her killed. Enter Delilah Watts. Now we were neck-deep in shit we had no business being in.

In other words, Delilah's answer mattered a great deal to Tex.

"No. The attack happened a few weeks after he got back to Virginia."

"And the other lease deals?" Garrett inquired.

"Aviv wasn't interested in anything in El Salvador except Alejandro Arias. And Croatia is for his..." Once again Delilah paused and her face paled.

"What's Croatia for?" Garrett prompted.

"His experiments," she whispered.

"Dr. Gates and his pig brain research," Garrett pushed.

"You know about that?"

Delilah rocked back and it dawned on me we were still standing in the middle of the room.

"Babe, let's sit down."

"No, I need to stand."

I heard Zane groan before he snarked, "And so it begins."

"Zane," I warned.

"And here I was worried you were gonna drag this shit out."

"Yes, we found Dr. Gate's papers on restoring brain circulation and function on decapitated pigs," Tex confirmed.

"And Myles told me you know Alejandro Arias found a new way to engineer brain cells by reprogramming skin cells to become stem cells."

"Jesus fuck," Zane growled.

"Abrams has two research programs running simultaneously. They're separate but they're connected. The cognitive radar contract Abrams won is merely to fund Aviv's true obsession." Delilah's gaze came to mine.

"It's all good, Delilah," I encouraged

"Aviv is fixated on artificial intelligence. He believes it's the way of the future."

"It is," Garrett cut in. "Today's military AI market is worth approximately six billion. In five years it'll be an eleven billion dollar industry. The Royal Navy has one of the most advanced AI-based threat identification systems ever made. The application monitors the air picture and can build a threat eval in milliseconds. The Air Force has been before Congress several times wanting more funding for their airborne warning control system. AI is a game-changer."

"Agreed," Delilah said sharply. "The military is enlisting a whole new generation of soldiers. These men and women were brought up in the gaming era. So why not give them the tools they're used to playing with? The battlefield is now on a screen. They're playing a video game and with that comes the disconnect. No emotions, no adrenaline, no feelings, no moral responsibility for your target. And the problem with the Air Force's advanced battle management system funding package is the part about weaponizing satellites."

"Yeah, there's no doubt there're some downsides," Garrett concurred. "But there's no denying AI speeds up information analysis. Soldiers can make informed decisions on the battlefield. I've used fire support tech. It was in its infancy but it worked. I could be sent out on my own without a spotter and still get my job done."

I could clearly see the frustration on Delilah's face. She was holding something back. Something important and she hadn't touched on with the experiments she'd mentioned.

"Delilah?" Her head snapped to mine and she frowned. "Baby, just say what you need to say."

There was a grunt over the line—presumably from Zane but he wisely kept his mouth shut.

"But *you* were pulling the trigger," Delilah spat. "Aviv's building unmanned systems. If drones can take over the air he wants robotics to take over the field. Spec ops teams replaced completely with enhanced soldier technology and robotics."

"Aviv can want all he wants but that shit is never gonna happen," Zane rejoined. "And if it were going to happen the Army's combat capabilities development command would never allow the civilian marketplace to own the tech. DEVCOM already has a program, IoBT— internet on the battlefield things—stupid name for a research and development program that's nothing more than theoretical bullshit."

"It's not bullshit," Delilah whispered. "It's happening or at least parts of it are. Autonomic systems, predictive processing, goal-driven decision making, and therein lies the big problem; these systems take away the human element. It makes the battlefield amoral. That's what Aviv wants, he wants to build a hybrid army. AI robotics and enhanced human soldiers. That's why he wants Dr. Gates and Alejandro Arias."

"Restoring brain function and engineering brain cells." Tex's statement hung in the air.

Delilah was shaking and looked ready to bolt. And now that we were getting into the thick of it I understood why. There was more she needed to explain, specifically the part about Aviv experimenting on soldiers but I didn't have it in me to rush her. Hell, I wanted to disconnect the call, take her on the run, and demand her to forget everything she knew. Unfortunately, that was an impossibility.

"What exactly does enhanced human soldiers mean?" Garrett asked.

Delilah didn't get a chance to respond before Zane took over the conversation.

"It means that Aviv Abrams was either involved with a program the IDF was running called Fear or he found out about the program, didn't care the science was proved wrong, found Gates and Arias and thought they had the answers. Am I right, Delilah?" Zane growled. "Is Abrams fucking with soldier's goddamn brains trying to remove their fear response?"

"Yes," Delilah squeaked.

"Motherfucker," Zane barked. "Garrett, find me all the

intel you can on the program. It was shut down in 2012 or it was supposedly shut down after ten men underwent brain surgery to remove their amygdala. Two died on the table and eight recovered successfully, however the surgeries failed to produce the desired results."

Delilah's head dropped forward and her shoulders slumped. The shaking had turned into quaking and she was wringing her hands.

Fuck. There was more.

"Baby, what are you leaving out?"

Without looking up she mumbled, "He knows the surgeries weren't a complete success but nor were they total failures. Removing the amygdala didn't stop the subjects from feeling fear but it was successful in dampening their harm avoidance response. The subjects reported that they no longer felt fight or flight. That gut feeling you get when you know you're in danger was missing, making them have a higher tolerance for acceptable risk. And they reacted slower and were less expressive to painful stimuli. Aviv's moved on from that, to attempting to rewire the brain. He wants to completely remove the fear response."

"Jesus Christ," Zane roared.

Delilah jolted, and when her head lifted and our gazes locked, confusion and fear warred.

"Baby, he's not upset with you."

"I'm not?" Zane snapped. "Because I'm feeling pretty fucking *upset* at the moment. Wait, no I'm not, I'm feeling pretty fuckin' pissed. How long you been sittin' on this, Delilah?"

"Since Alejandro Arias sent an unsecured email to Aviv with his research and his resignation. Which was about three months prior to me finding Evette snooping around Abrams."

Delilah's tone was full of indignation and ire but the wariness was still written across her face.

"Speaking of Evette, I'm curious how you figured her out."

That was Garrett and he knew exactly how Delilah had caught Evette.

"My first clue something was going on was when her IP address hit the Abrams website multiple times a day for weeks. She went through every page, clicked every external link, read every article on our News and Events page. She was easy to find, and once I had Evette London's name it was easy to connect her to Anaya, Kalee, and Piper through social media and professional profiles. It was then I understood why Evette was poking around and I hoped I had an ally, one who worked in media and could expose Abrams."

"When did you know someone put tracking software on your machine?" Garrett continued.

"How do you know that's how I got caught?"

"Because I didn't believe someone with your skill would be so careless."

Delilah sighed and seemed to relax the smallest fraction, but then her posture stiffened and her eyes narrowed on me.

"I thought you all thought I was setting Evette up."

"We did," Zane joined. "Garrett's a tech geek; he thinks that fellow tech geeks are smarter than I think they are. So no one was listening to Garrett when he told us he didn't think you'd fuck up and send Evette intel using your office email. Obviously, since you *did* send her emails using your Abrams email account, I was right and you fucked up. Evette's got a soft heart, that is, when she's not trying to shoot me. She went to bat for you if that makes you feel better."

"I think I like Evette," Delilah muttered.

I heard Garrett bark out a laugh and before I could stop my chuckle I joined him. It was an unfortunate error on my part, a mistake that meant I was on the receiving end of a saucy smile complete with a sassy wink.

A smile that was different than any of the other ones she'd given me.

Before I could recover Tex broke in.

"How much of this can you prove?"

"All of it if you help me find Alejandro Arias," Delilah returned.

Shit, fuck, and damn.

"Arias is dead," Zane informed her.

"No, he's not."

"He is," I gently told her. "He died in a car accident."

Her smile remained in place when she proudly announced, "No, Myles, Alejandro didn't die in a car accident. I helped him fake his death. He's alive and has everything we need to take down Aviv."

"How did that happen?" Zane demanded.

"Just curious, Mr. Lewis, do you have any tone other than jerk?"

There was a beat of silence, then my boss answered honestly, "Yep. Supreme asshole."

"Welp, that explains why Evette tried to shoot you," she mumbled.

I shot her a grin and Tex again interjected, "Who else knows Arias is alive?"

"No one."

"How sure are you?" I asked and Delilah lost her smile.

"We were careful. We planned it right. At first, Aviv thought Alejandro ran and he sent a team to look for him. But when they got to Santa Ana the team found out he died in a car accident. There was a funeral, there's a tombstone, his aunt and grandmother mourned."

"Damn that's cold," Garrett mumbled. "Did he stay in El Salvador?"

"The plan was for him to go to Jalapa, Guatemala."

"How were you supposed to make contact with him?" That was Garrett followed by Tex asking, "Did he take the evidence with him or is it in El Salvador?"

"Does anyone care I asked a question?" Zane grumbled.

Jesus with the rapid-fire questions.

Delilah started to fidget and her gaze slid back to the floor. A look that conveyed uncertainty. And I didn't think it was Zane's new tone that conveyed he could and did often slip into supreme asshole.

"Give her a minute."

"Actually," Tex said gently. "I think she's given us enough to start with. One last thing; to help me locate Arias, do you know the alias he was planning on using?"

"Juan Lopez."

"Let me guess—Juan Lopez is the most common name in Guatemala."

"Yes."

"A challenge," Tex returned. "Myles, I'll be in touch."

"Appreciate it."

Tex didn't reply before he disconnected.

"How much longer do you think it will be before Tex stops taking Zane's calls?"

Garrett's question was aimed at me.

"Shocked he still answers," I returned.

"That's only because Ivy sends Melody and his girls Christmas gifts."

"My wife is a damn smart woman," Zane broke in. "She knows what's what and added birthday gifts after Brooks found Tatiana and the writing was on the wall that none of you fuckers were going to listen."

Garrett was joking, of course. Tex did not help because Ivy sent his wife and kids Christmas and birthday gifts. Though, it might make all the bickering he has to sit through easier to listen to. But likely after all these years Tex just tunes that shit out.

"No one listens because your advice sucks," I pointed out.

There was a commotion on Zane's end before he cursed a blue streak that had Delilah's eyes going wide.

"Goddamn, I have to go. When I find this fucker I'm pulling his balls out through his asshole. Check in later."

Zane disconnected and Delilah stared at my phone.

"He's joking," I lied.

"He didn't sound like he was joking."

That was because he wasn't but I wasn't going to tell Delilah that. Zane was gruff, sometimes rude, mostly sarcastic, and fiercely protective—he was an acquired taste—you either loved him or hated him and he didn't give a fuck which way you fell. If he liked you, you had his loyalty for life. If he didn't he didn't give you another thought. If you crossed him he'd pull your balls out through your asshole and not think twice.

That was Zane.

He'd also give you anything you needed. He'd lay down his life for you. He'd keep and protect his men's families.

Delilah's gaze slid around the room then settled on the window.

For two days we'd been in the hotel room, for days before that she was locked in a shitty rundown house, and for months before that either on the run or held captive. She needed fresh air and a break from everything swirling around her.

"How are you feeling?"

Not taking her eyes off the ocean she answered, "I don't know how to answer that."

"There's no right or wrong answer."

She still hadn't moved when she said, "In a way, I feel better now that it's out there. But I also feel vulnerable and anxious. Your boss scares me and if I would've talked to him while I was in California I wouldn't have trusted him. I want Aviv stopped and this to be over but I'm scared of how it ends. I'm worried about the repercussions. I'm worried I have nothing to go home to. I'm worried about what Aviv is doing and planning. I'm seriously freaked out about Tamir and where he is and if he's planning on coming back to take me. I'm worried for Alejandro and I hope he's okay."

When Delilah paused I took the opportunity to set her straight.

"I get you're worried about Tamir and Aviv and I get why, but I promised to keep you safe. So you worrying about what they're doing and planning is in vain. Neither of them are getting anywhere near you. Whatever repercussions come about at the end of this will not touch you. However that comes about, Delilah, it isn't on you. Aviv's bought his ending, he either goes down ugly and permanent or he goes down a different way that leaves him breathing but not free. As far as Zane goes, the man doesn't do warm and friendly. What he does do is bust his ass every day to make sure the people he cares about are taken care of. He lives by an ethos that most people would find offensive."

She turned from the window to ask, "Offensive?"

"Safety comes at a cost, one that Zane doesn't blink an eye to pay. Zane is a man who lives with the weight of his decisions heavy on his shoulders yet still stands strong. He barks and bitches and is nosy as fuck. He has zero filter and he says the most obnoxious shit. But make no mistake he would protect you with his life."

Her brows pulled together and I wished like hell she was closer so I could smooth the wrinkle and worry away.

"I don't understand."

No, she wouldn't understand. Growing up the way she did, her mom putting man after man ahead of her, she wouldn't understand why someone would offer safety and shelter. She wouldn't understand being on the receiving end of help though she'd offered it to an El Salvadorian scientist and to a woman who was looking into her friend's capture and torture.

Then I wondered why the hell I was still standing across the room. So I closed the distance, got close. When she stepped into me and put her head on my chest and her arms slid around my waist I had my answer.

An answer to a question I wasn't fully aware I'd been asking and one she certainly didn't understand she was giving nor did she understand the implications. She couldn't have a clue what I'd been pushing down and holding back. But her arms sliding around me, her cheek on my chest, there was no denying what I'd felt within hours of meeting her.

No, that was a lie. The feeling started from a picture. Every day, ten times a day, I'd look at that picture and be drawn to something in her eyes. I didn't know it then but knew now, the cause of her pain. The sadness under the smile.

My mind filled with all that Delilah never had. Five years ago—hell, two years ago—where my thoughts were at would've had me out the door. But now, seeing good men all around me find good women, and knowing there is so much beauty in what they have, I wasn't running for the door as I thought of all the ways I wanted to fill her life with all that she should've had.

I abandoned her statement, knowing I couldn't explain something to her that she needed to experience and feel in order to understand, and instead asked, "What's going on?"

"I don't know," she whispered and burrowed deeper.

Then it dawned on me. The way she was holding tight, getting close—she was searching for something no one had likely given her.

Affection.

"Later we're gonna get out of the room, go for a walk on the beach, and get you your greasy fries. But first, we're gonna rest. Couch or bed?"

"Is it safe to go out?"

It wasn't but I'd make it so if it meant she got some sunshine and fresh air.

"Absolutely. Couch or bed?"

"Bed."

No hesitation.

Good choice.

Delilah didn't take her arm from around me when I moved us across the room, though she did turn just enough to walk. When we hit the room, she disconnected to climb onto the bed, not stopping until she scooted into the middle. As soon as I got on and settled she rolled and pinned me to the mattress.

Something about that was unsettling. Not her pinning me to the bed; that felt really fucking great. I'd kissed her twice—yes, one of those times we were in bed and I was on top of her. And yes again, I didn't hide the fact my dick was hard enough to pound nails, and Delilah hadn't hidden she was turned on and getting more so by the second. But right then, this was not about that. This was about something else.

"Babe?"

"Huh?"

"What's going on?"

There was a long pause of silence but during that lull, Delilah's body was stringing tighter and tighter. And the stiffer she became the more unease settled in my gut.

"Sor-sorry. I shouldn't've—"

I rolled, reversing our positions, and balanced my weight on my elbow.

"Wrap your legs around me." Her eyes flashed, reading the situation wrong. "Want you holding on to me baby, that's all."

I waited until she wrapped her legs and hooked her ankles.

"Now, tell me what's going on in your head."

"I don't know."

"What don't you know?"

Her eyes came up and it was like I was looking into a pit of despair.

"I don't know what's going on in my head. I don't know why I did what I did. I just wanted…I just needed…" Her words were hollow. Broken. Disjointed. "I feel…weird."

Delilah abruptly stopped and shook her head.

Yeah, she'd been so starved of affection she didn't fucking understand what she was feeling and why. Thirty-five years old and didn't understand after the morning she'd had, the stress she felt, the anxiety she admitted to, she needed a *hug*.

A fucking hug.

Human interaction. Touch. Kindness.

She'd burrowed in and held me tight, needing that connection, needed to feel close.

Goddamn, her mother was a bitch.

"I know what you need," I told her and shifted off her.

Her legs fell away and I heard her mewl of protest. I ignored that and rolled her to her side, fitting my front against her back. I found her hand and threaded our fingers together, then brought them to rest high on her chest.

"Early morning. A lot going on," I murmured.

Delilah nodded and I continued.

"Been bottling all that shit up. A lot to keep in. A lot to worry about. A lot to carry. That's done for you, Delilah. You let it out and gave it to us. We'll take it from here. I suspect there's more to share. You give that to us and we'll handle that, too."

I felt her body sag but her fingers that were twined with mine tightened.

"You keep trusting me, baby, I promise you won't regret it."

"I know I won't."

I let that burn through me and shoved my face into her hair. I inhaled and the smell of flowers permeated my senses.

Weird.

It had been days since I'd found her. Hours since I first kissed her, but lying in that bed with her holding her tight it felt longer—much longer, years longer.

Being as I wasn't stupid, I was going with that feeling, the one that told me the number of days or amount of hours didn't matter. What did was the rightness I felt down to my bones.

CHAPTER 12

The warm Pacific was lapping at my ankles, the sun was shining on my face, the smell of sand and sun and salt surrounded me.

It was divine.

Just what I needed.

It was early in the day but the beach was busy. Umbrellas, chairs, coolers, towels were laid on the sand. People everywhere—in the water, on the shore, asses in chairs.

It was beautiful. But the real beauty was the man standing next to me holding my hand. That was the kind of beauty you didn't lose when the clouds rolled in and the sea turned stormy. It was the kind that became more so when the storm hit and the waves threatened to take you under. I would know, a squall had snuck up on me and when I felt the force of it and started to go under, Myles pulled me through.

He'd held me until the feeling of helpless subsided.

He'd surrounded me with his presence and that was all I needed for the anxiousness to fade. Never in my life had I felt so out of sorts, not even when Tamir had me, not even when I thought I was going to die. I couldn't put it into words and explain to Myles what was wrong. It wasn't fear, it was a bone-deep restlessness, an unease that made me feel exposed and defenseless. It was without thought and on impulse, I sought comfort in Myles.

But something changed when I had my arms around him and he didn't hesitate to hold me in return. Realization struck, it wasn't impulse that drove me into his arms —it was instinct. At that moment I was exactly where I was supposed to be. I was where I *needed* to be.

"You ready to get that burger and fries?" Myles asked.

"Yes."

It was no surprise that Myles had been right, it had taken until last night for my stomach to get on board with food. I was starving all the time but a handful of bites into my food and I was full only to be starving an hour later. But last night for dinner he'd ordered me fish tacos and I'd cleared my plate. It wasn't a three-course meal but I finished and ate the tomatoes, mushrooms, and cucumbers Myles had picked out of his salad. Which meant he didn't actually eat a salad, he ate lettuce and croutons smothered in blue cheese dressing. Thankfully he'd picked out the veggies before he doused his lettuce; blue cheese is nasty.

"Joe's Hamburger Shoppe or Carl's Jr.?"

I adjusted the backpack Myles had insisted I carry and tipped my head back to clear the brim of the baseball cap —ditto on the insisted-on part—and looked up at him.

"There's a Carl's here?"

"Yep. Burger King is about a mile down if you're up for a walk."

"We can't eat American fast food while we're in Mazatlán."

Myles's lips hitched up into a semi-smile. His amusement became audible when he asked, "We can't?"

"No way. It's the golden rule of travel. Why go someplace new and exciting and eat something you can get back home? It's like buying a pair of Nike sneakers as a souvenir. Why would you do that when you can go to your local mall and pick up a pair?"

"No clue."

"Right. Because it's silly. Souvenirs are just that and they have to remind you of where you've been."

"Joe's Burger Shoppe it is," Myles declared.

It happened right after I finished chewing the last bite of my greasy, delicious hamburger. I was squirting ketchup on my plate when Myles called my name.

The instant my head came up and my focus shifted from the mound of ketchup to his face I braced.

"Listen to me carefully and do everything I tell you to do."

Myles's tone, his expression, his body language all demanded my complete obedience. Though he didn't wait for me to concede before he calmly gave his next directive.

"I'm gonna throw some bills on the table, we're gonna

stand, grab our stuff, and walk out like normal. Easy like, baby, no attention drawn to us. We're just two tourists finished with lunch. Don't look around, don't make eye contact, just walk. You with me so far?"

I did my best to follow his lead and keep my face neutral and nodded.

"Good. When we get outside we're turning right. One block down there's a parking structure. That's where we're headed. Here's the important part, Delilah; in your pack, there's a gun. You also got your new passport and a phone. If I tell you to run, you run. You don't hesitate or ask questions. Get yourself someplace safe, heavily populated, and you call Zane. He'll tell you what to do and where to go. Got that?"

"What about—"

"No time for questions. Did you get everything I told you?"

"Yes."

"Alright. Here we go. Slow-like, baby. No rush. Two tourists leaving a restaurant going back to the beach."

It was hard, extremely so, keeping my body under control and not bolting for the door even though I had no idea what I'd be running from. Myles did what he said he was going to do and reached into his wallet, pulled out money, and tossed it on the table while I awkwardly slid my backpack over my shoulder.

We simultaneously stood and Myles tagged my hand, halting my movements. He leaned down and placed a hard, closed-mouthed kiss on my lips. When he was done he pulled back but not far and muttered, "I got this, Delilah. Slow and easy."

"I know you do."

His hand holding mine convulsed and he straightened.

I never knew how hard it was not to look around a restaurant while exiting, especially when you've been instructed not to. I had no idea where to keep my eyes so I pretended to concentrate on fixing the straps of my pack. That meant I had to rely on Myles to guide us out. I figured that was better than me accidentally screwing up.

We hit the sidewalk, hooked a right, and Myles quickened our pace. He used the hand not holding mine to reach into his pocket and pull out his phone. Again, one-handed, he used his thumb to tap the screen before he put it up to his ear.

"Garrett, need you to stop what you're doing and track me. We're being followed." There was a pause then, "Correct, north on Calle Rio. There's a parking garage called Rico's; they have cameras so we're gonna dip in there. Male, brown hair, brown eyes, fortyish, don't know height, he was sitting but he's got some heft, easily pushing two-fifty. He was alone at the table, didn't clock anyone else with him but he was taking pictures." Another pause then, "Copy."

Myles shoved his phone in his pocket and I struggled to keep up, mainly because I was concentrating on not hyperventilating.

"Pictures?"

"Almost there, Delilah, everything's good."

The hell it was. It was distressing enough someone was taking pictures—that freaked me out. But Myles's reaction took distressing straight to unnerving.

I decided not to remind Myles I didn't react well to danger, I tended to freeze up and panic. Thankfully, the decision part was made for me since Myles was pulling me along and I had to take twice as many steps to keep up with his long strides.

I saw Rico's garage just up ahead and I felt extreme relief. A few more seconds and we'd be there. It was naïve really. I, of course, had no idea what Myles's plan was, why we were going to the parking structure, and what was happening after we got there. But not being out in the open on the sidewalk seemed like a good idea.

I was wrong.

Once we entered the garage things went from unnerving to downright scary as hell.

"Behind me," Myles barked but didn't wait for me to comply.

My backpack saved me from slamming into the concrete wall Myles shoved me against as he positioned his big body in front of mine.

"You get ready to run if I tell you to."

I didn't answer, hell, I barely breathed before Myles stepped away from me and had a man in a chokehold. I was stunned immobile. It might've been minutes or seconds—I wouldn't know because time stood still—but finally, Myles laid the man down on the ground. I thought after that we would run but we didn't. Myles knelt and searched the man's pockets coming up, with his wallet and phone. After that Myles surged to his feet, grabbed my hand, then we slowly meandered out of the garage.

I didn't ask questions, I didn't make a sound, I just followed Myles.

We made it across the street, down that side about half a block before he ran—okay he was jogging at a slow pace, I was running to keep up—into another parking lot and up to the SUV. He had his backpack pulled around, hanging at a weird angle because he was still holding my hand, and he was digging through it with his other hand. He came out with car keys then let go of my hand, rolled his shoulder forward, so his pack slid down his arm, and he handed it to me.

"Hold this and stand right here. Do not move."

That wouldn't be an issue. Without Myles pulling me I had a feeling I would've been rooted back at Rico's.

Myles lay down on his back with his torso under the SUV, which I vaguely recognized as the Mitsubishi.

"One more minute, Delilah," he said as he hauled himself up.

Again, this was not a problem. I was only capable of standing in one spot. Then it dawned on me I should probably be looking around making sure no one was… what? Following us, running at us guns-up, ready to shoot, sneaking up to slice our throats?

I heard something slam shut and turned in time to see Myles walking towards me from the front of the SUV.

"It's all good. Come on."

What's all good?

I didn't ask. I wasn't sure I wanted to know.

Myles unlocked the passenger door—with the key, not a clicker—and helped me in. He rounded the hood and I watched him scan the area. For what or whom I didn't know. I still had my backpack strapped on and his lying on my lap, and it must be noted his was twice as heavy as mine. And he'd jogged with it on his back like it was nothing.

"You're doing great, baby. Hang tight."

I was doing nothing and I wasn't hanging tight. I was

hanging on a string and that string was gonna snap at any moment.

Slowly, normally, like everything was peachy keen, Myles backed out of the parking spot and pulled out of the lot. Once he was on the busy street he drove the speed limit, stayed in one lane, didn't attempt to pass any cars.

And I again remained quiet.

We'd gone four blocks, and yes, in an effort to settle my racing thoughts I counted. We'd gone through four intersections when Myles spoke again.

"Toss my pack in the back and swing yours off."

I wasn't sure I could heave his into the back so I put it on the floor by my feet and twisted and shimmied until I had mine free. I threw mine in the back, righted myself in my seat, and belted up.

"Here." Myles passed me a wallet and two phones. "Go through his wallet and check for ID."

I did as I was told and sure enough, there was a U.S. driver's license.

"Caesar Stockholm," I squeaked and cleared my throat before I finished. "Houston, Texas."

"Can you take a picture of that and text it to Garrett?"

"Sure."

I had a hundred questions running through my head, none of which I asked. I took a picture of the ID and with shockingly steady hands I managed to text it to Garrett. No sooner did I hit send than the phone vibrated and Garrett's name flashed.

I hit the green icon to accept the call.

"Hello?" I was staring at the phone and could barely hear a muffled voice. "Shit. Hold on." I found the button to put it on speakerphone and repeated, "Hello?"

"Got the text. I'm running the name. I'll have something for you in a few minutes. Where are you?"

I looked around for a street sign but Myles answered before I found one.

"In the car, south on Calle Rio. I need to put some distance between us and Mazatlán. Tell me where I'm going."

There was a beat of silence then, "If you're up for a five-hour drive we've got a contact in Guadalajara. If you want more distance, next one's in Mexico City."

"Guadalajara for today," Myles answered. "But set up Mexico City for the day after. We need to keep moving."

"Copy that. Clean up?"

"Negative."

"I'll text the location."

Garrett's name disappeared off the screen.

"What's clean up?" I asked.

When Myles didn't answer right away I glanced over at him and my already pounding heart went into overdrive. I could see the muscle in his jaw ticking. My gaze dropped to his shoulder then his arm. I noted he still had my teeth marks on his forearm. My eyes went to his other arm and the black ink of his tattoo was stretched tight over his bunched muscle.

Never Again.

I wanted to ask why he'd tat those words into his skin but obviously, they meant something important or he wouldn't have had them permanently inked on his arm and I sensed now was not the time to ask. Something else was going on, something else that was important, I just didn't understand *how* important.

"Myles?"

"He was asking if he needed to send someone to clean up my mess."

"Oh."

There was another moment of silence before he clarified, "Mess being a dead body."

Eek.

"Right," I mumbled. "What about our stuff at the hotel?"

Everything of importance was in our backpacks, Myles made sure of that before we left the room but I'd left behind the clothes he bought me and all the toiletries Ivy had sent.

"You don't want to know if I killed him?"

"What?"

"You're asking about our stuff, which boils down to your shampoo, conditioner, and lotion. But you're not gonna ask if I killed a man?"

My not asking seemed important to him, and perhaps I should've cared but after the last few months I'd had, I didn't have it in me. As far as I was concerned everyone was out to kill me. And if Myles killed a man who was taking pictures of us, a man who'd followed us, by my way of thinking a man who meant us harm, I trusted that Myles didn't have any other options.

"You were protecting yourself and me."

"Babe—"

"He freaked you out enough for us to leave the restaurant. He followed us. What were you supposed to do? And I left more than my shampoo, conditioner, and lotion. I left razors, shaving cream, candy bars, chips, and two pairs of my shiny, blue, ruffle butt briefs that give me a wedgy with every step I take. They might be the most ridiculously ugly undies I've ever owned but I was attached to them."

"Good thing I got you a three-pack. Unless you're going commando you still have a pair."

I was in a sundress, I certainly was not going commando.

"Thank you for taking care of me," I muttered.

Myles's burst of laughter took me by surprise and my eyes snapped back to his face.

"I take you out to lunch when I knew it was safer to stay inside and you're thanking me for taking care of you even though I fucked up and put you in danger."

I wasn't sure if that was a question or a statement but either way, I felt it deserved an answer.

"You bought me clothes. You were gentle with me when you had to cut my hair even though I told you it was just hair and would grow back. You knew I was blowing smoke up your ass and I was struggling. Not with losing my hair but *why* I was losing it. You've been patient with me and you've insisted I be patient with myself. I know it's not normal, needing to shower every hour to feel clean, but you give it to me. You've humored me when I've ordered way too much when you knew I would be able to eat half of what I got but you still gave it to me. You've given me time to be alone in my head and you've pulled me back to the present before I spent too much time there dwelling. You've talked to me. You've listened. You held me when I felt weak. You've given me two of the best kisses of my life. You've made my belly flutter. You've made me feel safe. Every step, even when I didn't have you next to me you've been taking care of me. You've given me months of your life.

If that's you fucking up, Myles, then I don't know what to say."

I petered out then I remembered something else. "And you bought me gum in the wee hours of the morning for no other reason than I wanted it."

Suddenly the air in the cab turned stagnant. Thick and humid until it coated my skin. The longer the silence stretched the clammier my hands turned and the faster my pulse pounded. I was looking right at him, so I didn't miss it—his jaw clenched, his body turned to stone. Then there was a rumble like rolling thunder.

Hearing that rumble, my breath caught.

"Baby, you got a five-hour drive to think on what you just said to me."

"Think on what?"

"That green light you just gave me."

I stopped looking at his profile and glanced out the windshield. We were leaving the more populated area of Mazatlán, called the Golden Zone. There were fewer cars on the road and as far as I could see no stoplights.

"Green light?"

"You gave me something back at the hotel when you stepped to me looking for comfort. I suspect you didn't realize what you were giving me. But just now, you giving me all a' that on top of what you've already given me... baby, straight up you gotta know what you handed me."

I didn't know what I handed him but it was true I'd turned to him for comfort. Something he gave me and it felt damn good—not only the giving but the taking.

"I'm a little lost," I whispered.

"No, Delilah. You were lost, but now you are found. Lost and alone and my guess starving. None of that having to do with Tamir. I'd bet you've felt that your whole life. Cold and starving for the attention you deserved." Before I could confirm he was indeed correct, that I'd been alone and cold and starving, he went on, "I've known you days. That's all it took for you to pull down that wall you built. I didn't have to do a damn thing. When you were feeling lost and out of sorts, you walked straight to me, put your arms around me, laid your head on my chest, and gave me you. You gave me more when you followed me into the bedroom, and more when you admitted you didn't know what you needed and you trusted me to give it to you. Was gonna wait until all this was over—take my time, let you get your bearings, give me time to get in there, get your trust, let you breathe a minute. But what you just said, baby, you bought yourself a five-hour drive to decide if you'll let me keep what you gave me or if you're gonna take it back."

Did he…

Was he…

With my thoughts scattered, my heart pounding, my breathing erratic, and the English language evading me, Myles carried on.

"But let's just to say in the next five hours, you decide to take back what you've given me. I'm gonna fight to keep hold. You remember that belly flutter and those kisses and you do that knowing I'm gonna give you more a' that. I'm gonna give you everything you never knew you needed. All you gotta do is keep trusting me and I swear to you, I'll do the rest."

Holy smokes!

"Now, baby, sit back and get comfortable. We got a long drive ahead of us."

I said nothing, not because there wasn't a lot to say; I just couldn't find the words to explain all that I felt.

I didn't need five hours to think about what I wanted.

I wanted him.

But as the five hours dragged on, doubt crept in.

The familiar feeling of being close to something I wanted only to have it yanked away invaded my thoughts. Lessons I'd learned young, and as the years went on until I'd stopped wanting anything and pulled further inside of myself until there was nothing left to want or feel. Until I was so totally empty and unbelievably lonely. I didn't know the first thing about being with a man. I was too afraid to connect or become attached so I stayed distant, cold, remote.

Just like Myles said, lost, alone, and starving.

Hours into the drive as I was turning all of this over in my mind, pondering, wondering, contemplating if I could give myself to Myles it hit me—everything my mother had stolen from me. I'd thought she robbed me of a happy childhood. I thought it was normalcy she'd taken from me. I thought it was my ability to form lasting connections.

It was all of that, but more.

She'd stolen Myles.

The woman had made me unlovable.

I was stupid for thinking I could have something I wanted. I was dumber for wanting it knowing it'd never be mine to have.

"Better than I thought."

"What is?"

"Watching you laugh."

I let the pain of that memory burn through me.

Then I let other memories invade—all of them, every-thing he'd given me in the last two days. All the ways he'd taken care of me. The months he'd searched for me. I let the pain rip through me unbridled and ugly, reminding me I was not a woman who got anything she wanted.

CHAPTER 13

Five hours had turned into six.

Six hours of fucking torture. I would've said it was fascinating witnessing Delilah shift through whatever it was she was sorting silently in her head except it wasn't fascinating; it was goddamn torture. I'd catch a wince or glance over and see her hands balled into fists so tight her knuckles were white. Once I'd heard her whimper. Another time her body jerked in the seat.

The only conversation had been to check our route or plan our next stop or speak to Garrett when he called to give updates. Surprisingly, Caesar Stockholm wasn't an alias. He was from Texas and had ties to BZ Systems. The ties were loose but Garrett found them. Bryan Zaslow grew up in Connecticut but he spent summers—not many but a few—in Texas visiting his uncle's ranch. Caesar's mother was a cook and his father a ranch hand for Spirit Ranch. But other than the long-ago connection there was nothing else.

Now we were in an upscale, gated neighborhood on

the outskirts of Guadalajara and almost to our destination and her time was up.

"Wow," Delilah muttered, as I drove by a manmade waterfall. "Casa Club. Holy crap, look at that pool."

I clenched my teeth at the excitement I heard. Six hours of fucking torture and she was happily babbling about a clubhouse and swimming pool.

"Whoa! That golf course is huge."

Again I said nothing.

"And these houses. Holy smokes, they're like mini-mansions."

I found the address Garrett had given me and pulled into the driveway, stopped to punch in the code for the gate, and waited for it to slide open. I glanced around and noted the perimeter wall was seriously lacking as was the guard sitting in the booth at the entrance of the community. Not that it mattered. We'd be here twenty-four hours tops. With it being just me, I had two choices—keep moving or take her back to the States where Zane had secure locations.

The gate was almost open when my phone rang. Delilah had long since stopped asking me if she should answer, she just did it and put it on speaker for me.

"You're there," Garrett's voice came over the line.

"We are. Anything more on Stockholm?"

"Negative. I'm still looking."

"What about the earlier situation?"

"More stupid shit. There was a rock on the hood of Natasha's car when she came out of Dunkin with her coffee. Zane is on the warpath. Be happy you are not here."

Garrett had already filled me in on the rock incident

before we'd left the hotel for lunch. No note was left. Just a nice-sized rock on the hood of Nat's car.

"Know about the rock, anything new?"

"Nope. That's the problem. Whoever's fucking with us is doing just that and giving us nothing to go on. Zane's ranting and Ivy's threatened to shoot him with a tranq. Fun times, brother."

I slowly pulled into the courtyard of a clay-colored stucco house.

"What do you think?"

"I think Zane pissed someone off."

"Well, no shit, Sherlock."

"I'm telling you we got fucking nothing. Just a name of a guy in Canada that has fuckall to do with any op the company has ever been on. The guy has no connections to anyone employed by Z Corps or the women. I even checked if Delilah had a connection. Nothing. We're gonna have to send someone up north to pick him up. Zane's making those arrangements now. But with you in Mexico, everyone else on alert watching their families, that leaves Kevin and Cooper. I can't go because I'm still playing catch-up after being gone. And there's only so much we can ask Tex to do when he's running shit for fifty other people. The man is practically Superman but fuck even he needs to sleep."

I put the Mitsubishi in park and suggested, "Kevin's the best tracker, he should go to Canada and let Coop stay behind. He was a cop, he can help you with the investigation."

There was a beat of silence, then another. When Garrett didn't speak up I prompted, "Garrett?"

"Why don't you get in the house and settled? Call me back and we'll finish."

Fuck no. When I got Delilah into the house I would be unavailable the rest of the night, maybe the next morning as well. My unavailability was dependent on how long it was going to take for me to pull Delilah out of her head and get her to share why she'd spent the last six hours looking like she was in extreme pain. And after that, I was taking her to bed, upon which time she was going to become intimately acquainted with what she called a belly flutter. Though if I played it right she'd get acquainted with my mouth as well.

"Tell me now, G."

"Don't freak out and kill the messenger, brother."

Nothing good came from a statement like that, therefore, I braced.

Just not enough.

"Zane's thinking about sending Kevin down to Mexico to take your back. He wants you going down to Guatemala to—"

"Fuck no."

"We need Arias and his research."

"We do and will get it. But what we're not gonna do is drag Delilah into an uncertain situation. Uncertain but dangerous."

"I told him that's what your response would be. Owen, Gabe, Kevin, and even Cooper backed me up on that. But as I said, Zane's ranting, talking about the employee handbook and mating rituals. He's in full-on beast mode and you know him. When he's on a tear you just gotta let him burn out."

Fucking Zane and his goddamn employee handbook.

"He thinks he's funny," I returned. "But he's not."

"I seem to remember Gabe saying something along those lines. And before him, Thad, Leo, maybe even Colin. The only one Z didn't fuck with was Declan."

That was because Declan Crenshaw was a cold motherfucker. Zane was a formidable opponent; the man could and did outplay anyone who butted up against him. But Declan? The man would slit your throat in your sleep and you'd never hear him coming.

"Tell Zane that Delilah is off-limits and before you ask, that means what you think it means."

I heard Garrett sigh and Delilah inhaled a sharp breath.

Needing to get this done, I finished, "You feel me, G?"

"I feel you, brother. But I think after you think on it, you'll realize that you're a two-day drive away from ending this for your woman in a way that will free her to move on. Which means you'll be free to move on with her. You delay this, you're prolonging your end goal. Get her safe and back to Maryland."

I felt Delilah's hand come to rest on my jaw. The sensation was so overwhelming I fought to keep my body's reaction under control.

Yes, from a touch.

What the fuck?

"If you don't stop grinding your teeth you're gonna give yourself a headache," Delilah whispered.

She wasn't wrong.

"Before I let you go," Garrett started. "Don't forget to—"

"Swear on all things holy, G, don't say it."

"What? I was going to tell you not to forget to lock up and set the alarm."

"Right," I grunted. "Because I often forget to lock up."

"You haven't, but you've never had your head full of beautiful woman before."

Delilah's hand fell away and I wanted to punch my friend for making an inappropriate conversation uncomfortable.

"You know you're on speaker and she can hear you, right?"

"I'm fairly positive your woman's seen herself in a mirror and knows she's a beautiful woman."

"Garrett—"

"Touchy. Touchy. Get inside and lock up. I'll check in later."

The line disconnected and I vaguely wondered when Garrett turned into a mini-Zane. But those thoughts were fleeting. I did have a beautiful woman to get inside the house.

I scanned the courtyard then settled my gaze on Delilah, which I purposefully had not done while I was talking to Garrett. As soon as my eyes hit hers they demanded all of my attention, something I couldn't give her while we were sitting out in the open but something I couldn't prevent myself from giving, either.

"Ready?"

"Yeah."

I reached into the backseat to grab her pack, the lightness reminding me mine was much heavier than hers.

"Can you carry mine into the house or do you want to switch?"

"I can carry yours."

Yep, Delilah had spent six hours pulling into herself. The woman sounded more defeated now than she did when I found her.

"Wait for me, I'll come around."

I opened the door and the muggy humidity hit me. Overcast skies and it smelled like rain mixed with the sweet smell of citrus. I took in all the shrubs lining the driveway. Smaller flowery bushes gave way to taller bushes attempting to camouflage the six-foot cinderblock wall that fenced in the property. The wall offered some protection but not much. I could easily scale the wall which meant someone else could, too.

By the time I made it to Delilah's side I had her pack unzipped and was rooting through the contents until my hand hit on the Glock I'd hidden at the bottom. Her sandaled feet hit the concrete pavers and the sight had my insides clutching. Back in Mazatlán, I hadn't taken into consideration she was wearing flip-flops. Which meant I dragged her behind me, running in goddamn sandals.

"Myles?"

"Come on, let's get inside."

Delilah astutely took me in and even though we didn't have time for her studious perusal I allowed it until I didn't, then I tagged her hand and slowly, carefully pulled her to the portico very aware she was in crappy shoes and was carrying a heavy pack.

"Take this." I racked the slide, chambering a bullet before I held out the Glock. "Remember there is no safety, the gun is ready to fire. Barrel pointed down until you're ready to use it."

"Ready to use it?" she squeaked, taking the weapon.

"Just a precaution. I need to clear the house and while I

do that, you're gonna wait for me by the door. No one should be inside. If someone is, shoot them."

I hated the way her eyes flared as the fear crept in, but I had no choice. Her safety was more important than me sheltering her emotions.

I punched in the code to unlock the door, heard the deadbolt disengage, and asked, "Ready?"

"Yeah."

Shaky and full of concern. I hated that, too.

"Everything's gonna be fine, Delilah. Get behind me and follow me in."

"Right," she murmured and I pushed open the door.

Sterile, was my first thought.

Stark white walls, tinted concrete flooring, chrome accents, ultra-modern furniture. The only color in the large room was navy blue. My gaze went beyond the living room to a large glass table with six upholstered navy blue chairs that delineated the dining area. Beyond the table was the kitchen, navy cabinets, white countertops.

Boring as fuck but thankfully the living space was one large rectangle with no place to hide.

"Back to the wall. Keep my pack on."

Delilah did as I asked and with seconds to spare I punched in the alarm code and stopped the beeping. Once I had the door shut, locked, and the alarm reengaged, I turned back to the freaked-out woman looking around the room.

"Two bedrooms, two baths, four closets, and the indoor pool area," I rattled off the house specs. "It won't take me but five minutes, baby. If you hear something you don't like, get back in the car and drive away and call the office. If someone comes into this room, you shoot. No thoughts, Delilah, shoot them. If someone comes through the front door shoot them."

"Okay."

"Okay," I repeated. "Be back."

I tamped down my need to keep her with me and forced myself to focus. Room by room I cleared the house. The bedrooms were no less boring. The bathrooms were small, the closets filled with linens and provisions. It wasn't until I made my way into the indoor pool area that the house held some appeal. The pool was small but inviting. However, it was the warm tropical feel that made it spectacular. The blue theme continued to this room, but the multi-hued tiles on the wall gave the illusion the water danced up the walls. Soft lighting and potted ferns added to the ambiance.

Delilah was going to love this room.

On that thought, I made my way back to the living room. She was right where I'd left her; wild, fear-soaked eyes snapped to me as I entered the room. The relief was instantaneous; everything about her calmed.

And after six hours of being in her head, unable to hide her doubts, I needed to see that. But moreover, she needed to recognize it.

"How you feelin', Delilah?"

"Better now that you're back."

Perfect.

She was making this too easy.

"Why do you think that is?"

Cute lines formed between her brows and her head tilted ever so slightly when she said, "You came back."

"Yeah, I came back. Did you think I was going to leave you?"

"No."

"But you did when I first met you. You asked me not to leave you. You didn't trust me and thought I was going to drop you off somewhere. I didn't."

Those lines between her brows got deeper and her body went on alert. Her gaze also dropped to the bite mark she left.

"I didn't know you then."

"Right but you know me now. You trust me to keep my word."

"I do but I don't understand why we're talking about this."

Very aware she was standing with my pack still on her back and my extra gun in her hand I continued.

"We're talking about this because I warned you, you had five hours to think on things. That turned into six. And during those six hours, I watched you struggle. I let you have that knowing when we got here and it was safe for me to do so, I'd make that struggle worth it for you. So tell me, what'd you come up with?"

"I…um…can we sit down?"

"Nope. Right now we're getting this straight. Tell me, Delilah, what were you thinking about?"

"Can I at least put this down?" She waved the gun in her hand, careful to keep it pointed in a safe direction.

"Nope. Want you armed. Want you to know that you are fully capable of protecting yourself. You don't need me for anything. You got the keys to the car, a phone to call for help, you have a Glock in your hand, and if you can figure out how to assemble it you've got my rifle on your back. You have everything you need to protect yourself. You can walk away at any time and take care of yourself. Yet until I came back into the room you didn't feel safe."

"You are more capable than I am," she snapped.

"I am, but that's not why you were relieved."

"I don't get the point you're trying to make."

"My point is, since I found you I've given you choices. Yet you've chosen me. You chose to trust me. You chose to believe in me. You chose to stay with me. I'm asking you to forget whatever's clouding your mind and keep choosing me."

From across the room, I watched Delilah jerk in surprise, then I watched the tenseness creep in.

Her eyes bore into mine and I impatiently waited for her to make her choice.

This would be the last one she'd have to make. After this, I wouldn't ever again stand across the room removed from her, putting her on the spot to force an answer. But I needed this. I needed to know that she was choosing me of her own free will. That everything I'd been feeling since I first saw her picture and definitely after I met her was real.

I needed her to choose me.

"You don't understand," she whispered.

"Then educate me."

"I don't know how to do this. I don't connect with people. I've had three boyfriends. I'm in my thirties and I've slept with three men. All of them broke up with me. All of them touting the same reasons—I'm cold and distant. I was not torn up when any of them left me. I felt nothing. Not when I was dating them, not during sex, and not after they broke up with me."

It was hard but I ignored the pain that inflicted.

"Baby—"

"That's what I was thinking about. I wasn't struggling, I was remembering. I have nothing to give."

Right, that was bullshit.

"Seems to me when I have my mouth on you, you know how to connect in a big way."

"No," she denied. "That's you. *You* know how to connect. And besides, you're a good kisser and I get lost in the moment."

"You ever get lost in the moment with any of those three other guys?"

My stomach tightened in preparation for her answer. I didn't know which would be worse, Delilah telling me she hadn't which meant she'd never had a taste of something good, or that she had and I wouldn't have the honor of being the first to give her sweet.

"No."

"Right. Your belly ever flutter when you were with them?"

"No."

Thank fuck.

"You ever turn to them and burrow in when life kicked you in the teeth?"

"No."

"Two days and two kisses. That's what it took for you to pull down that wall. Six hours to rebuild it. I told you I was gonna fight to keep hold of what you gave and if you get rid of the garbage in your head you'll remember you

RILEY EDWARDS

gave it free and clear and admitted I was putting your heart back together.

"If I had something to give I would give it to you," she whispered.

As sure as if she'd sunk a blade into my heart I felt those words.

That was all I needed to walk across the room and end the standoff so that's what I did. And when I got to Delilah I reached for her right hand and took the Glock. I dropped the magazine and racked the slide to clear the chamber, heard the bullet clatter on the floor, and didn't bother to pick it up. Instead, I shoved the now-empty gun into the waistband of my cargos and the magazine in my pocket, pulled my heavy pack off her shoulders, and explained what was going to happen.

"I got enough to give for the both of us. But I say that, knowing you're wrong. You've got something to give and you've been bottling it up for so long that when it finally explodes there's gonna be so much of it I'm gonna happily drown in it. Until then, all I need is for you to keep trusting *me*, keep choosing *me*, and believe in *me*."

Those hazel eyes flashed and panic seeped in.

"And when this is over?"

"When what's over?"

"Abrams and Tamir and BZ Systems. When all of this is over and I get to go home what happens then?"

"When *we* get to go home," I corrected. "I say this cautiously, Delilah, but you've got nothing to go back to in Virginia. The choice is yours like it's always been, but I want you coming back to Maryland with me. But you have to want that, and I have until Abrams is taken down to convince you that coming home with me is the right place, the only place you wanna be. If I haven't successfully done that, then when we get back I'll keep at you Delilah until you know down to your soul that choosing me will buy you a lifetime of happiness."

Her frame went solid and panic turned into fright.

"She lied to you," I bit out. "Everything she told you was utter shit. All of it. How she made you feel was shit. I get you're scared. I get you've got doubts. This is where the trust comes into play. This is where you believe me when I say you are safe. Physically and mentally you're totally and completely safe with me."

We were standing close enough that I could hear the short, choppy breaths coming out in fast puffs. Her frame was rigid, arms hanging loose at her sides.

So close.

Not close enough.

And I had a feeling I'd never be close enough.

I'd always want more.

"I trust you."

The words that meant everything to me.

"Good, baby. Now kiss me, Delilah."

She didn't kiss me. Her hands came up and she framed my face before she attacked my mouth.

Fucking perfect.

I let her have her kiss for approximately five seconds then I pushed her tongue back into her mouth and took over.

She tasted like cinnamon and sadness. The first I liked, the second I would work my ass off to abolish.

The kiss went from wet to heated to deep and claiming. Delilah moaned and my cock jerked to life reminding me we were nowhere near a bed and we needed to be.

RILEY EDWARDS

I broke the kiss and my cock stiffened further when Delilah leaned closer and made a disgruntled noise that sounded like it came from the back of her throat. A cross between a frustrated growl and sexy mew.

Oh yeah, we needed a bed.

Delilah's hand fell away, I grabbed it and started for the small hall that led to both bedrooms. I veered right, then we were in the master. While Delilah was taking in the room with wide-eyed wonder I closed and locked the door, divested myself of both backpacks, walked to the nightstand, pulled her Glock out of my pants, and set it down. Next was the magazine in my pocket and my holstered Sig.

When I turned around my breath arrested.

Full stop.

Delilah's hair still fell well below her shoulders and right then it hung loose in front of her, the tips skimming the bottom of her full breasts. I was happy I hadn't attempted to guess her cup size, I would've been wrong. I wasn't a woman but I suspected a too-small bra didn't feel all that great. Her cheeks were pink and the pretty blush dipped down to her chest. Her lips were swollen from our brief kiss.

"You're beautiful," I said on my way to her. "Every night I would look at your picture and ask you where you were."

Her eyelids grew heavy, her lips parted, the blush deepened. When I got close I didn't wait; hell, I didn't even pause before I hauled her close, folded my arms around her, and dipped down to take her mouth.

It took less time to pull those sexy-as-fuck groans from her. Then we were moving. Mouths still connected,

I backed us to the side of the bed. I let go of Delilah only to pull the sundress she was wearing over her head which also, unfortunately, necessitated breaking the kiss.

Delilah let out a surprised cry.

My mouth slammed back onto hers, and even faster than the last time she was into it. Her hands yanked at my shirt, then dove under and started roaming. My hands went to her ass and were met with ruffles. Delilah melted closer, and since I was a sucker for the noises she made, when her whimper slid down my throat I ended the kiss just to hear disgruntled mewl.

She gave it and my cock twitched.

She gave more when her lips hit my throat. That lasted a good long while, her working my neck—licking, sucking, grazing her teeth, groaning against my skin. Delilah in my arms, her mouth on me, sexy-as-fuck-all sounds coming faster and faster, my cock at a near-constant throb. I disengaged and it was my turn to give back, doing the same to her until her hands came out of my shirt and slid into my hair while she arched. I took that as a demand for more so I went in for another taste, only this time lower. The tube-top-style bra was pulled up exposing the bottom swells of her tits.

Fuck, yeah. I bent and ran my tongue along the bottom curve of one then moved to the other. Shifted lower and ran my tongue down her belly until I encountered fabric. My hand on her ass glided up, and up, and up. It was mid-back before I met skin.

Pale blue, up to her belly button, granny panties. I pulled back to get a better look and even in my present state of turned-the-fuck-on I smiled. I quickly turned her so I could see the back. What looked to be a string of elastic gathered the satin material between her ass cheeks. Accentuating two round globes. Ugly as fuck ruffles went from hip to ass crack.

Start to finish they were hideous and weirdly sexy as fuck.

But they had to go, so they went.

I rolled the top down until fabric gathered at her hips, then I yanked them over her ass, let the material slide down her legs and fall to the floor. Delilah stepped out of the highly offensive undergarment and I stood riveted. Smooth, unblemished, creamy flesh. My hands went to her hips then split one went high, pushing her down until her forearms were on the bed. The other moved to grip a firm cheek, then my mouth followed. I had an overwhelming urge to mark the flawless skin under my lips so I did that too and sucked hard. With a mouthful of Delilah's ass, her moaning filling the air, I went to my knees.

My mouth disengaged and once again I was captivated by the sight before me. Craving hollowed out my insides. Desire snapped my focus to the pretty, wet pink folds before me. Hunger burned for a taste.

So I did that, too.

I dove forward, let the rest of the world fall away, and devoured Delilah's pussy. My tongue dipped and fucked deep.

The taste of her coated my tongue—unbelievably sweet. Her thighs shook, her moans now continual and growing louder by the second. I lifted her right leg and shoved it up and forward until her knee was resting on the side of the mattress. Fully open to me. Ass and pussy. I wanted both.

"Myles."

Impatient and needy.

Fuck, yeah.

I dipped my thumb into her soaked pussy and my cock wept.

"Myles."

Breathy and insistent.

And just in case I missed what she wanted she rocked back.

Oh, yeah.

Fuck, yeah.

I pulled my thumb free, gave her back my mouth, and circled her tight hole.

"Oh my God." Delilah's hips pushed back to greet my tongue and circled deeper. "Holy shit. Myles."

I barely pushed the tip of my thumb in her ass but that was all it took for Delilah to ignite. She hitched her leg higher, bucked back in a hungry attempt to get more, and when I reached around to tweak her clit the burn that had sparked to life combusted.

"More," she panted.

Oh, yeah.

I gave her more of my thumb, tongue, and worked her clit faster.

"I think I'm gonna…" she trailed off.

There was no thinking about it. With my thumb lodged deep in her ass, my mouth eating her pussy, she screamed her orgasm.

It tasted un-*fucking*-believable.

It sounded just as good.

When she stopped trembling I surged to my feet, flipped her to her back, yanked the tube-top up, took half a second to appreciate her full tits and pebbled nipples, then dropped my head to taste those too. I freed my stiff cock and fisted it. Oh, yeah, it was weeping. A steady bead of moisture leaked and coated the head. I sucked a nipple into my mouth and stroked. I moved to the other side, stroked faster, and dragged the head of my cock over her clit.

"Inside," she groaned.

I dipped lower, glided the tip up and down her slit, and asked, "Birth control?"

"No."

Shit.

"Fuck it."

I surged forward and in one hard thrust, I was rooted deep.

Rooted.

Tight, sleek, and wet.

Un-*fucking*-believable.

Delilah's back came off the bed and her legs went around my hips.

"More."

My gaze roamed. All of her laid out in front of me. Dirty blonde hair fanned out on the comforter. Hazy, hooded, pretty hazel eyes staring at me full of hunger. Rosy nipples peaked in desire.

"You feel connected?"

"Yes."

It sounded like a hiss.

"You feel what this is?"

I pulled out and pushed back in.

"Yes."

"I wanna hear it, baby. With my cock rooted deep. The

taste of you still in my mouth. I wanna hear you tell me you know what you gave me."

"I know what I gave you."

"I'm gonna take your ass again, you up for that?"

"Yes."

Fucking hell.

I bent forward, lifted her up, climbed onto the bed, then twisted and fell to my back.

"How'd you do that?"

Full of breathy wonder.

I wasn't going to tell her that she weighed less than my backpack when it was fully loaded with gear. I wasn't going to clue her in that I was bigger, stronger, and could overpower her. Instead, my hands went to her hips and I slid her up my shaft and pushed her back down.

"Ride me, baby."

The shutters started to drop as panic neared.

Hell no.

One hand left her hip, traveling up her back until I had a fist full of hair, and I yanked her forward until I had a nipple between my lips. Her body jolted and instinct took over. She tentatively glided up and dropped back down. I sucked hard and she went faster. I brought the fingers of my right hand to her lips. They parted and she licked, then practically swallowed them when she took them into her mouth.

Good Christ.

I pulled them free, reached behind her, and toyed with her hole until she was grinding and rocking, taking me so close to the edge I needed her to finish. I dipped a finger into her ass and she went wild. She threw her head back, her body bowed, and she rode my cock.

"More," she panted.

Christ.

I fingered her ass, going deeper and harder.

"Let go, baby," I pleaded.

"So close," she whined and ground down.

Fucking finally her pussy clamped around my cock and my vision blurred. Not since I was a teenager had I had to count backwards from a thousand to stop from blowing but right then I started at a million and started counting. The tighter her pussy clenched the harder it became until I could take not another second.

"Off," I growled but didn't wait for her to comply. I yanked her off my cock, found her hand, and wrapped it around my shaft. "Jack me off."

Her tiny hand fisted my cock and stroked as I pumped into her fist.

"Fucking, fuck," I grunted and shot off.

Euphoria swept over me chased by pure ecstasy.

Delilah's head was bent forward watching in fascination as she milked stream after stream of come out of my cock. She kept stroking even after the last of it hit my stomach.

"You drained it, baby."

I put my hand over hers to slow her down and suddenly her eyes snapped to mine.

I braced for the fallout that would necessitate another talk about where we were at and where we were going when instead I saw nothing but sweet wonder.

She glanced back down, and when her gaze came back to mine it was almost smug.

"I did that," she whispered.

"Fuck, yeah, you did that."

Alarm hit and it was time to move this along.

"Shower, baby, then we'll check out the pool and have a swim."

"I don't have a suit."

"Baby." I smiled. "I think we're past a bathing suit."

Her head tilted to the side, confusion clear. It was cute a fuck.

"I'm thinking after the last hour's festivities you can handle straight," I started. "I've had my mouth between your thighs. And as a side note, the way you sucked my fingers down your throat I'm seriously looking forward to the time when those fingers are replaced with my cock. Knew you were good with your mouth, but fuck, baby, you swallowed them. You're sitting on me naked with a fistful of my come and what's not dripping in your hand is on my stomach. I've finger-fucked your ass and as another side note, I wanna claim that with my cock, too. I want all of you. Everything there is to take. Every way a man can claim his woman I'm gonna take and that includes my cock up your ass while you're fingering your pussy for me." I paused only because Delilah shivered and her eyes turned lazy yet they were full of fire. "You want that, Delilah? You wanna feel my cock in your ass?"

"Yes."

Fucking brilliant.

"You wanna feel me claim you as mine?"

"Yes."

Fuck, yeah.

"Now, do you think you need a suit to go swimming, or are we beyond that?"

"Beyond that," she rapped out.

"Good, baby. Swing off so I can clean you up."

She didn't swing off. She kept her eyes glued to mine.

"I did that," she repeated in a whisper.

My gut tightened at her tone.

"Delilah, you're beautiful. You're sexy. You feel fucking phenomenal. And with the slightest push, you're fucking wild. Two seconds after I got inside of you I was ready to explode. So, yeah, baby, all of that is for you."

Sadness prevailed and I felt that skewer my heart.

"She lied. They all lied. It wasn't me."

"No, Delilah it wasn't you."

"The whole time I was connected. It was you and me. I felt it."

"Good, I'm glad you felt it."

She blinked and her head lulled forward.

"It wasn't me," she whispered again.

I curled up, wrapped my arms around her, and rolled us to the side. Front to front I held her close. She shoved her face into my neck and for the second time, I felt the swell of pride she'd turned to me for comfort.

If today proved nothing else, it was that I was going to fight tooth and nail to bring Delilah home with me—where she belonged.

CHAPTER 14

We didn't get to swim but we did shower together.

Nothing happened but at the same time, *everything* happened.

Something deep inside of me cracked open, or perhaps it mended.

I stood silently under the spray while Myles washed the evidence of his orgasm off my stomach. He washed my arms, my chest, between my legs, thighs, calves, feet, every inch of me he washed. He shampooed my hair, rinsed it, conditioned it, and rinsed it. It wasn't a long shower but a lot happened.

So much happened, I was locked in my head and Myles gave me the time to sort through my thoughts.

That was when *everything* happened.

It was a rebirth, reinvention, restoration, reincarnation—and this recreation was a better version.

I wasn't baggage, I never had been.

A child wasn't meant to sit quietly and act like a piece of furniture more than a human being. They were meant to be loved. A young adult was meant to be taught and shown grace, not turned away. A daughter wasn't meant to be discarded when she was of majority; she was meant to be cared for.

It was not me who'd committed those heinous acts, it was my mother. She was at fault, not me.

So the rebirth began.

And it happened in the most peculiar of ways —with sex.

Whoever said sex wasn't the answer had only been partially correct. It was sex with the *right* person that was the answer. It was not the driving of his cock. It wasn't the orgasm. It was the connection. The intimacy. When caution is thrown into the wind, and the most vulnerable parts of you are exposed. When you give yourself over to someone—truly and completely give everything inside of you to another person—that is everything.

It's healing in a way I never knew.

It brought clarity.

It relieved deep-seated insecurities that lied to me every day and told me I was broken. Self-doubt that had turned ugly, lying to me, telling me I was a loner who wasn't good enough to find companionship—friendship or otherwise.

So many lies I told myself over the years. So many lies I convinced myself were true.

And, yes, I learned all of that during sex.

I learned that I could open up and connect.

When it was right.

When I felt safe.

Yes, sex was the answer I needed.

After our shower, Myles dried me off and we found

the house had come fully stocked—*thank God*—along with toiletries a fluffy white robe was folded neatly in the cabinet with the towels. Myles had barely wrapped a towel around his waist when his phone rang.

That brought us to now. Myles in a towel with his fantastic chest and torso on display. I'd be remiss if I didn't mention his back and shoulders that left me wondering which view was better. His front won out only because it included his handsome face and great smile. Though, the back included his ass which was high and tight—in a nutshell, *spectacular*.

Myles scowled at his phone before he answered.

There was a series of grunts before Myles said. "That'd be cool, she'd appreciate that." Then he paused and went on, "Yeah, I'll put it on speaker."

He pulled his phone from his ear and did that while saying, "It's Zane. Evette's there. She wants to talk to you."

My heart soared then plummeted.

"Is she mad?" I whispered.

"Why would I be mad?" a woman's voice asked.

I gave Myles big eyes before they narrowed.

"Sorry, baby, I thought you knew I had it on speaker already."

There were a few masculine chuckles but only one female giggle.

Two hours ago I might not have been able to pluck up the strength to talk to Evette. In the beginning, after Myles had rescued me I'd wanted to speak to her but that was before I knew what happened to her and Gabe because of me. Before I knew she'd thought *I* was trying to kill her or at least part of the planning.

"Because I scared you and then almost got you and Gabe killed," I told her.

"BZ Systems tried to kill Gabe, not you. And just so you know, we found what they want from you."

"Alejandro Arias's research," I surmised.

"For sure they want that. But they also want your laptop."

"Tamir Cohen has my laptop."

"Well, that's what they want. From what Garrett was able to find out and Tex confirmed…wait, you know who Tex is, right?"

"I know of him, yes."

"Okay, so Tex confirmed that before you sent me the first email you loaded a program onto your computer to not only mask your IP but also send any emails from that machine through different proxy servers. But someone loaded a patch rendering your application useless. That same person also gave Bryan Zaslow access to your machine. He was in your machine when Tamir nabbed it. But just because the network connection was lost doesn't mean the breadcrumbs aren't there. Because the laptop was taken offline and has not been put back online, Bryan has not been able to delete his footprint."

"BZ Systems has a mole at Abrams?"

"Yep."

"Then why do they keep losing contracts?"

"Apparently this is recent, after they lost the radar contract. But then they found the good stuff, the research you intercepted. That's what happened, right?"

She sounded hopeful and proud and a touch nosy.

"Yes, with Alejandro's resignation he'd also attached all of his research. He didn't have any idea he was sending an unsecured email. I downloaded the files then took them off the network so my colleagues wouldn't find them."

"Any idea who the mole could be?"

Again Evette sounded hopeful.

"No. I wasn't close to anyone. I went in, did my job, and left. I couldn't even tell you who was married and who had kids."

"It's time to get the show on the road."

That was Zane.

"Zane." Myles's voice was an angry growl.

"I knew you'd have issues with my decision. Hell, I'm not happy with it either, but this is our only option. Kevin is flying down. He'll meet you in Guatemala in two days."

Myles's body went taunt—totally still. Then a tremble started in his hand that slowly worked its way up his arm until he was vibrating with anger. The air around us turned stifling, foul, menacing, and for the first time since he'd found me, I saw him truly angry.

"You found him?" I asked.

"Abrams did."

"How?"

My question was drowned out by Myles's very pissed-off outburst.

"Abrams found him and you want me to take Delilah straight to him, what the fuck?"

"Kevin is on his way to the airport. He'll be there tomorrow morning. Your choice is, leave Delilah there and get on the road first thing in the morning or take her with."

Fear infused my body quick and fast, taking over all rational thoughts.

"You can't leave me here alone," I pleaded.

"Can Cooper—"

"Cooper is right now trying to talk his brother off the ledge. Jaxon is pissed as all fuck that his wife and child have been targeted by some rock-throwing-motherfucker. I got all the men watching their women and children until we can suss this fucker out. Kevin was helping Garrett but I need him down there to take Delilah's back. I feel where you're at. I *know* where you're at and I wouldn't make this call if it wasn't the last resort."

"We have other resources," Myles returned.

"We do. But it will take time to get Ghost and his crew or Wolf and his team mobilized and up to speed. Ghost, Fletch, Coach, Truck, and Beatle are all making moves to get themselves freed up in case you need them. Holly-wood and Kassie are out of town. Blade's out because he and Wendy are on a cruise. If I send all five of them to South America and shit pops off here with one of the five things I'm juggling I leave all three teams vulnerable with no backup. Fish had offered to come down but you know how he feels about leaving Bryn and his boy alone, which means he's gotta stop off in Texas to drop them off, which means more time."

"Fuck!" Myles exploded.

Zane went on, "Kevin's bringing one of Tex's locators for Delilah. It's in a watch. You're chipped and Kevin will have a tracker. This should be an in and out. With Delilah there to talk to Arias, it should go faster. Grab his research and offer the man protection. He doesn't want it, then he walks and you bring back what he has."

"And if Abrams and Tamir are there?" Myles snarled.

"Then kill them and take the research."

I felt an unpleasant quiver rush over me.

Myles turned slightly. His eyes came to mine then bore deep. His right eye twitched and his jaw clenched.

He was not angry, pissed, or mad. It went far beyond that. Way far beyond.

"It's gonna be fine," I told him.

His body tensed further.

"You know everything's gonna be fine."

I didn't think it was possible but he looked even more furious.

"Yeah, baby, is it gonna be fine? Me taking you straight into the lion's den. You realize that's what's gonna happen. I'm gonna drive you straight back to Tamir. There is no doubt he's on his way to Guatemala to grab Arias."

"Then we better hurry and get there before him."

Wrong thing to say.

"That motherfucker took you," he roared and I hoped the house was well-insulated and the neighboring houses were unoccupied. "Then he left you for dead."

"No, Myles, then he left me for you to pick up. And you did. You were close and you came and got me. As long as I'm with you I know I'll be okay. The only time I won't be is if you leave me by myself. I couldn't take that, I can't be locked in another house. Not even one as nice as this. I can't do it, Myles; you have to take me with you."

His hand came up and tore through his hair.

"Fuck," he clipped. "Fucking shit. We'll leave in the morning."

"Now for the bad news. The POTUS has requested a meeting. A civilian DoD contractor that works at the Pentagon somehow managed a face-to-face with Graham. The president didn't like what he heard and now he's requesting a sit-down with us. To his extreme displeasure,

I have put him off a week. That gives us seven days to have this shit wrapped up and us at the White House."

There was a brief pause that did not give me enough time to process that the President of the United States had called Zane Lewis.

"The seriously fucked news is, Linc's brand new SUV is fucked. Side of it keyed and four rocks on the hood. It is of my opinion that out of my brother and his wife, the fucker chose the right person to fuck with. Linc's got patience and uses his time to plot and plan. Jasmin shoots first and sorts her shit later. But now that's three team members in three fucking days and everyone is dangling by a thread."

"Jesus."

"Yeah, you should probably start praying, brother. Shit's getting ready to go nuclear and this time I'm not sure I can control the blast zone. Get that research and get you and Delilah home. I need you here."

The line disconnected and I stood there stunned.

"Who's Jasmin?"

"Lincoln is Zane's brother. He's married to Jasmin. Linc and Jasmin are both on the Red Team. They have twin sons, Asher and Robbie."

"She's a mom and shoots people then sorts her shit out later?"

"She's a badass who doesn't take shit from anyone, a great teammate, loyal, and competent. Now that she's a mom she takes badass to a whole new level. She won't shoot someone who threatens one of her boys. She'd do that up close and personal and slit their throat."

"Seriously?"

"Yep."

My chest turned tight but instead of feeling scared or horrified this unknown Jasmin would kill someone, I felt happy for her boys. They had a momma bear to protect them.

Moving along.

"What's a locator and what does chipped mean?"

"Tracking devices. Over the years Tex has provided the teams with trackers, and not just Zane's. He also works with SEAL teams, Delta units, private security companies. He sets them in jewelry and monitors them. Though Garrett monitors ours. As for chipped, I have the tracker embedded in my arm. One too many times shit's gone sideways and it's taken time to find a location. Tex wasn't a hundred percent how long the capsule would last so only I got one. I'm the test dummy. If it works, then the rest of the guys will get them. But the women all wear Tex's jewelry."

"And he sent a watch for me."

"Yes. But baby, it only works if you're wearing it. So it's a safety net but not a hundred percent."

A net was better than nothing.

I'd take it.

"Zane knows President Graham?"

"Yes. Before Tom Anderson left office, Anderson introduced them."

"Zane knows former President Anderson, too?"

Myles cracked half a smile and answered, "Yes, Zane and Tom are good friends. Tom's daughter, Erin, married my teammate Colin. And Jasmin is Tom's niece. Before he left office we did a lot of contract work for the government. Things that they had to be able to deny knowledge of. As I said, Tom introduced Zane to President Graham.

Graham hasn't been in office all that long but this is the first time he's requested a face-to-face with the team."

I wish I would've known how connected Zane was in the beginning. If I had, none of this would've happened. I would've taken all of the information I'd found straight to Zane and he could've taken it to the POTUS. I didn't trust the regular government channels because Aviv had connections, he had DoD contracts, and not being versed in the who's who in Washington I was afraid I'd take my intel to the wrong person. So, I played a dangerous game and almost lost. Hell, I did lose, but Myles found me before that loss became the six-feet-under kind.

"I wonder who at Abrams is working for BZ Systems. And why does Bryan care so much if Aviv finds out? Competitors do that crap all the time. Corporate espionage is commonplace."

"Because unlike say, Microsoft or Dell being infiltrated, Aviv will employ his mercenaries. Microsoft would allow the court system to handle any breach. Abrams will send Tamir to kill the person. Zaslow knows this, so he wants that laptop. Though if he were doing more than poking around your machine and accessing the network, getting your laptop doesn't do dick to save him."

"We have a lot of security protocols on our laptops. Layers and layers of protection to prevent something like this from happening. Any system can be hacked, it's just a matter of time and expertise of the hacker. BZ Systems doesn't employ anyone with that capability. Part of what I did was research our competitors' tech teams. Bryan didn't have the money to outsource the work, so it makes sense he'd go at it from the inside. It would be cheaper."

"You weren't close to any of your co-workers?"

I shrugged and answered, "Couldn't connect, remember? Not with anyone. I used to have friends outside of work, but they all slipped away because there was no real bond to keep the friendships going. And employees, they come and go. I never got close to anyone at work because I knew there was a possibility they or I would get a different job and leave so I didn't bother."

Myles's eyes went soft and he murmured, "I hate that for you, Delilah."

It was on the tip of my tongue to lie. To tell him it was fine, but it wasn't.

"I was lonely. I just didn't know how to stop it. I had some friends but I'm a workaholic and the more plans I had to decline, or worse had to cancel after I committed, the less they called, and when that started to happen I felt them slipping away. To protect myself, I closed down and stopped answering their calls altogether. I thought that if it was me who walked away from the friendship it would hurt less. But it didn't and in the end, I was all alone and lonely so I worked more and became a total loner."

"I *really* fucking hate that for you."

There it was Myles giving me more. Concreting my rebirth. He didn't feel sorry for me; he simply hated I'd lived through it.

And I hated it too.

But I'd been reborn, reinvented, restored, reincarnated, and I wasn't going to let my second chance go to waste.

* * *

"Dinner was good, baby." Myles broke our kiss to tell me.

We were naked in the pool. He was standing in chest-deep water and my legs were wrapped around his waist, my arms draped over his shoulders. Myles's hands were on my bottom and his fingertips were kneading. It felt great. All of it.

This was after we'd gotten dressed. After he'd pulled the pieces of his rifle out of his pack and assembled it. After I'd taken the only pair of undies I had and hand-washed them in the sink. At which time Myles wandered into the bathroom to tell me they were the ugliest things he'd ever seen but he found them sexy and never wanted me to get rid of them. I didn't understand that but filed it away as being a guy thing and moved on. I cooked dinner and he made calls. We ate, cleaned up, then he took us into the pool room—bringing our packs and all three weapons—and locked us in.

"It's near impossible to mess up chicken, rice, and broccoli."

"Well then, thankfully the impossible didn't happen," he teased.

I liked that. No, I loved that even though he was on edge about us leaving in the morning he still had it in him to tease and smile.

"Thank you for not leaving me behind."

"We're not talking about that right now," he said as he walked us to the side. "Right now I'm gonna fuck you. After that, I'm gonna take us back to the shower, rinse you off, eat your pussy, fuck you again, and if I still have it in me, get your mouth around my cock. We'll see how that last part goes."

I shivered. Then his lips were so close to mine I could

feel his breath feather over them when he said, "Reach down and guide me in, baby."

Another shiver as I reached between us and did as he asked.

The head of his dick slipped inside and he went back to ordering, "Arm back up and hold on tight."

I did that too.

With one solid thrust, he slid deep.

After that, he gave me the best gift anyone had ever given me. He didn't hide a single emotion from me. His eyes rolled to the ceiling and when they came back to me they were hooded. His face was gentle like I was precious. His arms were tight around me like he never wanted to let me go. His movements were sure and strong but he wasn't fucking me. We weren't having sex. We weren't even making love.

We were fully connected.

And later when we lay spent in bed, Myles pulled me close so my head rested on his chest, my arm over his stomach, his arm tight around me, he kept that connection.

Oh, and for the record, he'd rallied and finally got my mouth wrapped around his dick, but he didn't let me finish him off. He decided he wanted a different ending, one that was extremely happy for both of us.

CHAPTER 15

"Whoa, this is the biggest mall I've ever seen," Delilah breathed.

I wasn't a mall kinda guy. None of my clothes since I was old enough to purchase them had come from a mall, and it was a safe bet to say I hadn't entered a mall in the last ten years.

"I'll have to take your word for it. Do you see any store that'll work?"

Delilah looked around, making sure the brim of her hat obscured her face, and I hoped like fuck she found a place that worked. This bitch was four stories and I didn't want to spend the next four hours tramping around a mall after being on the road for eight hours, and if Delilah was up for it, another eight hours after this. No, scratch that; I didn't want to spend four hours in a mall, period.

"Every American name brand I can think of is in here."

"Babe, Mexico City is a wealthy, major metropolitan area. Population eight-point-eight million. That's higher than New York City."

"I know that," Delilah snapped. "I'm just surprised most everything's in English."

She was correct about that. It was one of the reasons we were at a huge, four-story mall, taking an arguably stupid risk being caught on surveillance cameras.

"There's fine." She pointed to a store that had a row of mannequins in the windows wearing clothes meant for a woman twenty years her senior, which wouldn't have mattered if they weren't so unattractive.

I glanced around, saw a storefront that was two-stories tall painted black—Abercrombie & Fitch. I recognized the name but didn't know fuckall about the store.

"What about that?"

"Abercrombie is too expensive."

Perfect.

"Do they have clothes you like?"

"Sure, everyone loves—"

"Let's go," I cut her off.

"Myles—"

"Baby, you're not wearing clothes that are too old for my mother to wear."

Her eyes slid from the boutique back to Abercrombie and I felt it, she was gearing up to argue.

"You got one pair of the be-all-end-all grannie-panties, one tube top bra, one pair of sleep shorts, one tee, one dress, and a pair of flip flops. I reckon getting you kitted on a couple days' worth of clothes is gonna take a minute so can we please get on that and get back on the road?"

"Fine, but I'll warn you when all of this started I had two-thousand and some change in savings and four hundred in checking. I don't know the state of my finances or my credit at this point. So it is doubtful I'll be able to reimburse you for clothes and I know I can't afford the hotel we stayed in or the house."

Fuck. I hadn't told her about her home.

"You're checking and savings are intact and what you had is still there. But, Delilah, there wasn't much left of your apartment when Kevin and I got there. Someone had broken in—couch, bed, TVs, all trashed." I watched her face get tight, so I quickly went on to inflict the pain as fast as I could. "Your landlord had a cleaning crew go in and clear it out. Garrett said when he called to get your stuff shipped to Maryland he was told there were five boxes. He paid the back rent, the storage fee, and shipping. He hasn't opened the boxes so I don't know what was salvaged."

"Of course, someone broke in and trashed my stuff," she replied indignantly. "Whatever, it wasn't all that great anyway. It's not like I had any special family heirlooms or anything."

Come again?

"Baby, it's okay to be—"

"To be what, sad? I had nothing important or expensive. What's the worst they found, my vibrator and tampons?"

At the mention of her using a vibrator my dick twitched.

At the mention of tampons, I remembered I needed to buy condoms. We were playing a dangerous game not using protection. Something else unpleasant struck. She'd been gone two months, that was two cycles, or at least one. I couldn't bring myself to ask what she'd done to take care of that while she was with Tamir. I already wanted to rip the fucker's intestines out through his throat and it was highly likely her answer would send me over the edge. I shoved that to the back of my mind and vowed never to think about it again even if I wondered if that was why she still didn't feel clean. I wasn't a woman, but I also wasn't a moron and I understood that a woman on her period needed feminine products, and a daily shower during that time of the month would most likely be appreciated. I knew Delilah hadn't been afforded very many showers.

Tamir Cohen was a dick.

"Hey," Delilah called and I felt her hand stroke the side of my jaw. "Where'd you go?"

"I was thinking about how when I find Tamir I'm gonna gut the motherfucker for what he did to you."

"Seriously, Myles, it was just stuff. I'm not sad about it. What happened is an aggravation. One that will cost me some money to rectify but other than that, my stuff was cheap. It's no big deal."

Right.

She had no connections and no attachments.

Until now.

"Let's get you some clothes." I tagged her hand and started to walk toward Abercrombie. "Zane's paying. Actually, no, Abrams is paying since Zane will take this out of the five-hundred K Abrams paid him."

Delilah tipped her head back and smiled.

Christ.

Beautiful.

"Suddenly I feel like a shopping spree."

Thirty minutes later we walked out of the store, bags in hand. Delilah hadn't gone on a spree but she did get a few days' worth of clothing. Unfortunately, we had to carry our belongings in backpacks and those packs had to stay with us at all times.

But when we got back to Maryland, I was taking her shopping and it would be a spree. Only it wouldn't be an Abrams-sponsored event. It would be me taking care of my woman.

This would happen right after I convinced her to move in with me.

* * *

"Myles," Delilah moaned.

Christ. Hot.

"You're there, baby, let go."

Her hands parted, one going low to grab ahold of my ass, the other going high, skimming up my spine until she reached her destination and curled her fingers around my shoulder.

Her hips surged and she groaned.

"Myles."

Good Christ.

Breathy and full of wonder.

I hitched her leg higher and rode her harder.

Her back arched, her tits pressed harder against my chest, and her head tipped back.

I was done.

"Baby, let the fuck go."

My mouth took hers, my cock pounded, her legs squeezed, and fucking finally her pussy convulsed, triggering my orgasm.

Delilah stayed wrapped tight as I shot into a fucking condom. She stayed wrapped tight as I gently slid in and out. She stayed wrapped tight as I kissed down her neck, her throat, anywhere I could reach without disconnecting. She stayed wrapped tight as I naturally started to soften and had to pull out. She stayed wrapped tight when I gave her more of my weight, lowered my mouth to her ear, and licked the shell before I asked, "You good, baby?"

"I don't wanna let go."

Fuck, yeah.

"I don't want you to let go."

"Not ever, Myles. I don't ever want to let go. And that scares me."

"It shouldn't scare you."

"It doesn't scare you?"

"It guts me to say this, but I've gotta take care of this fucking condom."

Delilah's lips twitched before she smiled.

"You sound very disgruntled."

"I'm more than disgruntled. I like the feel of you bare. I like feeling you wet on my cock. I like being able to hold you when we're done and not have to get up to toss a condom. No, I fucking love those things. So, yeah, baby I'm disgruntled I gotta hit the pause button on our conversation and lose you wrapped around me so I can deal with a condom."

"When we get home, I'll get on birth control."

Home.

She said when *we* get home.

"Unlatch so I can take care of this and come back to you."

Her legs unlocked and fell away and so did her arms. I dropped a kiss on her lips before I pushed up and got out of bed.

I disposed of the condom, washed my hands, and glanced around the hotel bathroom. It was not as nice as the first two places we stayed, but it was nice.

We hadn't made it another eight hours in the car. We made it seven and stopped in Coatzacoalcos. Another waterfront touristy area on the Gulf of Mexico. I wanted to rent a beach bungalow but this wasn't a vacation and safety was the priority so we were on the top floor of a hotel. It was nice and had a great view but we wouldn't be there long enough to enjoy it. It had been dark when we arrived and would still be dark when we left in the morning.

I made it back to the bed and Delilah was exactly how I'd left her—naked, wild sex hair splayed across the pillow, faint red marks on her tits from my whiskers, and I knew if her legs were spread I'd see the same on her inner thighs. Lips puffy, face relaxed, eyes soft. She looked well-loved and thoroughly fucked.

Absolutely stunning.

"You're beautiful, Delilah."

She started to move to cover herself.

"Don't. Every part of you is beautiful." I got to the side of the bed and reached down and traced the darkest abrasion I'd left. "Every part of you is perfect but knowing it was me who marked you here, knowing how I marked you, is sexy as fuck."

My hand trailed to the other side and I watched her nipples pebble, and since that was equally sexy I bent and pulled one into my mouth until she started to squirm. Then I pulled off and went to the other and laved it with the same affection.

"Myles."

186

Needy and breathy.

That was all it took.

She'd had four lovers including me. The three before me couldn't get her off. The three before me were total dumbfucks. I wasn't going to give headspace as to the whys and wherefores of their stupidity or their lack of talent. The only thing I was going to be was grateful it was me who got to show her a side of herself she never knew existed. Delilah was sexy, beautiful, and with the tiniest provocation, she ignited and went wild. The mere fact she didn't know this about herself was a testament to how closed off she'd kept herself. It sucked. It hurt my heart she'd lived so long lonely and alone but it didn't suck it was me who now had the honor of showing her all that she could be.

In and out of bed.

She was coming home with me and once she was there she'd learn the meaning of friendship. She'd understand what bonds and connection really meant. She'd learn the beauty of commitment.

The first thirty-five years of her life might've been about isolation and being remote.

But the next thirty-five and beyond would be about in-your-face family. Loud, nosy, well-meaning, obnoxious —because Zane would be a part of her inner circle— loving, kind, loyal family.

"Myles," she called again and I lifted my head to look at her.

Hot and hungry.

Two of my favorite looks on her.

"Right here, baby."

"How many condoms do we have?"

187

Hell, yeah.

I smiled when I told her, "Eleven."

"Do you think we can make that ten?"

"You up to using your mouth?"

"Yes."

Good Christ.

"Scoot over and get on your knees."

Delilah scrambled to do my bidding.

Once I was on my back I tapped her thigh and instructed, "Swing your leg over me, mouth to my cock, ass to my face."

Her eyes flared and she hurried to do that as well.

When she was settled astride me, the view was phenomenal but when her warm, wet mouth enveloped my cock, phenomenal went straight to miraculous.

My hands went to her ass and she moaned around my cock, sending shards of pleasure up my shaft.

I dipped a finger into her pussy, gathered her excitement, and rimmed her hole.

"Gonna take your ass and pussy while you suck me off, baby."

On an upward glide, she increased suction then tongued the tip until she slid back down and took me to the back of her throat.

Oh, yeah.

Fuck, yeah.

She was down with me taking her ass and pussy while she sucked me off. Not only that but she wiggled her ass in my face as an invitation. Or maybe she was telling me to get on with it. She also seemed to get off when I talked dirty to her, which was good because I was going to take it up a notch.

I pulled her hips back, rolled up, and with a long swipe of my tongue I licked her from pussy to ass. Once she was nice and wet and losing concentration I settled her back down. Two fingers went to her clit, my thumb to her ass, and I pushed in.

The moan around my cock was fucking heaven.

"Jack me while you suck, baby." Without delay, she fisted my cock. *Spectacular.* "Christ, your mouth. Not sure what's better—you blowing me, how wet your pussy gets when you're doing it, how the harder I go at your ass the wilder you get, the feel of your hair brushing my legs as you bob." I paused and leaned slightly to the side and groaned at the sight. "Seeing your tits sway and your lips around my cock. All of it so goddamn hot I need you to stop now before I come."

I reached out and tagged a condom off the nightstand, tore it open with my teeth, and stopped toying with her pussy.

"Up, Delilah, you're gonna ride me."

My cock came out of her mouth with a pop and I seriously mourned the loss.

"Shift forward and lift up." She followed my instructions and in record time I was sheathed and guiding her down.

"Oh, God," she whispered.

Oh, God was right.

So fucking good I had to clench my jaw and close my eyes.

"Ride, Delilah."

She rode.

Hard and fast. With my hands on her hips and hers on my thighs, she slammed herself down, swiveled her hips, rocked, glided. Hard and fast and fucking wild. It took everything in me to hold on and enjoy the sounds that filled the room, enjoy the way her pussy hugged my cock, enjoy the sight before me, enjoy the feel of my woman getting the fuck off being herself, being who she'd locked away.

"Close," she whined.

"Finger your clit, Delilah."

One hand left my leg but she didn't go at her clit. She grazed my balls with her fingertips then she took them in her hand and rolled.

"Fucking hell," I groaned. "Harder."

Delilah, *my* Delilah, the woman who let go and got wild gave me harder. She fucked me harder, rolled and pulled at my balls harder, breathed harder, moaned louder.

"Other hand at your clit. Now, Delilah. I'm gonna come."

"Don't need it. Come with me." She slammed herself down, I felt her inner muscles tighten and she growled, "Now, Myles, come with me."

Good Christ.

I shot into another condom while her pussy quivered and constricted around me.

Totally spent.

Best damn orgasm of my life.

I don't know why, didn't fucking care, though I suspected it was because facing away from me, riding me hard, Delilah in full control, she gave me the last part of herself she was holding back. She'd found the confidence she didn't know she had. She'd demanded my orgasm and took her pleasure along with mine.

She'd *taken* what she wanted.

The woman who never asked for anything.

Fuck yeah, she felt secure enough with me to take and command.

Brilliant.

"Condom. Hop off."

I didn't miss her whine of irritation when she had to move.

"Hate those things," she complained, and I smiled.

"Me, too."

She rolled off and I waited until she righted herself then I kissed her before exiting the bed.

I repeated the process of ridding myself of the condom, stopping to turn off the light, and got back into bed.

Before I could tell her to, Delilah curled up close— head to my chest, arm over my stomach.

Only twice we'd slept like this but I couldn't remember a time when she wasn't next to me. It was as if the time I'd lived without her was erased and my life had begun when I first saw her.

"So," she started. "You're an ass man."

I was not.

Never before did I have an overwhelming need to claim a woman, every part of her. That wasn't to say I hadn't had anal, but it was more out of curiosity than an insistent need to take it. And I found it did nothing for me. For it to be done right, taking that part of a woman was intimate in a way I'd never wanted to be with another woman.

"Nope. Not an ass man. Long legs have always done it for me. Which, in case you're wondering, you have spectacular legs and when they're wrapped around me they're even better. After that a pretty smile, and again in case you're wondering, your smile is so fucking pretty it makes me want to work my ass off for the rest of my life, to do whatever it takes just to earn another one. After that eyes —not the color but how expressive they are. And yours say everything, every emotion you feel shines in your eyes."

Delilah burrowed closer.

I closed my eyes and relaxed, relishing in the feel of her naked body pressed against mine. Nothing between us.

There was a long stretch of silence. Delilah's breath had evened out, her arm sagged heavy over my stomach, her legs tangled with mine, and I was close to sleep when her whispered words filled the darkness.

"I never had a type. I never thought about what kind of man I was going to spend my life with because it felt like a wasted effort. I never thought about what I was attracted to because I was attracted to nothing. By that I mean, I'd lived a life that made me want for nothing because I knew I'd never get it. And it hurt so damn bad to want things, wish for something more, dream about a life where I wasn't lonely so I stopped doing it. I watched my mother go through men at an alarming rate but I also watched them go through her. Man after man. They dumped her and divorced her. Some of them I think she really loved and those are the ones who broke her. Each time one left she lost more of herself. I never wanted that and I think that's another reason why I closed myself off."

It sure as fuck was.

But I sensed there was more she wanted to say so I

didn't confirm her suspicions were corrected and I waited for her to continue.

"Now I have a type," she whispered and I braced. "He's tall and strong. He's gentle and wise. He's protective. He thinks I'm beautiful and makes me believe I am. He's trustworthy. He's giving. He can be sweet and dirty—sometimes at the same time. He gives me strength and confidence. He makes me want everything—to ask for it, to demand it, to be worthy of it. I never could've dreamed for you. I never could've wished for you. I never could've needed and wanted you because I didn't know you existed. But now that I know, I have a type—you.

"You can claim me any way you want as long as you know you don't need to claim me because I'm already yours."

Jesus Christ.

The left side of my chest burned while the rest of me chilled. Hot and cold collided, electrified, and lightning ricocheted through me charging my nerve endings, shocking my muscles, electrocuting my insides.

"More," I ground out and rolled her to her back.

"More?"

"You keep giving me more and I hope to fuck you understand what you just gave me because I sure as fuck do. I knew the first time you gave me a piece of you. I've known what it means each time you've given me more. But now, you've given me the rest. You've given me all of you. And I hope to God you understand I'm not giving it back."

"I don't want it back," she whispered.

"That's good, baby, but you've never had the option to take it from me. And for the record, I'm never, not *ever*, gonna stop claiming what's mine. But more, I'm never, not until I leave this earth, am I gonna stop giving you me. I'm gonna give you everything. I swear it. Promise it. Vow it. You will never again go without."

I didn't give Delilah a chance to respond. I slid my tongue in her mouth and let our connection tell her everything she needed to know.

The next morning there were eight condoms left and neither of us got much rest.

And ten minutes into the drive Delilah was asleep.

Fuck yeah.

She knew she could rest and I'd keep her safe.

CHAPTER 16

I was not a road trip type of person.

I'd learned this when I was with Tamir and spent hours upon hours in the car with him. The whole time I was with him I was scared out of my brain, and the hours of quiet time in the car only fueled my fear. It gave me nothing to do but dwell on my situation.

I thought being in the car with Myles would be different, and it was, for all the obvious reasons. However, sitting in a car for hours and hours and more freaking hours was not my thing. Good company or lunatic-bad-guy company.

My ass hurt, I was fidgety, and I wanted the drive to be over.

We'd been driving for ten hours and still had four more to go. I stared out my window seeing the same thing I'd been seeing for that hour—nothing but trees and farmland. It was pretty but there were only so many fields I could look at before I was out of my mind with boredom.

"What's the tattoo on your arm mean?" I asked.

Myles shifted his left forearm.

Never Again in bold, black ink. Under that, there were smaller letters: JLA.

"It's a reminder to never again listen to someone else when my gut tells me it's wrong."

That didn't sound good but the dead tone he spoke in sounded worse. But I still asked, "And the JLA?"

"Jeremy Lee Alderson. My teammate who paid the price for my fuck-up."

Oh, yeah, it was worse.

I thought back to an early conversation about why Myles had left the Army.

"Is he the reason you think you became ineffective?"

"One of the reasons."

Myles didn't elaborate and since the vibe in the car had gone from natural and happy even if some boredom had been sprinkled in there to straight-up unhappy, I ceased questioning him.

I had never been close to a single person, thus I'd never lost someone I cared about. Myles obviously had cared about his friend if even after all that time had passed he still sounded mournful and angry about his death.

I wanted to know more. I wanted to know everything about him but not at the cost of upsetting him.

"Tell me about your parents," I changed the subject.

"Grew up in the Springs, lived in Denver, Fort Collins, then we moved south to Durango."

"That's a lot of moving."

"My mom's a lawyer. We'd move somewhere, settle in, and a few years later she'd get a job offer and we'd move. Dad loves her so he didn't mind following her around as long as she was happy. And looking back I think he got off on it. Other firms recognizing her talents and recruiting her. Them seeing in her what he'd always known, her getting the accolades for her intelligence. He's proud of her and she knows it."

That was sweet.

"So your dad taught you how to be a good man."

"My dad taught me a great many things. How to love a woman, certainly. How to be a man of honor and integrity, absolutely. But it was Mom who taught me by example that I can do and be anything I want to be. There are no such things as limits, no heights I cannot reach. She didn't struggle, work hard, claw, fight, and put in an ungodly amount of hours because she thought as a woman she needed to. For her, being a woman has no relevance in any conversation. It was about work ethic and she taught that to me."

"You believe you can do anything?"

"Abso-fucking-lutely. If I don't believe I can do anything, then who will? If I set a limit to what I can do and achieve then how will I succeed? A limit means a stopping point. Believe this, Delilah, there is nothing you cannot accomplish if you are willing to fight for it. It's all about how much of yourself you're willing to give to get it."

He was right about that.

Two women, very different—opposite actually.

Yet they had something in common.

My mother never stopped going after what she wanted, she fought for it, and was willing to give up pieces of herself and me in the pursuit of finding a man to fawn all over her and fill the holes the previous men had left. And in doing so she taught me I was worthless.

Myles's mother never stopped going after what she wanted, either, but in her pursuit, she'd taught her son a strong work ethic and self-worth. He honestly believed he could do anything. I heard it in his voice; he wasn't blowing smoke, making some abstract, theoretical argument about success. I also heard extreme pride and I loved he thought so highly of his mother.

"Wish I had that growing up."

"Lucky for you when we get home and I invite my parents out to Maryland to meet their future daughter-in-law they'll be on a plane so fast it'll be a miracle if my mom's hair doesn't catch fire. After that, she'll give you all she gave me. The woman cannot help herself, she inserts herself wherever she feels needed. And don't twist that in your mind as something bad. It's her way. It's her nature to give, to protect."

Future daughter-in-law?

"I see you learned that from her, too."

Myles smiled and shook his head in the negative.

"No, baby, my dad taught me that. He showed me the way. Taught me that the best gift you can give the woman you love is to prop her up until she soars. Until she's secure in the knowledge that you will protect her at all costs, making her free to be anything she wants to be."

My belly felt funny. Not queasy but rumbly. Not butterflies but fluttering. Everything that Myles had said and done floated through my mind. He'd been propping me up. He'd been coaxing me out of my shell until I felt free to be me. And I did. I felt free. He'd given so I could learn how to take.

"I think I'm falling in love with you," I blurted out.

"You think?" Myles smiled.

"I've never loved anyone," I reminded him.

"Right. Take your time, baby, I'll be waiting to catch you."

He'd protect me at all costs so I could soar.

Yeah, I was falling in love with him.

"We're coming up on another toll booth. Put your hat on, baby."

I grabbed the hat off the floorboard in front of me and put it on. I also did what he hadn't asked and scooted down in my seat and turned my face toward the passenger window in preparation to curl up, tuck my chin, and feign sleep so the cameras in the toll booths wouldn't get a clear picture of my face. Myles had to pay the toll, but he knew how to angle his head to disguise his identity.

There were a few minutes of silence before Myles said, "Jeremy died because of bad intel. We knew it was bad, something felt off, but some asshole sitting behind a screen with a silver bar on his shoulder thought he was smarter than his men on the ground and made the call to kick in a door we shouldn't've. I knew it, felt it so deep I was contemplating disobeying a direct order. I didn't get to make that choice. We weren't even in the village when we were attacked. One second Jeremy was standing next to me, the next he was at my feet with an AK round through his throat. That's not a quick, painless death. It took minutes for him to suffocate."

Myles stopped and inhaled deeply before he went on, "After that, I went with my gut. No matter what. That's frowned upon in the Army, especially at the level I was at.

We're trained to carry out orders. I didn't agree. My way of thinking was, the Army trained me to be a lethal fighting machine, and to be that they had to trust me to critically think on the battlefield. They didn't agree and since we were at a stalemate because never again was I going to follow an order I knew was wrong, I left the Army."

Myles pulled up to the toll booth, I tucked my chin and closed my eyes. The previous times I'd done this I'd been paranoid, like the person accepting the money would magically know who I was and who I was running from. It was silly; they had no way of knowing, but the illogical thought had been there. This time I pictured an unknown Jeremy with blood oozing from his neck. Even if Myles hadn't said it, I'd imagine he would've been fruitlessly trying to stop the bleeding.

Myles didn't become ineffective. He just wouldn't be swayed from his convictions. That led me to think about his reaction to Zane telling him to bring me to Guatemala to find Alejandro. Myles was vehemently against it. He wasn't going to back down until I begged him not to leave me behind.

Damn.

He'd been swayed.

Never Again.

I waited until he was driving again then I waited another few minutes before I opened my eyes and uncurled.

"I'm sorry," I whispered.

"For what?"

"I should've stayed behind. You didn't want me to come. I pushed it and I shouldn't've."

"I wasn't going to leave you there by yourself. It's a lose-lose situation. We're spread thin and I understand Zane needing to keep assets close in case he needs them. Any other time I'd have my team with me. That would mean more protection for you even if you had to come with us. I was also caught off-guard. But I trust Kevin. He'll have our back."

I said nothing to that because now I was controlling my panic as it started to bubble.

Myles reached over and put his hand on my thigh before he picked it up and turned it over palm up. I stared at his big rough hand before I set mine in his. Immediately his fingers curled around mine.

"Everything's gonna be fine."

"What if Kevin doesn't like me?"

Myles's bark of laughter filled the car and my eyes shot to him.

He was beautiful when he laughed, some of the hardness slid out of his features and deep grooves lined the outsides of his eyes.

"Kevin will love you. But just to warn you, he's got zero tact and a warped sense of humor."

"What's that mean?"

"Zero filter. Some of the stuff that comes out of his mouth can be downright shocking. But he doesn't ever mean to be mean. He and Gabe are a lot alike in that regard; both lack subtlety. But on occasion, Gabe knows when to keep his trap shut. Kevin does too; he just chooses not to. He likes to egg on a situation."

"Okay."

Myles chuckled.

"Seriously, baby, you have nothing to worry about.

Kevin's gonna like you, which means he's gonna tease you. He'll also take one look at you, read the situation correctly, and he'll start flirting with you to press my buttons and piss me off. When I lose my shit, he'll pretend to be surprised even though he'll have worked hard to irritate me. And before you ask why I'll lose my shit even though I know what he's doing, I'll tell you the answer. It's a guy thing, it's a brother thing, it's stupid, but it is what it is."

"Tell me about Evette," I prompted.

Myles gave my hand a squeeze and he told me what he knew about the woman. By all accounts from his team-mates back in Maryland, she was awesome. Perfect for Gabe in every way so even though Myles hadn't spent any time with her he said he was happy she was in what he called the family.

Then he told me about Natasha, a woman who was a mob princess and had narrowly escaped the life she hated. She'd also been sold into human trafficking. That was scary as all hell, so I pushed that out of my head. He also told me she was strong and resilient.

By the time he finished telling me stories I was no longer nervous about meeting Kevin and I was looking forward to meeting the women. And I had to admit, there was a teeny tiny sliver that wanted to meet Zane Lewis in person, too.

He'd called a few times in the hours we'd been on the road. With each call, he sounded a little more grumpy. The last call he'd cursed so much, he ran out of cuss words and started making up hilarious combinations. But under all his gruff humor I sensed he was getting worried.

He didn't want Myles and Kevin home—he *needed* them there.

Soon.

As soon as we got the research from Alejandro we'd be on our way home.

CHAPTER 17

"See you in five," I told Kevin, and Delilah disconnected the call for me.

"What's that?"

My gaze followed where she was pointing then went back to the road.

"Cemetery."

"No. The place going up the mountain with all the green, yellow, pink, and orange structures."

"Cemetery. In Guatemala, the afterlife is celebrated. Those aren't structures, they're tombstones painted the favorite color of either the deceased or something bright and cheery that the family chooses."

"How do you know that?"

"I'm a documentary geek. Spent a lot of time on merchant ships. For the most part, maritime security is pretty boring so I watched documentaries."

"Have you ever seen Shoah?"

"Too easy. Best documentary on the holocaust ever made."

There were a few moments of silence before she asked, "Don't look back."

"Bob Dylan."

"Damn. What about, Man with a Movie Camera?"

Impressive.

She knew her docs.

"A silent Russian film that in my opinion was boring as fuck. But I suppose with today's technology we all know the tricks of good editing. Back in the day it might've been fascinating but in today's world not so much." I found the small restaurant where we were meeting Kevin and pulled into the gravel lot. "I take it you're a fan of documentaries."

"I find TV boring as a whole. But when I watch it I like to learn something, so I do lean towards documentaries or true crime shows."

Brilliant.

"Invisible Monsters," I supplied.

"Serial Killers in America."

I parked next to the white Toyota pickup, circa Marty Mcfly, complete with the light bar on top, and looked over at Delilah. She was looking out her window staring at the truck I knew Kevin was not in because he was already inside waiting for us.

"We've gone back to the future," she murmured and turned her smiling face towards me. "It's like it's nine-teen-eighty-five all over again."

"Baby, I think Marty's was black."

"I've never seen one in person."

"You've never seen a Toyota pickup in person?"

"Not one that's thirty-six years old and in mint condi-tion. Seriously, it even has the yellow KC light covers on it. That thing is so totally rad I might want you to steal it for me and smuggle it back into the U.S."

"I'll see what I can do for you."

Her smile widened when she said, "I think if there was a way, you'd actually do it."

You're damn right I would.

"Now you're catching on."

"I think I'm ready for you to catch me now, Myles."

Jesus.

"Then jump."

"I think I just—"

Delilah didn't finish; my hand tagged her around the back of her neck and brought her face directly to mine.

"You love me?" I asked against her lips.

"Yes."

Three letters that slammed into my heart. One word that meant the world.

"You gonna move back to Maryland and move in with me?"

"Yes."

Elation radiated through me.

Fuck, yeah.

"I promise I'll make you soar."

"I know you will because you already do."

Good Christ.

"Are you gonna kiss me, Myles, or make—"

I kissed my woman and I made it deep and wet while I claimed every inch of her mouth. When we broke apart and her eyes opened they were hazy and hungry.

Two looks I loved.

But we needed to get into the restaurant.

"Grab your Glock out the glove box. Remember how to rack the slide to chamber a bullet?"

"It was just this morning you taught me and it's only been fourteen hours. I haven't forgotten."

It'd been fifteen and a half but I wasn't going to remind her. She was over the car ride three hours after she'd woken up.

"Good. I want you to keep it in the front of your shorts. It won't be comfortable but it will be accessible."

"Copy that," she sassed.

Oh, yeah, fuck yeah, she was opening up and it was goddamn beautiful.

"Smartass."

She smiled and I got out of the SUV, rounded the back, and helped her out. Then I opened the back and grabbed our packs.

"You know what the best part will be when we get home?"

"I could think of a few."

"Not having to carry a backpack all the time."

"Suck it up, buttercup. With any luck, we'll be heading Stateside tomorrow."

I gave her hand a tug and walked towards the small eatery.

As soon as we cleared the door I saw Kevin sitting at a carefully selected table. He had a view of the room plus the two exits.

I didn't wait for the hostess to seat us. I took Delilah directly to my smiling teammate.

"There she is, in the flesh," Kevin said by way of greeting and I braced. "And even more beautiful—"

"If that Marty Mcfly Toyota is yours I'm driving with you," Delilah interrupted.

Kevin blinked, looked between us, smiled, then belted out a laugh.

"Ready to ditch the grumpy beast already?"

"Great Scott, no. I'm keeping Myles but I will use you for a ride."

"Did she…" Kevin sputtered. "Did she just Great Scott, me? I think I'm in love."

"I think you'd find my foot up your ass if I wasn't afraid you'd like it," I returned.

I started to pull out Delilah's chair when Kevin cleared his face and asked, "What's wrong with a little ass play every now and again? As long as she trims her nails that shit feels—"

Delilah tipped her head to the side and busted out laughing. I'd seen her laugh, but never that hard. The sight was absolutely stunning and I knew Kevin thought so, too, because he was staring at her with what looked like approval.

His eyes came to mine and he muttered, "You did good, brother. Real good."

* * *

Delilah did not get her ride with Kevin when we drove to the small house on the outskirts of town. Though by the end of dinner Kevin would've given her the keys or alternately stolen it for her and put it on a cargo ship for export back to the U.S.

Now Kevin and I were sitting at a small table with a map in front of us while Delilah showered—a place I wanted to be with her but Tex called and we had plans to go over.

"I don't have a lock on Cohen or Abrams." At Tex's information, I felt like I'd sustained a blow.

"Any indication either are in Guatemala?" Kevin asked.

"No. But something else you should know, I confirmed Caesar Stockholm didn't get any of the pictures he took to Bryan Zaslow. He reported he found her, but hadn't sent confirmation. It's also going around that Tamir Cohen killed Delilah."

"What does 'going around' mean?" I inquired.

"Aviv Abrams has investors he reports to and it's been reported that, and I quote, the Watts problem has been permanently resolved, end quote. This part is a gut feeling, but I think that's why Cohen instructed you to keep Delilah hidden. He stashed her then went back to Abrams and told him he killed her. Abrams would have no reason not to believe him."

"Why the fuck would he do that?" Kevin asked what I was thinking.

"Garrett and I have been looking into the Fear program. The test subjects were given identification numbers. Neither of us has been able to dig up names but we know that the program pulled from the Yamam unit."

"Tamir's brother's unit. That's why he left Shayetet 13," I surmised. "Do you think his brother was a test subject or just knew about the program and was taken out to keep him quiet?"

"I don't know," Tex admitted. "The Israeli Defense Force doesn't fuck around with classified intel. It's not like in the U.S. where top-secret information has a way of leaking out. That does not happen in the IDF, period. The

Cohen family is respected in Israel but after Isaac Cohen died a country that loved three siblings took that up a notch and now they are revered. It was a sad day for the IDF when Tamir left and went to work with Abrams. By sad I mean, Aviv Abrams pissed a lot of people off by poaching Tamir. I'm not convinced that Tamir hasn't turned, but I will concede that something is off."

"Agreed," I put in. "If Tamir wanted to kill Delilah she'd be dead. But that doesn't mean that if she resurfaces before Tamir's ready he won't take her out to cover his ass."

My gut tightened at the thought.

Tamir had an objective, a course of action, a mission to see through and just like me, the man wasn't a quitter. He wouldn't stop until he succeeded. However, the same questions remained; what was his plan and why hadn't he killed Delilah?

"How'd Abrams get a lock on Arias?" Kevin asked.

"Arias contacted his grandmother. It's a reasonable guess that Abrams was watching his family. Delilah deleted the research off the Abrams servers. Aviv Abrams had made big promises to very powerful men, he needed Arias's research to give to Dr. Gates. Again, it's a guess but an informed one. Abrams was hoping someone in the family had the research. Maybe they didn't know what they had but he wanted to be ready to take it—and take them out—should it surface."

What an idiot.

"So, all this time in the clear and he calls his granny. Now, he's gonna get popped if we don't get to him first," Kevin concluded.

"Yep. You have his location. My advice, don't delay.

Tamir and Abrams could be anywhere. I've got facial rec software running day and night, no hits. I know Garrett's doing the same, but his time is being pulled in a hundred directions. Watching out for Myles and Delilah getting caught on camera somewhere and what's happening at the office. Zane's on edge so everyone is on alert. It'd be good if you two get this done and back to Maryland before Zane loses it. Zane pissed is one thing. Zane on the warpath can mean anything—none of those things good."

Tex was not wrong.

The sooner this was done and we could go home the safer the unsuspecting population of Annapolis would be.

"Thanks for all your help, Tex. Couldn't have done this without you."

Tex made a disgruntled sound and not for the first time I wondered if the man could take a compliment and gratitude gracefully.

I doubted it.

"Your planes are on standby," Tex continued. "Kevin, you're going east to Chiquimula. It's a small airfield with a trusted pilot in case you have to incapacitate Arias. At this point, I don't think he has the luxury of choice. If Abrams gets him he'll be in Croatia performing whatever experiments Abrams and Gates can think up and that's not safe for anyone. Myles, you and Delilah take the research and head west to La Aurora."

"Copy and thanks again," Kevin said.

"Be safe."

Tex disconnected and I stared at the map.

Alejandro Arias was close—ten miles to the north close.

"What's your gut telling you?"

I glanced from the map to Kevin and answered, "Abrams and Tamir are here."

"Yep, that's what I think."

My eyes went to my watch. It was nearing on ten.

"A quick snatch and grab," I started. "We roll up, you tag Arias and go. You can be at the airfield by midnight. Delilah and I will get the research and be on our way. My only issue is I gotta dump my weapons before I hit the airport. Saving grace is it's a large international airport; once we're past security we'll be clear of Abrams and Cohen."

Kevin was silent and I heard the shower go off, reminding me I *really* wished I'd been in there with Delilah.

"Don't like that, brother. I think I should stay until you and Delilah are on the road."

"We can't take the chance of Arias—"

"Worst case, he's not helpful. I'll gag 'im and bag 'im. Then help you search the house. But with Delilah there, I don't think we'll have a problem. He obviously trusts her, he'll give up the goods and leave with me."

Before I could commit to the plan my phone rang and Zane's name flashed across the screen.

"Before you answer that, I gotta tell you, Z's dangling close to the ledge. You know him, he'll take whatever's thrown his way. But this shit...no. His people are being fucked with and he's planning on fucking back in a big way. Brace, Myles, when Garrett tracks this guy —game on."

Fucking shit.

"Noted."

I swiped the screen and prepared for Zane's normal

biting sarcasm. However, what I got was not annoying banter. What I got sent a chill down my spine instead.

"You're on speaker," I said into the phone.

"Tex brief you?"

"Yep. We're all set to roll out in about thirty minutes."

"Cooper and Gabe are on standby for airport runs. Keep me updated on pick-up times."

All business.

No bullshit jokes.

"Anything new going on there?" I inquired with a good amount of trepidation.

"Got another note—those who live in glass houses shouldn't cast stones."

Dry. Calm. Devoid of emotion.

"Zane—"

"Mark this, the motherfucker wants to throw stones, they're gonna be met with bullets. He means to go after *my* house they'll be met with missiles."

The malice in Zane's tone couldn't be missed but it was what I didn't hear that concerned me the most.

Zane was a ballbuster. He could take any situation and infuse it with mockery and a heavy dose of hyperbole. Right then, his claim of bullets and missiles was to be taken literally.

Game on, was right.

Fucking shit.

"We'll be home in under forty-eight hours, Z."

"Great. See you then."

The line went dead and I locked eyes with Kevin.

"Fuck. He didn't even tell me to glove up."

"Job one when we get home is keeping Zane under wraps. He's freaking Ivy out. She knows what kind of man he is. And you do not back Zane Lewis into a corner and expect him not to fight his way out. His house is his to reign and anyone who thinks to overthrow the king will be met with heavy artillery. Ivy knows Zane will die before any of us take the hit. She understands that Zane's house is not the penthouse they live in but the people he loves. The women are rallying. And the men are doing what they can to circle around him."

"War," I muttered.

"War," Kevin agreed.

Fucking hell.

Our conversation was cut off when Delilah walked into the room, hair brushed and down around her shoulders but still wet from her shower.

"Didn't wanna mention this before, darlin' but you need a new hairstylist."

I tensed at Kevin's comment but Delilah's smile had me relaxing.

"I'll let Myles know you don't approve of his butchered attempt at a second career as a stylist," she returned.

"You cut her hair?" Kevin turned back to look at me. "What'd you use, a field knife?"

I grunted.

Delilah laughed then told Kevin, "I don't know if it was a field knife but my choices were the tiniest pair of scissors I'd ever seen which would've taken him a year to cut all the thick clumps of matted hair, or the knife. At the time the knife seemed faster and actually the cut's growing on me. I think I'm gonna start a trend, the angle cut. It'll be all the rage, like the off-the-shoulder, slouchy shirts that fit diagonal across a woman's chest. Now she can have hair to match."

I was pleased as fuck she was smiling. But what I wasn't happy about was the reminder her hair had been a tangled mess and how those tangles came to be.

I grunted again, wanting to move on from memories I wanted to forget but knew I'd never manage to erase. Those memories of a scared and dirty Delilah were forever branded onto my brain.

"Put your watch on, baby."

I held up the watch Tex sent down with Kevin.

"We're gonna roll out in about twenty minutes."

I hated the way her face sobered. I hated that she was in Guatemala with Tamir and Abrams still on the loose. And I really fucking hated that my choices had been limited and the ones available to me sucked.

Quick snatch and grab.

In and out then home.

Those were my thoughts.

Less than forty-eight hours and we'd be home.

I had something to hold on to. It wasn't much but it was all I had.

CHAPTER 18

It is a strange turn of events when I, Delilah Lynn Watts, with weapon in hand was getting ready to follow two heavily armed men into a house. What's worse, I had to pee. Like cross your legs, do a dance, turn in circles pee. I didn't know if it was because I was scared or from all the soda I drank at dinner but if I was ever involved in another rescue operation I wasn't drinking anything the prior twenty-four hours.

We'd gone over the plan, then the backup plan, then the fallback plan. And after that, we went over all three again and again until I could recite them to Myles and Kevin without pause. That had taken more than thirty minutes, so we were behind schedule by ten minutes. Both men had been patient and insistent that memorizing our course of action was more important than keeping a self-imposed timeline. However, I could tell they were anxious to get Alejandro and go.

So was I.

We were almost out of Guatemala. Soon we'd be back in the U.S. and I would go home with Myles.

Myles was in what he'd called "point." I don't know why he hadn't just said he would be in the lead because that's where he was. In the front taking the lead with Kevin at his back and me bringing up the rear. We all had our positions when we entered. Mine was to stand with my back to the wall closest to the door. I was to shoot anyone who was not Alejandro, Myles, or Kevin.

Never in my life had I ever thought I'd hear "shoot anyone." Thus I never thought I'd be happy to never hear those two words said to me again. But there you have it, I would be happy never to be told to shoot someone ever again.

We were in a not-so-nice neighborhood. And not so nice was putting it mildly. Both sides of the small two-way traffic road—and it was only open to two-way traffic because I hadn't seen any F-250s or Ram 3500 dually trucks in Jalapa. From the street, there was a sidewalk then the house with street-level doors. In America we would call them townhouses or Brownstones, only I'd never seen a one-story townhouse before and all of them were single-story with stucco exteriors. They all had terracotta tile roofs, all of them in major disrepair.

So, not a nice neighborhood. One I didn't want to be in for any longer than I needed to be even with Kevin and Myles with me.

Therefore I was happy when Kevin reached back and tapped my leg. That was the signal that Myles had picked the lock and we were ready to go in. As if we'd practiced it, which we had verbally but not otherwise, we entered the house as a unit. Even our steps were synchronized. Myles had his rifle up, the stock—he'd briefly explained the parts of his rifle, thus I now knew what a stock was—headed straight for the hall. Kevin moved forward to clear the main living space—which was extremely small—his rifle up and at the ready as well. I gently closed the door, locked it, and pressed my back against the wall, holding my Glock. I did not have mine up and at the ready, as usual—*when had holding a weapon become normal and usual?*—my barrel was pointed safely at the floor.

So far I'd been able to keep my heart rate under control but when I heard a crash then loud scuffling my heart started to pound. These noises didn't seem to bother Kevin in the slightest. He continued to open doors—even the pantry. Anywhere a person could hide he looked. Anywhere a weapon could be hidden he looked. He was fast but thorough.

Just when I thought I was going to come out of my skin, Myles came back into the living room with a disheveled Alejandro. I'd never met the man in person but seeing as he was a leading researcher in his field there was a lot of information about him on the internet and that included pictures. The bearded man standing before me looked nothing like the clean-cut young man who was too smart for his own good.

"Alejandro?"

I started to step away from the wall but halted when Myles's hand came up.

"Who are you and what do you want?" Alejandro asked.

"What's your name?" Kevin asked.

"Juan Lopez. Who are you?"

Kevin looked at me and I wasn't sure if he was giving me the go-ahead to speak or if he wanted confirmation that this was indeed Alejandro Arias.

I thought it best to clarify. "May I speak to him?"

"Yeah, but stay where you are."

"Remember me? I helped you—"

I got no more out before Alejandro interrupted. "I remember."

"We're here to get you to safety."

"There's no such thing as safety," he returned.

Cold dark eyes pinned me to the wall.

Boy, do I remember thinking that.

"There is and these men will provide it. Do you still have your research?"

I saw the unhappy flash in his eyes and the way his mouth tightened couldn't be overlooked. I didn't blame him; that research had cost him everything and if he wasn't careful it would cost him his life. But I could swear I also saw regret and I couldn't help but feel sorry for him. More than once Alejandro had told me he wished he never would've answered Aviv's first email to him. The one that promised riches and a better life for his grandmother and aunt.

"Yes, *Delilah*, I have it." Disdain dripped off each word.

Whoa. What was that about?

I wasn't the only one who heard it. Myles looked at Kevin, and like there was an invisible tether, Kevin immediately looked at Myles as some sort of silent man-team-mate-brotherhood communication happened and Myles jerked his chin and looked back at me.

"Why don't we get it now and get to the airport?" Kevin suggested.

Myles's gaze held mine even as Alejandro stepped away from Myles and walked into his kitchen. Kevin followed Alejandro and Myles continued to stare.

"Everything I tell you to do, you do."

"Okay."

"Without question or hesitation."

I felt it pertinent to start doing that now so I immediately answered.

"I understand."

He seemed to relax minutely. However, that was a mere shade down from high-alert so he was still wired. Which in turn made me wired—or more wired than I already was.

Something wasn't right.

This wasn't the Alejandro I spoke to all those months ago. That man was soft-spoken and kind. He was scared at what he'd gotten himself into. He wanted out and didn't want his findings to be used for bad.

The man in front of me now was hardened. Spiteful. Angry.

I could understand those emotions, I felt them as well. But Alejandro seemed to feel that way toward *me*.

Yet, I was the one who suggested he fake his death even if it was for a short time. Maybe the reality of what that meant was too high of a price. Maybe he'd changed his mind.

It sounded like pots and pans were banging around in the kitchen and a moment later Alejandro returned with a thick manilla envelope and Kevin behind him.

"Here." He handed the envelope out for Myles to take. "It's all there."

Alejandro's head turned in my direction and guilt clear as day shone in his eyes.

Yep. Something was wrong.

"Check in," Kevin muttered then turned to Alejandro. "Let's go."

Without question, Alejandro followed orders.

He didn't ask why he was going to the airport. He didn't ask who Kevin and Myles were and they hadn't introduced themselves.

That was strange.

Kevin and Alejandro walked out the front door and left.

That easy, they just left.

Myles quickly made his way to me and I let out a breath I didn't know I was holding.

"You did great, baby. Turn around and let me put this in your pack."

Oh, yeah, my backpack. Another thing I won't miss when we get home.

I turned and felt Myles tugging at the zipper.

"That was weird, right?" I asked.

"Yep."

"He just left with Kevin. No struggle, no questions, nothing. Did he fight you in the bedroom?"

"If you're asking if he bit me, no. And no again, he didn't fight me once I had him on his feet."

Thankfully Myles's arm was healing nicely. Unfortunately, he'd bear a few scars.

"He sounded pissed at me."

"That he did."

"Is that why Kevin left with him so quickly?"

"Yes."

Myles zipped my pack back up and used it to turn me around. Once I was facing him he bent and gave me a sweet kiss.

"Let's get home."

Home sounded wonderful.

Blissful. Divine. Heavenly.

"Before we go, may I use the bathroom real quick?"

I could see he wanted to say no but he gave in.

"Yeah, but hurry. We need to roll."

"Okay."

Myles guided me to the bathroom but before I closed it I handed him my gun. "I won't need it in the bathroom." He didn't look too happy, but after a moment, he took it.

I, on the other hand, was happy to hand it over—thankful that would be the last time I'd ever be in a situation to possibly need it. Myles gave me a smile and shut the door.

I dropped my pack, and as fast as I could, unbuttoned and unzipped. I did this praying I didn't get stage freight. I knew Myles was on the other side of the door and I knew he'd be able to hear me pee.

It was an idiot thing to think about; he'd done all manners of wonderful, filthy things to my body but I still didn't want him to hear me pee.

In the end, it didn't matter.

"Do not leave that bathroom," Myles's angry declaration came through the door.

"Okay."

My ass was halfway to the seat when I straightened

and pulled up my shorts. I didn't bother with the zipper but buttoned them.

"No matter what you hear, baby. Promise me you won't leave the bathroom."

What the hell is going on?

"Promise, Myles."

I don't know why I did it but I stepped into the shower stall and slowly closed the plastic curtain that would offer no protection whatsoever.

A few seconds passed and when I heard nothing I started to relax.

Then I heard him.

"Myles Simms."

Aviv Abrams.

The man that wanted me dead.

The man that would kill Myles.

"How nice of you to come into town. Saves me the effort," Aviv went on. "Where's Kevin and my scientist?"

Wait, how did Aviv know Myles and Kevin? And how did he know we were in Guatemala?

"They left," Myles calmly said.

My hands started to shake so violently I clasped them together.

"Left?" That was Aviv.

"Left," Myles confirmed.

"Check the house," Aviv demanded.

No.

Oh, fuck.

I unclasped my hands and used one to cover my mouth to stifle a groan.

Myles has my gun. Why didn't I keep the damn gun?

The bathroom door opened and I stood paralyzed

with fear. I heard footsteps, then the shower curtain opened.

Tamir.

Face-to-face with my worst nightmare.

My torso swayed and I fought to keep my feet. His eyes filled with what looked like compassion.

Compassion.

What the hell?

He slowly shook his head, brought his gloved hand up, extended his pointer finger, and brought it in front of his mouth.

I was frozen in fear.

When this shit was done, I was seeking help for my inability to react properly in a life-or-death situation. Clearly, my instincts were fucking broken. I should be attacking. Clawing his eyes out, biting, kicking, punching. *Something!*

Tamir lowered his hand, dipped his chin, and in a crime against the universe attempted to give me a reassuring look.

What the hell?

He backed out of the bathroom, closed the door, and a moment later I heard him say, "There's no one here."

What?

I heard the front door slam, then silence.

Total silence, which made the pounding in my chest echo in the small bathroom.

I stood in the middle of the room and waited.

Then I waited longer and longer and longer.

No matter what you hear, baby. Promise me you won't leave the bathroom

So I waited longer.

Finally, when I heard nothing for a very long time I unzipped my pack and found my phone.

First I called Kevin but it went straight to voicemail.

Next, I called Zane.

He answered on the second ring.

"Tell Myles he's driving in the wrong direction."

"Aviv has Myles," I whispered.

"Where are you?"

"Still at Alejandro's house."

"All right, darlin'. Are you safe?"

"I don't know. I was in the bathroom so I couldn't see but Aviv was here. He knew Myles and Kevin's names. Aviv asked where Kevin and Alejandro were, Myles told him they left, Aviv told Tamir to check the house and when Tamir found me in the bathroom he told me to be quiet. Not with words, he used the universal hand gesture and shushed me. Then he lied and told Aviv there was no one in the house. The door slammed and now it's quiet."

"Did you get all that?" Zane asked.

"What?"

"Not you, sweetheart, I was asking Garrett. He's tracking Myles now and he has your location, too."

Right. Myles is chipped. Thank God.

"Stay put. Let me get the ball rolling and I'll call you back."

"No!"

"Delilah—"

"Please don't hang up. Please, just keep the line open. I won't talk. I promise I'll be super quiet, just don't leave me alone in this house."

God, I was weak. So damn weak but I didn't give one

single shit Zane now knew what kind of woman I was. I was too damn scared to care.

"All right, sweetheart, I'm gonna leave you on speaker. Garrett's with me now and in a few minutes, I'm gonna gather the team. You'll hear lots of voices, and we'll all be here if you need us."

"Thank you," I whispered.

"Anything you need, Delilah."

CHAPTER 19

The funny thing about time is whether you want it to or not it passes. Some moments seem to go in the blink of an eye, others seem to drag on and on making seconds feel like minutes and minutes feel like hours.

Twenty-six minutes had passed since I called Zane. Twenty-six that felt like an eternity.

And once again I was alone. Different house, different country, same feeling.

Fear.

I could hear Zane and the others talking. In an effort to distract myself from my current situation I concentrated on memorizing who was who by their voices. Zane, Garrett, and Gabe were easy; I'd heard them before. Owen, Lincoln, and Cooper were new. It had taken me a few minutes to be able to tell the difference between them. Lincoln's voice was deeper than Owen's and Cooper's. Owen spoke quickly. Cooper had a hint of Southern California Valley in his voice. And since Ivy was the only woman in the room she was a no-brainer.

Every once in a while Zane would stop what he was doing to ask me if I was still on the line. Once he had my confirmation he'd get right back to it. They were tracking Myles's location in real-time, something that should've made me feel better but it didn't. And they had my location thanks to the watch Tex had sent. Neither did that do anything to calm my nerves.

"Kevin's calling in," I heard Zane say.

The line went silent for a moment and my panic increased ten-fold until suddenly Kevin's voice boomed in my ear.

"We got a problem," Kevin announced.

"I'd say we have multiple fuckin' problems," Zane barked. "Where are you?"

"Forty miles east of Jalapa. Arias bit it."

"What?" I whispered.

"Is that Delilah?"

"Fucking hell," Zane grunted and ignored Kevin's question in favor of his own. "How'd that come to be?"

"Five minutes ago he started rambling on about what a disgrace he was to his family. How he messed up. From what I could piece together from his barely coherent mumbling Abrams has his grandmother and aunt. Then he starts apologizing and pulls Tic-Tacs out of his pocket. I don't think anything of this until he starts foaming at the mouth."

"Why'd you leave before Myles?"

"Arias was hostile towards Delilah. Myles and I didn't like the vibe. Now, why's Delilah on the line. What's going on?"

"Dump the fucker on the side of the road and get back to Jalapa. Abrams tagged Myles."

I thought I heard the screeching of tires. I couldn't be sure but it also sounded like a car door opened. But what I did hear was Kevin cuss a blue streak. He was almost as creative with his profanity as Zane was. There were lots of grunts and groans. Then it hit me; Kevin was literally dumping Alejandro's body on the side of the road somewhere.

Granted, Kevin didn't kill him, but still.

He was a human.

"Maybe Kevin should take Alejandro—"

"Evidence is suggesting he sold you, Myles, and Kevin out," Zane started. "You said Abrams walked in and it sounded like he knew Myles and Kevin would be there."

"Well…"

"And because of that, you're sitting in a bathroom alone, and I got a man whose body is moving but I got no way of knowing if he's breathing. Remembering that, do you still care where Kevin puts Arias's dead body?"

Um…

"And before you answer that, evidence is also suggesting that Abrams has his aunt and grandmother, yet the fucker kills himself instead of telling Kevin everything he knows so his family can be rescued. That's the man you're feeling sorry for."

Well, when you put it like that…

"I no longer feel sorry for him. But just so you know, I stopped feeling any twinge of human decency for him when you brought up him selling out Myles and Kevin. And that's all it was, decency."

"Good to know."

This was not sarcastic; he actually sounded like he was

happy to know I cared more about Myles and Kevin than I did about Alejandro.

"Where's Myles?" Kevin asked and a door slammed.

"Traveling southeast on CA19. The last town they drove through was Monjas."

"Fuck me, service sucks here. I'm north of him just outside of San Pedro Pinula."

"Figured that was it," Garrett said. "We've been trying to reach you for over twenty minutes."

"The mountains are hell on my service. Where am I going? Looks like in another twelve miles I intersect with JAL-1 and that will take me south to meet up with CA 19."

"Head back to Jalapa and get to Delilah," Zane told Kevin.

"No. Go get Myles."

"Delilah—"

"No. No way. I'm fine where I am. Go get Myles from Aviv. Tamir's with him. I don't know who else. I didn't hear anyone else talking. Just Myles and Aviv and I saw Tamir."

"Myles would not want that, sweetheart," Zane said softly.

Likely to calm the hysteria I heard in my voice.

"Kevin," I whispered. "Please go get Myles for me."

"Fuck."

That was said by a variety of different male voices.

"How do you feel about driving yourself to the airport?" Gabe asked.

I fucking hated it.

"I can...um...do that."

"No fucking—"

"Z, Kevin has to get to Myles," Owen put in.

"I can do it," I said stronger. "I have my pack with my passport and ID."

"Keys? Do you have the keys to the Mitsubishi?" Zane asked logically.

Fuck.

I didn't have them.

"No. But I can look for Alejandro's keys. Take his car."

"And how will you know which car is his?"

"Stop being fucking logical, Zane Lewis!" I shouted. "I don't know how I'll figure it out but I will. I'll leave right now and get to the airport. I'll go wherever you send me, I swear it. But please, I'm begging you; send Kevin to get Myles."

"Christ Almighty," Zane snapped "You women are a pain in my ass."

"I got this," I lied.

I didn't have it, but for Myles, I'd find it.

I didn't have any other choice.

"Without Myles, she shouldn't fly commercial," Garrett said. "I'll call Tex to arrange for her to use Kevin's plane. He was going to Houston with Arias and catching a connecting flight from there. We'll reroute and take her to an airfield close to Killeen. I'll call Ghost and get him on standby."

"Delilah, get something to write the directions on," Kevin said.

I froze.

I had to leave the bathroom.

My mind screamed for me to get a move on before Zane changed his mind and sent Kevin to get me.

Come on, Delilah, move!

"Delilah?" Kevin called.

"Yeah?"

"Where are you? Right now, where are you standing?"

"In the bathroom where Myles told me to stay."

No matter what you hear, baby. Promise me you won't leave the bathroom.

"You need me to come to you first?"

Absolutely not!

"No."

"Then make like a tree and get outta there."

It took me a second, then I got it.

"Did you just *Back to the Future* me?"

"Delilah, go into the living room and find something to write on. Do it now and do it quick. I gotta tell you how to get to the airport. Cell service sucks as soon as you get into the mountains."

Kevin was firm but not impatient. He needed me to move so he could get on the road.

I was wasting time.

Fuck it.

If someone was out there, I'd deal with it.

I picked up my pack, slid it out, and opened the door.

Before I could think, panic, or freeze like an idiot I marched into the living room and looked around.

No one was there.

No one.

I'd hidden in the bathroom like a fucking baby for *nothing*.

My gaze landed on Myles's pack and I rushed to it.

"His pack's here," I said into the phone. "Rifle and both handguns are on the table."

"Find something to write with," Kevin prompted.

I rushed to the kitchen, the epicenter of most houses,

and opened and closed drawers until I found the junk drawer. There was a pad and half a dozen pens mixed in with the other detritus.

"Tell me," I demanded.

Kevin quickly rattled off directions which included landmarks he'd passed up until he stopped—*to dump a dead body*. I was not going to think about that or Alejandro's betrayal.

Myles was all that was important.

"Got it."

"I'm disconnecting now," Kevin announced. "Garrett, keep me posted."

"Will do."

"Delilah?" Kevin called instead of disconnecting. "You need me, call me."

"Just bring Myles home and be careful."

"I will, Delilah. I promise."

Keys.

I needed keys. I folded up my directions and shoved them in my pocket and rushed to Myles's backpack and rummaged through it until I found what I was looking for.

Thank God!

"I have keys!" I shouted. "What should I do with the guns?"

"Leave them," Zane told me.

Leave them?

"Myles taught me how—"

"Myles isn't there," Zane reminded me softly. "You do not want to get caught with a firearm in a foreign country."

Damn.

I glanced at the Glock and thought about ignoring Zane.

"Zane's right, Delilah," Gabe said. "Myles could buy his way out of a situation. You can't. Don't chance it. Leave the gun and drive safely to the airport."

Shit.

Okay, Gabe was right.

I picked up Myles's pack and looked at the door.

I promise I'll make you soar.

I steeled my spine and walked out the door.

I lived in Virginia, we had mountains there. We also had mountain roads. But none were like what I was driving on right then. In America, there were these awesome things called guardrails. Apparently, Guatemala hadn't gotten the memo that guardrails were awesome, terrific, handy barriers that gave some protection from running off the road and rolling to your death. And Guatemalan drivers were possibly some of the bravest in the world. Oncoming traffic zoomed by. And I swear on all things holy a man who looked to be over one hundred pulled up behind me, swerved to pass me but slowed down next to my car, and shouted before he shook his hand at me and zipped ahead of me.

Kevin must've been crazy because I'd been driving for twenty-five minutes and I had not gotten as far as he did. I also had no cell service, which was not making the drive any easier.

Two days ago I would've laughed if Myles had told me I'd give anything to hear Zane's voice. That was if hearing

Myles's wasn't an option but since I didn't have that option, Zane was the next best thing. Hell, I would've laughed myself stupid if Myles had told me that under all the gruff and sarcasm Zane Lewis could be sweet and gentle.

Kevin told me the airport was a little over two hours away which meant it would be a minimum of a three-hour drive since I was driving well below the speed limit.

Soon.

I'd be there soon.

And Kevin would get to Myles.

He'd be all right.

I spent the next thirty minutes repeating my mantra—Kevin would get Myles. They'd both be all right.

Over and over until I was out of the mountains and my phone rang.

"Hello?"

"You doin' all right?" Zane asked.

"If I ever tell you I want to visit Guatemala remind me that I don't."

It must be said, the countryside was unbelievably beautiful. But the drivers were lunatics and the roads were shit.

"I don't remember the drivers being this insane when Myles was driving," I added.

I heard Zane chuckle.

Holy shit.

"You're making good time."

"How do you know?"

"The watch."

"Oh, right. I forgot. I think I have an hour and a half until I get to the airstrip."

"You're out of the mountains now, it'll be an easier drive."

Thank God.

"Where's Kevin? Does he have Myles? Should I wait for them at the air—"

"Not yet, sweetheart. The pilot is there and ready to take off as soon as you get there."

I closed my eyes—just for a moment; I was driving after all. When I opened them I pulled in a breath and fire scorched through me.

Everything hit me at once.

Absolutely everything.

Myles showing me I was more than I thought I was and coming to terms with the lies I'd been told. Falling in love, then falling deeper, then Myles catching me just like he said he would. Abrams and Tamir taking away the one good thing I'd ever had in my life and how that could end in a very final way.

My lungs burned and my breath hitched.

Zane was trying to be nice to me and not freak me out so I could drive safely to the airport. But it was too late.

Too fucking late.

"Please tell me where they are."

The silence that ensued crushed me.

I felt the terror unravel in my belly.

"Sweetheart," Zane murmured. "I need you to get to the airport safely."

There it was, the confirmation Zane was being a nice guy. I didn't want nice, I wanted the truth, I wanted his snarky, blunt, forthcomingness back.

"Tell me," I said with more vigor.

"Delilah—"

"Myles didn't shield me from the truth."

"Right, but he shielded you from the emotional fallout."

That was the damn truth.

"I can handle it. Tell me."

Again with the silence.

"They're still on the move. Kevin's about thirty minutes behind them. He's doing his best to catch up with Abrams and Tamir before they stop somewhere."

Right, because stopping somewhere would mean any number of bad things could happen to Myles.

"Thank you," I whispered.

"You're welcome. Do you want me to keep you company while you drive?"

I closed my eyes again, this time a little longer than I should've while behind the wheel but I couldn't help it. This new and sweet Zane was too much.

"You're busy—"

"I've got twelve men in the office right now that would be pleased as fuck if I stayed in my office and on the phone with you instead of bossin' them around."

"Will you tell me about Myles?"

"What do you want to know?"

"Everything."

"He's a crazy bastard." Zane laughed. "Did he tell you he's from Colorado?"

"Yeah."

"Did he tell you about the time in the dead of winter he snowshoed into the woods to set up game cameras after a mountain lion was seen roaming his parents' property, and he decided he wanted one as a pet?"

"What? A mountain lion as a pet?"

"He was six."

"Six?"

"Yes, six," Zane confirmed and laughed.

All the way to the airport Zane regaled me with stories about Myles. He kept them light and entertaining. He never touched on Myles's military career or the work he did for Z Corps. By the time I made it to my destination I had to agree—Myles was crazy-adventurous, crazy-brave, and crazy-funny. And the best part—and there were a lot of good parts—but, the best was learning about Myles through Zane's perspective. The pride and camaraderie I heard helped settle me.

But just talking about him gave me the strength I needed to push forward.

Myles was going to make it home, he had to, there was no other option and I wouldn't allow my mind to wander. He was strong and resourceful. He was smart and experienced. And he deserved nothing less than my full confidence that he'd be all right. And Kevin would help, he, too, was strong, resourceful, smart, and experienced.

Myles asked me to believe in him.

So I believed.

He could do anything.

CHAPTER 20

It had been a long fucking time since I'd been bound and hooded.

An un-*fucking*-pleasant experience I hadn't taken kindly to the first time I experienced it in Turkey. I wasn't enjoying it any more this time around.

I'd gone peacefully, walked out the door with Abrams, Cohen, and two other men that screamed former IDF.

Four against one in close quarters wasn't very good odds and would've ended bloody. Bullets would've torn through drywall as well as flesh. And with Delilah in the bathroom, blind to the situation going on right outside the bathroom door, she could've been riddled with bullets. A chance I wasn't going to take until Abrams told Cohen to search the house.

Tamir Cohen could not march Delilah into the room without exposing his lie. He'd told Abrams he'd killed her. It had been a gamble, a huge one, but one that proved to be the right call when Cohen lied again and told Abrams there was no one else in the house.

There was nowhere for Delilah to hide in the small bathroom and even if there had been, Cohen was well-versed in clearing a room, he would've found her.

Which meant he saw her.

And let her be.

If either of the other two men with Abrams had been sent to search the house, a firefight would've ensued. I wouldn't've taken the chance of Delilah being presented to Abrams.

So, I left peacefully, leaving Delilah behind, trusting my team back home would call Kevin and get him back to the house to get her.

That was the only thing that had kept me sane over the hours—Kevin was close. He would turn around and get her safe.

I trusted him to take care of her.

Then Zane would call in an extraction team.

It was all good.

Abrams hadn't killed me yet, proving he was a stupid motherfucker.

Four against one might've been shitty odds but I'd faced worse and now that Delilah was safely out of the equation four men were going to die.

Tamir would be last.

He and I had shit to talk about.

* * *

Kevin Monroe watched from a distance.

Aviv Abrams, Tamir Cohen, two unknown males, two unknown females, and Myles.

He could guess the females were Alejandro's aunt and

grandmother. Further, he could guess the two unknown males were also former IDF as were Abrams and Cohen.

Two against four—stellar odds—that was, if Myles wasn't hooded and cuffed.

The women had been ordered to their knees. Abrams's command was followed instantly and even from a distance, Kevin could see their fear.

"I'm going in."

"Check in when you're done."

Kevin disconnected the call, turned his phone on silent, but left it on so Garrett could track him.

Abrams had made a critical tactical error with his choice of locations. One that would be the death of him. Not only were they in a wooded area, outside in the open, but there were too many places for Kevin to use to take cover. Trees that he could use to hide his approach, dilapidated buildings to conceal his position once he was in place.

It was a mistake that was almost comical.

Abrams had gone soft, become complacent, thought he was invincible.

No man was.

And today Kevin was going to prove it.

* * *

The hood was yanked off and I blinked against the blinding sun.

Fields. Trees. Outbuildings. No homes. Two women.

Fuck.

Whoever they were, they were fucked.

"Where's my scientist?" Abrams asked.

"Please tell me you didn't drive me all this way to ask me questions I've already answered."

"Where is Alejandro?" Abrams repeated.

"You can ask a hundred different ways and my answer will still be the same. I don't know."

Abrams swung the barrel of his rifle to the women huddled on their knees and asked again, "Where is he?"

"I still don't know."

A shot rang out and my gut roiled.

Fucking, fuck.

High-pitched screams filled the quiet beauty of my surrounding.

I didn't look, I didn't need to.

"Shut her up," Abrams commanded one of his men.

I didn't pay attention to that either. My focus was on Tamir—jaw tight, eyes hard, biceps twitching.

Tamir Cohen wasn't down with his boss killing women.

His angry gaze came to mine and I kept mine neutral.

Stone cold—that was the only chance I had of getting out of this alive.

Patience and disconnect from the carnage.

"Do you now remember where he is?" Abrams asked.

Fucking Christ.

"I'm telling you, Abrams, I don't know where Arias is. But my guess is on a plane headed back to the U.S."

"Wrong answer." He swung his rifle back to the women—or woman as it were—and paused. "Where?"

"I still don't—"

My answer was cut short when he pulled the trigger.

Jesus.

The welcomed and familiar feeling of rage uncoiled and swelled.

"Get on your knees."

That was never going to fucking happen.

"I think you know that's never gonna happen."

Anger twisted his ugly face when Abrams shouted, "Knees, Simms."

"You're gonna have to kill me on my feet."

Abrams swung his rifle to his back, yanked a blade from the sheath on his hip, and stalked toward me.

Brilliant.

He was two steps away from me when a shot rang out and Abrams crumpled to the ground mid-stride. My eyes sliced to Cohen and he shot again, another man hit the dirt. But the third shot came and nailed the third man before Cohen could take aim.

What the fuck?

"Drop your gun, Cohen," Kevin shouted, coming out from behind the barn.

"I think you know that's never gonna happen," Cohen returned, using my earlier statement.

Though he did holster his weapon and moved in my direction.

"Turn around so I can cut you loose."

Again, what the fuck?

"I'll do it," Kevin announced.

"One of you fucking do it," I barked.

Kevin came up behind me and a moment later my arms were at my sides.

"Goddamn," I ground out, and shook out my arms as blood rushed back to my limbs. "You think maybe you could've done that back at Arias's place?"

"Not without Delilah getting hit in the crossfire." He told me something I'd already thought of.

Wait.

"Where the fuck is Delilah?"

"Her plane took off almost thirty minutes ago."

Relief so overwhelming I had to fight to keep my feet tore through me.

"Now, what the *fuck* was that?" Kevin asked.

"Arias safe?" Cohen inquired instead of answering.

"Arias is dead. I'm assuming that's his aunt and grandmother."

Kevin gestured to the two dead women.

Christ.

"The research safe?" Cohen pushed.

"Yes. Now start—"

"Lewis will dispose of it?"

"Jesus Christ," Kevin exploded. "Enough about the goddamn research. Start talking, Cohen."

"That research—"

I didn't let Cohen continue, I'd had enough.

"I'm grateful you saved my life but that shit's wearing off quick, Cohen. I haven't forgotten about you snatching my woman, scaring the fuck out of her, and treating her like she was a fucking animal instead of a human. You got five minutes to convince me not to yank your intestines out. No fucking joke, Cohen, five minutes."

A mean, nasty smile that would give small children nightmares for years tugged at his mouth.

What in the hell?

"I didn't hurt her," he said.

"No, but you scared the fuck—"

"Yeah, I know I did. I couldn't help that. But I did not

hurt her. I didn't put a hand on her. I got her as far away from that piece of shit as I could and once she was safe and hidden I called you to go get her."

"Yeah, let's talk about that—the part why you killed Abrams."

"He killed my brother."

Fucking shit.

CHAPTER 21

"Hi, Delilah, I'm Ghost."

The jet had barely stopped moving and the pilot hadn't even announced I could remove my seat belt when the cabin door was opened and a nice-looking dark-haired man appeared.

Zane had told me a man called Ghost would be picking me up. But Zane was clear I wasn't to leave the plane until I confirmed Ghost's identity.

I felt my cheeks heat even before I asked the question Zane told me to ask.

"Can you please show me your fairy wand?"

The man startled and his eyes widened.

It must be said that when Zane gave me these instructions I was half in a daze. I was out of my mind with worry about Myles. I was freaked out that the pilot who would be flying me to Killeen, Texas was heavily armed and he had practically dragged me onto the plane, shut the door, and had us off the ground in a flash. So when Zane was giving me his last-minute instructions before I had to power down my phone I wasn't really paying attention.

"Come again?"

"I'm supposed to ask you to show me your fairy wand," I repeated.

A loud bark of laughter rang through the small cabin. My gaze swung to the open door and a man so big he had to bend at the waist to clear the opening was laughing so hard his shoulders were shaking.

"Zane tell you to ask Ghost that, or did Tex?" the man asked, still chuckling.

"Um...Zane."

"She wants to see your *fairy wand*. That's hilarious. Hurry up and show her, so we can get on the road."

Ghost blinked a few times then smiled big and pulled up his right pant leg and shifted so I could see a tattoo of an eagle. There was a lightning bolt to the side and the eagle was holding a rifle in one of its talons and a fairy wand in the other.

I glanced back up and met his gaze.

Ghost dropped his pant leg and asked, "Ready?"

"Yeah, thanks for humoring me. I'm gonna kill Zane when I get home."

"It's no problem. I shouldn't be yet I'm still shocked Zane knows I have that tattoo."

I picked up my pack and Myles's but didn't get more than a step when Ghost held his hand out.

"I'll take those."

I stepped back and shook my head.

"No thank you, I got 'em."

Ghost studied me for a moment then read the situation wrong.

"Tex is a good friend of mine. I've worked with him a lot of years. Know Myles and Zane, too. Zane wouldn't've sent you to me if they didn't trust me. That means you can trust me, too."

"I know."

And I did know. Zane or Kevin never would've sent me to Ghost unless he knew Ghost would protect me.

"It's just I'm used to wearing my pack. And the other one's Myles's and…well…I just wanna keep it close."

"Okay." Ghost lifted his hands in surrender.

"It's not that I don't trust you," I rushed out.

"You want a part of your man close, I totally get that. It's all good."

Ghost moved to the front of the airplane and slowly walked down the steps in front of me which was a good thing because when I caught sight of the big guy from the doorway I stumbled and Ghost had to catch me.

Myles was tall. If I had to guess he had a good eight inches on me, placing him about six foot three. Ghost was tall, too, but the other man was humongous.

"Whoa. You okay?" Ghost steadied me.

"I've never seen anyone that tall before."

The man smiled, and out in the warm Texas sun, I could also see he had a gnarly scar that ran from his temple to the corner of his lip. Whatever had happened it looked like it hurt like a mother.

I wasn't tall neither was I short; at five foot seven I was pretty average. But never in my life had I felt small. And that was exactly how I felt when the man stopped in front of me.

"I'm Truck."

Truck.

MYLES (SPECIAL FORCES: OPERATION ALPHA)

Good name.

"Delilah," I introduced myself like an idiot.

"This way," Truck motioned to a big black SUV.

Now that the shock of embarrassment had worn off from asking Ghost about his fairy wand I was getting antsy.

The three-hour flight seemed to take forever. I'd never flown on a private jet before, and any other time I might've nosed around or maybe sat back and enjoyed the luxury ride. But I couldn't stop worrying about Myles, and now that I was here I didn't want to be rude. Ghost was there doing Zane a favor but I also sort of didn't care.

"I'm sorry to be rude, but I need to call Zane."

Truck tilted his head and looked from me to Ghost then back to me.

She lied to you. Everything she told you was utter shit. All of it. How she made you feel was shit.

No, Delilah, it wasn't you.

I promise I'll make you soar.

I felt wet hit my eyes then roll down my cheek.

Now was not the time to have a flashback of my shitty childhood and the lies my mother had told me. I quickly swiped it away and stood tall. I wasn't being rude. No one was going to scold me for checking in with Zane. I wanted to know what was happening with Myles and I was going to damn well do just that.

"Delilah—"

"I'm fine." I waved off Truck's concern.

"Get in, you can call him on the way," Ghost said and opened the back door.

I climbed in without taking off my pack. I didn't care

249

how stupid it was that I was using a backpack like it was a security blanket. I needed it close, mine and Myles's.

I pulled my phone out of the side pocket of Myles's bag and turned it back on. While I was waiting for it to power up I watched Ghost slide in behind the steering wheel. Then I took stock in my emotional state. When I found I was having trouble breathing I decided I was a basket case and I'd worry about that later. The good news was, I was so worried about Myles I hadn't thought about my crazy need to shower five million times a day. The bad news was, I was no longer thinking about getting clean because Aviv had taken Myles.

God, I hated him.

Aviv not Myles.

A vicious thought cruised through my mind and I felt no shame when I hoped Kevin beat Aviv to death. He was a sick, rabid monster. So was Tamir.

Ghost was pulling out of the gates when I dialed Zane.

He picked up on the first ring, "Are you with Ghost?"

I had the sweet Zane on the phone. The one who was worried about me.

"Yeah and when I get home I'm kicking you in the shin for having me ask about his fairy wand. I was too emotionally distraught to think about what else that could mean to a guy and how that might sound when I asked. How's Myles? Did Kevin find him?"

"Myles is fine and as of ten minutes ago, he's on a plane to Killeen. He'll be to you in a few hours."

The sob tore from me loud and painful. My shoulders shook and my head dropped forward.

"Kevin?" I croaked.

"All good, sweetheart. Both of them are fine. Kevin's on his way to Maryland."

"Delilah?" Truck called.

"He's fine. They're both fine," I cried.

"Should I stay at the airport if he's on his way?"

"No. Ghost is taking you to Colin and Erin's house. It's more of a vacation home so no one's there. Ghost will stay with you until Myles picks you up."

"Truck's with him," I told Zane.

"Good. I figured he'd bring backup."

Backup?

Oh no!

"What happened to Aviv?"

"Myles will tell you everything when he gets there. You have nothing to worry about. You are safe. Totally safe, I promise. It's over, Delilah."

I let go of the breath I was holding. Zane didn't strike me as a man who would make a promise he couldn't keep.

"Thank you," I whispered.

"Call me if you need me but Ghost and Truck will take care of you."

"Thanks."

My forehead dropped to the top of Myles's backpack and I wrapped my arms around it as tightly as I could.

Myles was on his way to me.

He was fine.

Kevin was fine.

It was over.

* * *

Things were not fine.

When we pulled into the driveway of a nice house in a nice neighborhood there were cars and trucks parked in the drive.

"My wife, Rayne, is here," Ghost said as he guided the SUV around the other vehicles and parked in front of a two-story garage. "Along with Truck's wife, Mary, Fletch and Emily, and Coach and Harley."

I didn't have time to ask why all those people were there. The front door opened and two men strode out to meet us. Both had an air of confidence about them, same as Truck and Ghost. Zane hadn't explained his acquaintance with the men but I'd guess they were all former military or maybe still active duty. Again I didn't have time to ask because my door was opened and Truck was helping me out.

"Delilah, that's Coach and Fletch," Truck introduced.

Holy moly what did these Texan boys eat? The man who'd jerked his chin when Truck called out, "Coach" was almost as tall as Truck. And the one named Fletch wasn't as tall but he was still big and broad-shouldered.

"Hi. Nice to meet you."

"Let me take your bags," Fletch said stepping forward.

"She's got 'em." Ghost came to my aid. "But let's get you inside so you can set 'em down."

We all trekked into the house and two things assaulted me at once—women chattering and the smell of food. My stomach took the opportunity to remind me I hadn't eaten since dinner…when was that? Last night? Two days ago? What time was it, anyway?

"Hey there, you're Delilah. I'm Harley." A tall woman approached with a huge smile on her face. Her black-framed glasses and cute bobbed haircut made her look like a sex-kitten nerd. She was stunning. "Welcome to Texas. Oh, and Coach belongs to me."

Harley paused as three women filed out of the kitchen.

"I'll make the introductions," she continued. "That's Rayne, Ghost is hers." Harley pointed to a pretty brunette with an Old Hollywood bombshell figure and I was instantly jealous of her fantastic curves. Harley went on pointing as she went. "That's Emily, Fletch is hers and this used to be their house until an RPG took it out. But don't worry, Fletch remodeled it and that includes reframing before he sold it to Colin and Erin. Anyway, over there is Mary and Truck is hers."

I must've looked like a deer caught in a Super Duty F250's headlights and if I didn't I was doing a damn good job of hiding my shock.

"You look like you're scouting out places to hide," Mary said.

There it was, I wasn't hiding anything.

"Mary! God, be nice," Rayne sighed.

"How am I not being nice? Look at her."

"Tex called Fletch and said you've had a bad night," Emily joined. "He wasn't telling tales or anything but Tex wanted to make sure we had everything you'd need. We didn't know—that is, us women didn't know—what time zone you were coming from or when the last time you had a proper meal was so we decided on brunch. Are you hungry? We didn't know what you liked so there's a little bit of everything in the kitchen."

I didn't say anything. I just stared. Then I glanced around the room. Four men taking time out of their day to help me. Four women welcoming a stranger and going out of their way to cook me food.

I used to have friends. I was never truly close to any of them. But I'd still had them. None of them would've ever gone out of their way for me. Not that I could blame them, I never actually connected with them on any deep level. But still, I'd never had what these four women very obviously had and I'd never been on the receiving end of this much kindness. No, that wasn't true, I had been. From the start, Myles had given me everything.

He'd shown me what true friendship was, he'd propped me up so I could soar. He'd made it safe for me to get free of the garbage I used to carry around. And in his absence, he'd given me Zane, Kevin, Ghost, Truck, Coach, Fletch, Mary, Harley, Rayne, and Emily.

And I was going to take it.

Unfortunately, since I was at the beginning stages of learning how to openly share my feelings I didn't hold back.

I just went for it and blabbed everything in the world's worst case of verbal diarrhea.

I locked eyes with Mary and admitted, "The last few months of my life have sucked. It started when I learned my boss was a psychotic maniac who wanted to build his own personal army of super soldiers. To do this he wanted to rewire their brains."

Mary's eyes got big and I heard a gasp but I sallied forth. "I know, crazy, right? And if that wasn't bad enough, he was also engineering wartime AI systems. I think he must've watched *Star Wars* one too many times as a child. So, anyway, he found out I knew about his crazy research which included experimenting on pig brains and it worked. He found a doctor who could essentially bring a dead pig back to life, or at least restore brain function after the pig had been totally brain-dead. Obviously, he didn't like that I knew this or that I was feeding this information to a reporter, because, hello, he was insane and needed to be stopped so he sent his top-dog head of security after me."

I paused to take a breath and looked at Harley. "So, top-dog head of security finds me, but he doesn't kill me, he kidnaps me and takes me on a two-month ride from California down through Mexico. Then he drops me off and locks me in a house...*with no running water.*"

"No," Harley murmured.

"Yes! I thought I was going to die. Then Myles finds me. But I didn't know he was there to save me so I fought him and bit his arm until I tasted blood. Now he has my teeth marks forever scarred into his arm."

I heard a masculine chuckle and my eyes sliced to the men.

"It was gross. I had a mouth full of blood."

"I bet you did," Coach muttered.

"Way to go," Truck added.

"So what happened next?" Rayne asked.

"Wait!" Harley called out. "Put your bags on the couch."

I reluctantly set Myles's bag down and shrugged mine off. As soon as I was free of the packs I finished my story.

"So Myles saves me but instead of coming home, he hides me. Then while we were eating lunch one afternoon, Myles catches someone taking pictures of us so we had to flee Mazatlán."

"Oh, Mazatlán," Emily cut in. "I've never been but I hear it's beautiful."

"It was so totally beautiful," I confirmed. "We left there in such a hurry I had to leave behind my shampoo. Oh, let me back up. I'd had about five showers in two months so when we got to the hotel I was so filthy and gross it took half a bottle of shampoo and a whole bar of soap to wash clean. But my hair was so matted, Myles had to cut it with his field knife."

"I didn't want to ask you about your haircut, but sister, you need a trim to even that out," Mary interjected.

"Yeah, Myles warned me he'd never cut someone's hair before and offered to take me to a barber."

"A *barber*?" Harley giggled.

"Where'd you go next?" Rayne asked.

"Farther south to a safe house. We spent the night there, then we got word that my ex-boss found out the scientist I'd helped fake his death was really alive and well, living in Guatemala, so we hightailed our asses to Jalapa. We got there and found the scientist but my ex-boss found us. Myles told me to hide in the bathroom and not come out no matter what. So there I was hiding in the shower with the flimsy plastic curtain closed because you know that will stop a bullet." I stopped and shook my head. "And while I'm in there hiding, top-dog head of security comes into the bathroom, looks me square in the eye, and tells me to be quiet. Then he tells my ex-boss that the house is empty and there's no one else there. I don't know what to make of that; the man kidnapped me and held me against my will for two months but he lied to protect me. Then my ex-boss and the top-dog take Myles. Now I'm here and Zane says that Myles escaped and is fine and on his way here to pick me up. And throughout all of this, I fell in love for the first time ever and learned that my man-eating bitch of a mother who already held the title for the worst mother in history was also a lying bitch."

"Holy shit," Mary gasped.

"How long ago?" Rayne inquired.

"How long ago did Myles save me?" Rayne nodded. "Um…a few days ago."

"A few days ago?"

"Oh, please, when it's right it's right," Mary said. "One hour, one day, or one month. Besides, you fell in love with Ghost during a one-night stand."

"I did not," Rayne denied.

"You did," Ghost contradicted. "How about we plate up some food, I'm starving."

Rayne swept her hand in the direction of the kitchen and a few minutes later we all had plates of food. The men took theirs to the back patio and the women sat at the huge dining table.

"Colin and Erin must have a lot of dinner parties to need a table this big," I mused.

"Do you know Erin?" Harley asked.

"No."

"Erin Anderson, President Anderson's daughter. She's married to Colin. The Andersons are from Texas so when the president left office he and his wife moved back. Not to Killeen but only about an hour away. So when Colin and Erin are in town, they host her parents. We also all come over on occasion. This table gets a lot of use; Erin loves to entertain and Colin loves to give Erin whatever she wants," Harley explained.

"Myles did tell me that. I'd forgotten."

"Right, like you didn't have more important things on your mind, like say, falling in love." Harley smiled.

"You have a cool name," I told her.

"Thanks, but it's not as cool as Emily's."

Emily was a pretty name but Harley was cool.

"She goes by Emily but her real name is Miracle," Rayne explained.

"That's a great name!" I told her, then looked back at Rayne. "I'm assuming your name is Rayne with a Y and N and E and not like the water dripping from the sky, rain."

"You'd be correct."

"Harley, Miracle, and Rayne," Mary grumbled. "Then there's plain old Mary."

"There's nothing plain or boring about you, friend. Besides, you need a common name to balance out all your attitude and sass." Rayne nudged her friend and smiled.

"Why is it when a woman is strong and independent she automatically has an attitude?" Mary snapped.

"And there she is." Emily giggled.

Mary narrowed her eyes on Emily and the rest of the women dissolved into fits of laughter.

It felt so good, I joined them.

I'd spilled my guts to four strangers. I'd opened up and they hadn't rejected me. They welcomed me into the circle.

Who knew it could be so easy?

Life wasn't about being alone and lonely.

It was this.

Connecting. Friendship. Laughter.

And most of all, love.

CHAPTER 22

From my airplane window, I saw Beatle leaning against the rental car Tex arranged for him to pick up for me. His wife, Casey, was nowhere in sight. The small private plane taxied to a stop and Beatle pushed off the car. By the time I'd thanked the pilot and opened my door Beatle was there waiting for me to jump down.

"Good to see you in one piece, brother," Beatle greeted.

"Good to be seen."

"I hear that. Tex filled us in."

I figured Tex would.

"How's Delilah?"

"Haven't seen her. Casey's on kid duty and I was dealing with picking up your car. But Ghost called a few minutes ago. Rayne, Mary, Harley, and Emily are keeping her company."

Fucking shit.

I adored those women just as much as I loved my teammates' women. They were good women. But Delilah wasn't used to having people poking in her business and those women would spend whatever time was required for them to suss out what had happened to Delilah. And they'd do it not because they were nosey but because their hearts were as big as Texas and they'd see a sister in distress and move in to help.

"She's kinda shy."

"Shy? Ghost said two minutes after meeting the women, she laid out her whole ordeal. Including falling in love with you. He also reported she's in the house laughing her ass off with the rest of the women."

Jesus.

I felt the smile tugging up the corners of my mouth and at the same time the throb on the left side of my chest that had started when she told me she loved me intensified.

"Let's get you to your woman," Beatle suggested.

We were on the road, Beatle driving, when he asked, "Do you need Truck to look you over?"

Truck was his team's medic and he was a damn good one.

"Nope. Hooded and cuffed, but Abrams didn't lay a hand on me. Weirdest shit ever. Don't know if he just wanted Arias and the research and planned on letting me go after, so he didn't catch the wrath of Zane or what. Considering he's dead, and he hadn't clued Tamir in on his plan I'll never know. Though he had no problem killing two helpless, unarmed women and he was getting impatient so maybe he was planning on killing me. At this point, I don't care. Just happy to get to my woman and do that without her having to see me beat to shit."

"I hear that."

The rest of the drive was spent with Beatle filling me in on what was going on in Texas. I'd never been on a team with him, Ghost, Truck, Fletch, Coach, Hollywood, Blade, or Fish but the 1st Special Forces Operations Detachment community was small. Over the years I'd run into them both during missions and stateside training ops. I'd liked them all from the time I met them and that hadn't changed over the years. All of them were married, devoted family men, and the happiness and pride in Beatle's voice as he talked about everyone's families couldn't be missed.

He'd just finished telling me about Fletch and Emily's daughter, Annie, when he turned into Colin's neighborhood.

"I bet she's giving Fletch a run for his money," I noted.

"The girl is a ball of energy and fire. She's the Colonel of the Kid Brigade. I swear to you, she's got the ones who can walk in formation, teaching them how to march. I think we're all a little scared since Annie's started training Hollywood's daughter, Kate to be her second-in-command. Her brother Ethan would've been a better choice; the little guy is already showing signs of being a natural diplomat. But not Kate, she's up for anything. She's the first one to yell 'charge' when they're playing in the backyard."

"I'm thinking you need to disband Annie's Army before you all find yourselves in the midst of a hostile coup. Then it'll be dessert for breakfast and vegetables will be a thing of the past.

"You're not wrong. We're on high-alert for the rebellion. Our problem is Annie just might be able to outsmart us."

Beatle was correct about that. Annie was smart and resourceful. She was also loving and kind so she might spare her parents in the takeover. Maybe.

We pulled into Colin's driveway. While Beatle was still negotiating around all the cars in the drive the front door opened and out flew Delilah.

Without me having to say a word, Beatle hit the brakes. I'd barely gotten my feet on the pavement when Delilah did a running flying leap into my arms. Her legs went around my waist, her arms around my shoulders, and with her face shoved into my neck she broke out into hysterical sobs.

"Hey, baby," I whispered against her ear.

Her body bucked and I held on as tight as I dared.

"You're home," she cried.

"Yeah, Delilah, *we're* home, baby."

Another sob tore through her and she nuzzled deeper.

"House," Beatle muttered.

When I turned I saw it.

Delilah had spent a short amount of time with these women but in those hours she'd won them over. They cared about her. Rayne and Harley were wiping tears off their cheeks, Emily's lips were pinched together, and even Mary, who was always watchful and the last to break down, but arguably the most fiercely protective out of all of them, was tucked close to her husband.

That didn't surprise me one bit, Delilah was sweet and likable. What shocked the shit out of me was that she'd let them in. Shocked and proud.

The couples were moving out of my way as I carried

Delilah towards the door when I heard Truck say, "I remember a time you used to welcome me home from a mission like that."

"I've never welcomed you home like that," Mary said.

"My point, baby."

He was teasing her, bringing her out of the heavy so she didn't break down.

"You're as big as a tree, Trucker. I'd have to be an Olympic high jumper to get my arms around your neck," she snapped.

Pure Mary.

The woman had attitude, lots of it, all of it good.

I didn't stop when I hit the living room, though I did notice my backpack and hers sitting on the couch. Instead of focusing on why she'd schlep my pack all the way to Texas and the reasons behind her motives I concentrated on getting us to Colin and Erin's bedroom.

We had less than an hour before we had to leave to catch our flight back home to Maryland but I needed time alone with Delilah before we had to haul ass to the airport. I knew what was waiting for us back in Maryland and I needed to prepare her for it.

I settled on the bed and gave her a few moments before I started.

"First things first, back in Jalapa you gave me something special and I didn't get a chance to give it back. I love you, Delilah."

Her breath hitched and a strangled moan fanned over my neck.

"Kevin filled me in on what happened after I was taken. Proud of you, baby. So damn proud."

"Aviv and Tamir had you and I was so scared what they'd do to you."

She didn't know that Abrams and Tamir had not been alone and there was no reason to bring it up. It was over.

"You did everything right. Kevin told me how brave you were."

"I wasn't brave. I wanted to stay in the bathroom and hide like you made me promise, but I didn't want Kevin to come back to Jalapa when he needed to be looking for you. All I had to do was drive to the airport."

No, she'd had to overcome her fear. And she had to find the courage to face an uncertain situation by herself. Something she'd admitted having a hard time with. Yet, she'd done it.

"Zane helped me," she whispered.

"Yeah?"

"He stayed on the phone with me. Him and Kevin at first. Then after I got service back Zane talked to me for a long time. He told me stories about you. So, you see, I didn't do it by myself. I had you and Zane with me the whole time. That was how I was able to do it."

I didn't know what got service back meant and I didn't care.

Delilah was safe and in my arms.

Nothing else mattered.

Even though Zane would disagree, I owed him huge. It was rare, but it happened; Zane would set aside his armor and his soft side would come out and he'd prove what we all knew—he'd do anything for any one of us. And that included our women and exposing a side of himself very few ever got to see.

"Delilah, baby, I need to explain to you what happened.

Can you handle it now or do you wanna wait until we get home?"

Delilah shifted in my arms and when her head came up, her eyes darted around my face and fresh tears started to fall.

"Zane said you were fine," she whispered. "Are you fine?"

"Totally fine. Not a scratch on me anywhere."

"I missed you."

I rolled, taking Delilah with me until she was on her back and I was balancing on my elbow, hovering over her. Her hands went to my chest and drifted up until they came to a rest on my shoulders. My hand went to her cheek and I thumbed a tear away.

"Abrams is dead," I told her gently and braced for her response.

She didn't have one so I went on.

"Tamir Cohen killed him and in doing so he saved my life. Though saying that, Kevin was in place and if Tamir hadn't acted, Kevin would've taken him out."

"What?"

"Tamir's brother Isaac was also IDF; he was in a unit called Yamam. When Isaac was killed Tamir asked to be transferred from Shayetet 13 to Yamam. Both units are highly trained but Shayetet is the tip of the spear; transferring was like a demotion. Tamir asked to be moved because he'd heard rumors about the Fear program and the last time Tamir saw Isaac he knew something wasn't right. Word was that the program recruited men from Yamam. It wasn't until after Abrams left the IDF and started his business did Tamir figure out what happened to his brother."

"What happened to him?"

"Abrams killed Isaac to stop him from going to the higher-ups and telling them Tamir had turned. Both men were in the Fear program. As you know it affected each man differently. The IDF shut it down as a failed experiment. But some of the men had adverse reactions. Abrams was killing combatants after they surrendered. It was no longer about protecting, it was killing for Abrams. Isaac witnessed it and was going to report him."

Delilah's fingers dug in and her brows pinched together when she asked, "Then why did Tamir go to work for him?"

"Because the man who came clean about what happened was murdered. And Tamir wanted proof, so when Aviv asked Tamir to come to work for Abrams he took it as an opportunity to get close to Aviv and get what he needed to take him down. And Tamir got what he needed. Then Evette started poking around and you started helping her."

"So he took me," she whispered. "But he didn't hurt me."

"Right. He took you and scared you and he knows what he did. But he was never gonna hurt you. I know you can't believe this and I didn't want to either, but from the beginning, none of us could understand how such an honorable man could turn into Abrams' personal death dealer, but he didn't. He held on to the pieces of himself that he could while he got the proof he needed.

"Tamir wasn't going to kill Abrams—he wanted justice. And for Tamir, the only way justice is served is if Aviv Abrams was discredited. He wanted everyone to know what Abrams did. He wanted him to be publicly shamed. The man that Tamir is, that was the vengeance he needed for his brother. In Israel, your family honor is everything and he wanted Abrams disgraced."

Delilah's eyes drifted closed.

"I don't know how to feel about all of this."

"You feel however you want to feel. Tamir's reasons aren't your problem. He might not have physically harmed you, but baby, he marked you. He had you for months. You were scared—"

"I was scared," Delilah cut me off. "But he saved your life."

"Baby—"

"He saved your life, Myles. I don't care if Kevin was there; Tamir saved you and in doing so he gave up avenging his brother."

"He did," I confirmed.

"Where is he now?"

"On his way to Maryland with Kevin to debrief."

Delilah's eyes flared and her head pushed back onto the mattress.

"You're not gonna see him. When we get to Maryland, we're going straight home. You won't—"

"I wanna see him."

"Delilah, that's not a good idea."

"I need to see him, Myles, and you'll be with me. But I need to thank him. He knew I was in the bathroom. He looked me right in the eye and told me to be quiet. Then he saved you. I want to talk to him."

Christ.

"Whatever you want."

Delilah's lips tipped up into a smile—a playful smile—and finally, after hours of crippling fear, I could breathe.

"Well, right now, what I want is for you to kiss—"

I didn't need her to finish telling me what she wanted.

I kissed my woman.

She tasted like tears.

It was the best kiss of my life.

CHAPTER 23

The last five days blew up in a whirlwind.

The first crazy thing happened before we left Colin's house. Rayne, Harley, Emily, and even Mary had all pulled me into a huge group hug. Then each of them wrote their phone numbers down—since I didn't have a phone and the one I was using belonged to Z Corps—and made me promise to call them when I had a new cell. Which I immediately agreed to, then I made myself a promise not to allow those friendships to drift. I wanted to get to know them better even if they lived in Texas and I'd be living in Maryland.

We'd flown home using our real names and I'd suspected but it was confirmed that Tex could do anything when he'd sent Ghost my driver's license and passport. They were new since my old ones were gone along with my purse, wallet, and credit cards.

By the time we touched down at BWI, I was dead on my feet. I'd been riding on waning adrenaline and was so emotionally spent that Myles got us a Lyft and we went straight to his townhouse. Upon which time he didn't bother with a tour of my new home but instead led me to his bed where I face-planted and fell asleep.

After that, we spent four days locked in the house with the phones turned off.

We lived in a bubble of surreal happiness. We ate, we talked, we told secrets and funny stories. I teased him about trying to tame a mountain lion and he laughed himself silly when I told him about my crazy fascination with mummies. That was something else we did—laughed. It felt so good to just be with Myles without the black cloud of Aviv looming.

We were free to just *be*.

And I ate up every second. So did he. I found that Myles was just as attentive at home as he was in Mexico. He looked me in the eye when I spoke. He asked questions, though studiously avoided anything having to do with my mother. Which worked for me because I'd given her as much of my life as I was going to give her.

Though we did talk about his parents and we agreed to call them after we came out of hiding. We decided this for no other reason than neither of us wanted anyone intruding on our time.

It was like a five-day, twenty-four-seven date.

It was awesome.

Better than awesome.

Further, I found that sex only got better. Sweet or dirty, the sex was so crazy-good he had me addicted. Which worked well for him because several times a day he'd take me and murmur he couldn't get enough. So the bed, shower, vanity, floor in the living room, kitchen counter, couch, and table were all christened.

However, all good things must come to an end. The bubble had burst and we were now on our way to downtown Annapolis. Tamir was leaving to go to Israel and I wanted to see him before he left. It was also time for Myles to get back to work. And I knew he wanted me to meet his friends.

Weirdly, I was excited about this. Normally I'd be dreading the obligatory meet-and-greet where small talk is exchanged. But not now. I was stoked to see Kevin again and finally get to meet Evette face to face. Then there was Zane; I couldn't wait to thank him for keeping me sane all those hours.

"If I didn't love you I'd steal your Bronco and go on the run," I told Myles.

"It's a good thing I love you because if you tried to steal my Bronco, I'd shoot you."

I busted out laughing while Myles continued to drive straight-faced. I felt his hand land on my thigh and I looked down to see it palm up. I set my hand over his palm and threaded my fingers between his and smiled.

He had great hands.

"Now that I've let you out of the house, do you want me to get your hair trimmed up?"

I hadn't thought about my uneven hair since Mary had brought it up.

"I'm not ready yet."

Myles pulled into a parking garage and my belly fluttered.

"Okay. When you are, we'll get it styled."

"I apologize in advance if I say something that embarrasses you," I told him.

"Why would you say that?"

"It would seem I now blurt stuff out. I never used to, so I can't be sure if Texas was a fluke or the new me, but within minutes of meeting the girls, I spilled my guts. It wasn't pretty, words were flying out of my mouth and I couldn't stop them."

"Good."

"Good? Did you hear me, it was like one huge run-on sentence. I didn't even take a breath, I just talked and talked and talked."

Myles parked next to a Lexus and cut the engine, the old-fashioned way by turning the key.

"Yes, good. I want you to feel comfortable around my friends. You should say whatever's on your mind, anytime you wanna say it."

What was on my mind right then was that parts of my life were up in the air and messed up but there was one part that was so perfect I didn't care that I needed to buy a new car or find a new job. I didn't care that all of my worldly possessions fit into five boxes. I'd learned that the good stuff life had to offer didn't come in boxes. Cars and jobs would come and go but Myles would be my constant.

"I'm glad you didn't quit and give up on me," I said.

"That was never going to happen."

"I won't quit and give up on you either. Everything's sunshine and roses right now, but when a rough patch gets in our way I promise I won't quit."

"I know you won't," he said quietly.

"How do you know?"

"I know because in today's world shit goes down all around us, yet people turn a blind eye and they go about their business. Either they don't care, they don't want to get involved, they don't have time, or they're too scared. But not you. You saw something happening, something bad, something that could harm a lot of people, and you stood up and did something about it. You didn't make excuses; you did something brave even though you were scared. If you'll risk your life to stop strangers from getting hurt, and in the pursuit of that you lose everything and come out the other side stronger, then what will you do for me? For us? For our family?"

I loved that he thought that about me.

I loved it so much I wanted to tell him but my words were stuck in my throat and all I could do was lean over the big center console and kiss him.

His hands slid into my hair and because I loved that too I moaned into his mouth. The consequences were fabulous and it was wet and deep and sweet.

My man could kiss.

"You ready to go up?" he asked when he broke the kiss.

"I was but now I wanna sit in your awesome Bronco and make out all day."

"Unfortunately, there are cameras in the garage. Best guess is if we're not up in five minutes someone will be down to check on us. Though, I'm game to test my theory if you are. Or we can hit the pause button, go up, you can meet everyone, have your talk with Tamir, then we can head home and I can kiss other parts of you."

I shivered and Myles smiled.

"I'll wait until we get home."

273

Myles was wrong; Kevin didn't wait five minutes to come find us, he was already walking out of the lobby as we were walking up.

"Make out on your time, you Delilah-hog," Kevin complained right before he pulled me into a bear hug.

"Thank you," I whispered.

"Nothing to thank me for, sweetheart."

I gave him a squeeze and before he let me go I told him, "You trusted me to be strong enough to take care of myself so you could go after Myles. That belief was what gave me the strength, so thank you, Kevin."

"You're welcome, Delilah."

Myles's arm swept around my shoulder and he tucked me close.

One could say it was an adventure to get up to the actual offices upstairs. Fingerprint pads, retinal scanners, and key cards. Abrams had top-notch security, or at least I thought it did. But walking through the maze of security checkpoints just to get to the elevators proved me wrong. Abrams was amateur compared to Z Corps.

"What happens if the power goes out?" I asked on the ride up.

"The powerplant kicks on," Myles told me.

"Zane didn't fuck around," Kevin picked up. "We have an armory in the basement that has to be secure at all times; the intel we have in the office has to be protected. Zane didn't put in happy homeowner generators—he built a powerplant that could service downtown Annapolis."

Why didn't that surprise me?

Zane struck me as a man who went above and beyond the minimum that was needed to get a job done.

The elevator doors slid open and my jaw dropped.

Oh, yeah, Zane didn't cut corners. The room was huge. No, it was cavernous. Grey walls, chrome accents, sleek and modern lines. There were desks scattered about but they were clean, like no one used them, and doors lining the walls. Probably offices. But what caught my attention was an enclosed glass structure. From where I stood I could see six monitors all actively displaying security feeds.

If I had to guess, that was Garrett's domain and it was cool as hell.

The space was also totally empty of people.

"I'll give you a tour later," Myles said and steered me toward a hall. "Everyone's waiting in the conference room."

I didn't know who everyone was but I was too busy looking around the coolest office space I'd ever seen to care.

Kevin pushed open a door and held it open as Myles and I followed.

Yep. Zane Lewis did nothing in half-measure. The table that dominated the space looked like it belonged in the war room at the White House. I didn't have time to count but at first glance, it looked like it sat at least twenty. And the other furnishings in the room were top-of-the-line, including the gigantic wall-mounted monitor.

Once the shock of the room wore off I took in the occupants.

Tamir Cohen stood in the farthest corner.

Our eyes locked and I waited for the fear of seeing the man who'd kidnapped me to settle in.

There was none.

Memories assailed—the days of silence, the grunting and pointing when he wanted me to do something. The times when he allowed me to shower and when I came out of the bathroom to find him standing by the door guarding it. The food he'd given me, the stops he made without me asking so I could use the bathroom.

He never touched me.

Nothing about the experience had been pleasant, but he hadn't hurt me.

Why hadn't I talked to him? Why hadn't I asked questions?

Then I recalled the last time I saw him.

Guilt and regret. I remember thinking that was what was in his eyes.

There was no fear seeing Tamir Cohen, only sympathy for a man who'd lost his brother. A man who wanted justice. I could understand that.

"Delilah. Welcome home."

I knew that voice.

My gaze went to the man who'd kept me sane during the hours I didn't have Myles. The man who'd given me comfort and strength. The man who'd financed my rescue.

I ducked out from under Myles's arm around my shoulder and made my way to Zane Lewis ignoring the other five men in the room I didn't know.

I stopped in front of Zane who was almost as tall as Truck—which, by the way, Mary had informed me that Truck was six foot seven—cocked my leg back, and kicked Zane as hard as I could.

There was a collective gasp, but since they were all men it sounded more like strangled grunts.

"You kicked me," Zane unnecessarily noted.

"I told you I was going to kick you in the shin," I reminded him. "It's not my fault if you're forgetful. You should've been prepared."

"Woman—"

"Fairy wand? Really, Zane, you had me ask Ghost to show me his fairy wand!"

Zane smiled, and when he did it transformed everything about him. It did not escape me that he was a good-looking man, but when he smiled two dimples dented his cheeks and his beautiful blue eyes gentled. I could see his wife, Ivy, falling victim to that look.

"What's this?" Myles asked from behind me.

"Actually, you can thank Tex for that. I had no idea Ghost had a tattoo of a fairy wand on his leg, but now that I know, I won't forget. I already had Ivy FedEx him a princess sparkly wand."

So, that was kind of funny. Rayne and the rest of the women would think it was, too. Ghost, seeing as he was a man, not so much.

"Thank you for everything," I whispered.

Zane's smile waned but didn't go completely away when his face went slack and he gently said, "Don't mention it, sweetheart."

His eyes were dazzling.

"Wow," I muttered.

Zane's smile returned full force and his dimples once again appeared.

"Here we go," a man I didn't know said.

"Don't be jealous, brother," Zane quipped.

"Hard not to be when every woman you smile at, taken

or not, is momentarily spellbound by your damn dimples," the man returned.

I glanced at the man who called Zane 'brother' and deduced they were indeed brothers. That had to be Lincoln. Similar features, similar blue eyes, though Zane's were dark as was his hair.

"Dimples?" I asked. "I was talking about his eyes. They're a crazy-cool shade of blue."

I jolted when Lincoln howled with laughter. Confused by his outburst I glanced around the room and all of the men, sans Tamir, were busting a gut. Correction: Zane wasn't laughing either, he was scowling.

"Finally, a woman immune to the dimples."

I knew that voice as well. I turned and came face to face with Garrett.

"Hey, Delilah, I'm Garrett. Good to finally meet you."

Whoa.

He was hot too.

It was then I decided now was a good time to start paying attention. Thus I did and by the time I took in each of the men, I realized that Myles's co-workers were all nearly as hot as he was.

Aviv Abrams wanted to build a brigade of super soldiers.

Zane Lewis had amassed a platoon of deadly sexy soldiers.

Jeez.

"Good to meet you," I returned.

Myles came to my side, slid his arm over my shoulders, and tucked me back to his side. Back in Mexico, Myles had been affectionate, but he was more so now that we were home. I loved that if I was close he was touching me in some way.

I tilted my head back to smile at him and he dipped his to kiss me.

"Let's get the introductions out of the way," he said and pointed to a man with grey streaks at his temples. "That's Owen." Next was a tall, lean man who looked a little younger than the rest. "That's Cooper. That's Gabe." The last man had a pair of soulful brown eyes and big, broad shoulders. "And that's Linc."

"Nice to finally meet you all."

"Great," Zane unhappily snapped. "Now that I've been physically assaulted, Delilah's been properly introduced to the team, and my self-esteem's been crushed, maybe we can get on with it."

"It's called your ego, boss, and it's too big to be crushed. Deflated a touch maybe, but crushed? No," Gabe said then added, "But I agree, let's get this part out of the way so we can let the women in before they come in whether we're ready for them or not."

Did they still not trust me?

That thought made my belly cramp and body tighten.

"Baby," Myles murmured. "They're giving you privacy to talk to Tamir. What you choose to tell the women is up to you and only you. And they're not gonna learn about it until you're ready to share."

It was good to know Myles could read my thoughts. Though I was unsure he understood the meaning of privacy since the room was filled with men.

It was also strange that throughout the introductions, Tamir had stood stoic and silent in the corner. For some reason I didn't like that; it was like he was in the naughty chair and everyone was ignoring him. Including me.

"I'm sorry about Isaac."

The impossible happened and Tamir's already blank expression turned dead.

"I'm sorry you spent so much time putting the pieces together and gathering what you needed to give your family peace and it was all for naught. I understand the need to find peace and you gave that up to save Myles. I'm forever in your debt."

Tamir remained quiet, arms loosely hanging at his sides, feet planted shoulder-width apart and I thought back to the times I'd seen him in the Virginia office. He'd never spent a lot of time there. Abrams's main office was in Haifa. And where Aviv went Tamir went which meant he traveled a lot. But I'd never seen him smile. Not one single time. I'd always thought it simply went with the position as head of security.

But now, I knew.

He never smiled because he knew he was in the presence of scum. He walked beside the man who'd murdered his brother. How much self-restraint and discipline did it take to breathe the same air as the man who took something so precious from your family and keep your silence?

"You didn't hurt me—"

"I did," Tamir contradicted. "I hurt you, Delilah and you know it."

"You scared me."

"Fear is hurt."

"No, fear is fear. I was scared and if you would've told me why you were taking me I would've understood. I would've gone with you and done anything you needed me to do. I would've kept your secret. But I also understand you couldn't trust me with something so important. I just wanted Aviv stopped—however that came about I didn't care. But what's done is done. It's in the past. And in the end, you gave up everything so I wouldn't have to and for that I am grateful."

Tamir's stone exterior began to crack. I wouldn't call it a smile or even a grin but there was a hint of amusement on his face.

"Your man didn't need my help. Aviv was arrogant and stupid and the program he went through made him more so. He lacked what every good soldier has—discretion and wisdom. He allowed his conceit to guide him. He's driven by pride and underestimates his opponents. As the saying goes, Aviv brought a knife to what should've been a gunfight. And Myles being a worthy opponent waited for Aviv's ego to show up. If I hadn't taken out Aviv when I did, Myles would've, then he would've taken me down next. You've mistaken me for a good man, I killed Aviv to save myself."

It was sad he didn't think himself a good man after the sacrifice he'd made to find justice for Isaac. Sad, but not something I could fix.

"Whatever your reasons, I appreciate them."

Tamir tipped his head, effectively ending the conversation.

"Myles? Do you have anything to add?" Zane asked.

"Nope. Said what I had to say in El Salvador."

Wait. What?

I tilted my head back to look up at Myles to ask what they'd talked about when I saw his clenched jaw. Then I thought better about asking. If Myles wanted me to know, he would've told me. He hadn't mentioned it, thus, I could take it as a read he didn't want to share.

"Then we're done," Zane announced and I glanced back over at him.

"We're done? What about Dr. Gates?"

"Dr. Gates' brain bucket research was already under investigation by the National Institute of Health and the Food and Drug Administration. Yesterday, the NIH received proof Dr. Gates has not halted the experiments and has gone as far as experimenting on other animals. With Abrams gone so is Dr. Gates' funding."

Well, that was good. The doctor was creepy, his research creepier, even if it was not illegal just unethical.

"His lab in Croatia?"

"Gone."

"Bryan Zaslow wanted the research," I reminded him.

"BZ Systems has bigger issues with the IRS and ATF. They've lost the last five contracts to Abrams and were damn near bankrupt before they paid me off." Zane stopped to smile. "Now Tamir is going to ensure that when the new CEO takes over Abrams, Aviv's Super Soldier program is squashed and the research is destroyed. As well as all future plans to develop AI tech is done responsibly. Any other questions?"

I had about a thousand questions but I settled on, "How can you be so sure what the new CEO is going to do?"

"Meet the new CEO." Zane tipped his head toward Tamir.

"Tamir?"

Zane didn't confirm. Instead, he said, "I hope you don't

mind, but while you and Myles were love-shacked up I negotiated your severance package."

"Severance package?" I asked.

Zane once again ignored my question in favor of hearing himself speak, "However, I declined you keeping your position at the Abrams Corporation, seeing as they're closing the Virginia office and will be working full-time out of Israel. Long-distance relationships suck."

I looked up at Myles and inquired, "Does he ever answer a direct question?"

"Not the ones he doesn't want to."

"Maybe I should've kicked him harder."

"No maybe about it."

"I negotiated a two million dollar deal for the woman and she threatens bodily harm," Zane huffed.

Two million dollars?

What the hell?

"You didn't negotiate anything," Tamir started. "You just told me to write Delilah a two million dollar check. There was no discussion."

Zane rolled his eyes and waved a hand in front of him. "Same thing."

Myles chuckled. I was too stunned to find the humor in anything.

"I have a flight to catch," Tamir announced. "Delilah, the money will be wired into your account immediately."

"I'll be in touch," Zane told Tamir.

"I can't wait," Tamir returned with enough Zane-style sarcasm I couldn't stop my smile.

And that was when it happened.

Tamir smiled.

"Be well, Delilah."

"You, too, Tamir."

Tamir left the conference room, followed by Lincoln, and something stole over me. A feeling of finality.

It was over.

All of it.

Now there really was nothing left but me and Myles and all the goodness that came with him.

CHAPTER 24

I heard them before I saw them.

The women were fast approaching.

I only had a few seconds left.

"You okay, baby?"

"Yeah."

"Did you get everything you needed from seeing Tamir?"

I watched her face change and her eyes go soft, the way they did when I said or did something she liked.

"I did. Though the two—"

"It's not enough. He owes you more than that and he knows it. It won't change what happened but you lost everything and he knows that, too. He's also giving you that money to make himself feel better, and since you hold no grudges, give him what he needs to move on."

"Okay."

That was it.

Just, okay.

But then that was Delilah.

Easy-going.

She was strong when she needed to be and easy the times besides.

She was my all-or-nothing.

The room filled with voices and a woman I barely knew threw her arms around me and Delilah.

"I'm so happy you're both home," Evette cried. "I was so worried."

"I'm so happy you're alive," Delilah returned.

"We did it," Evette whispered.

"We did it," Delilah agreed.

Evette let us go and her pretty tawny eyes sparkled.

"I mean, we might've had a little help from the guys, but mostly *we* did it."

"Just a *little* help." Delilah laughed.

The two women stared at each other.

Whatever silent communication was passing between the women must've been good because they both broke out into huge smiles.

I vaguely wondered if Delilah finally accepted the truth about the lies her mother had told her. The abuse she'd endured. But I figured she did by the way she'd opened up to Rayne and the other women. And now getting to witness her giving Evette the gift she was giving her, I knew she got it and as the years went on, Venessa Hudson would fade further and further until the memories were so distant they be empty.

"Jeez. Can I have a turn?" Natasha chirped.

Talk about a difference.

Natasha Cullen.

Night and day.

"Hey, Myles," she greeted me like an afterthought.

Oh, yeah, the woman had gone from a scared woman who didn't speak to an outspoken woman who loved her friends.

"We're having a moment," Evette clipped.

"Too bad, I want a moment," Nat complained and stuck her hand out. "I'm Natasha. But everyone calls me Nat."

Before the women got too deep into whatever it was women got into I needed to extradite myself.

"Babe? You good?"

"Of course."

Of course.

I wanted to snort at the puzzled look on her face.

I was wrong. It wasn't going to take years for Venessa's bullshit to fade. It was gone.

"Great. Then I'm gonna go talk to the guys and leave you women to it."

"That's code for he's already bored," Evette put in.

She was incorrect; it was code for I wanted Delilah to bond with the women without me around. It was also code for I needed a brief on what had been going on around the office since I'd been gone.

"I'll be—"

"I'm fine, Myles."

Fuck yeah, she was.

I bent and gave her a swift kiss and joined the men on the other side of the room.

"Welcome home," Coop greeted.

"I have to say, I'm totally disappointed," Owen said. "You got off so easy."

"By the looks of it he's gotten off a lot," Gabe mumbled. "And he had the luxury of doing it in private."

RILEY EDWARDS

"Sorry, G-man, it's hard to ratchet down all this sexiness." Cooper gestured to his chest and stomach. "I didn't mean to cramp your style when you were wooing your woman."

G-man? Hilarious.

"Your comebacks are about as bad as your brother's," Gabe returned.

Damn, it was good to be home.

It felt like I'd been gone forever. I totally missed out on Gabe, Evette, and Cooper living together at the safe house. I bet Cooper gave him hell.

"You keep it up, Coop, and when it's your turn they'll give it back ten-fold," Garrett added.

Accurate.

"Coop's turn? What about you, old man? If you're not careful your balls will be shriveled up and you'll be spitting dust by the time you find a woman to put up with your ass," Kevin joined in.

A cloud of regret passed over Garrett's expression.

The kind of regret that ate at a man when he knew he'd fucked-up and lost huge.

And Garrett had lost huge. He was in love with a woman he'd never have because he'd never go after her.

"I signed Zane's contract and had that shit notarized," Coop said. "I'm currently living my best life sampling all of life's beautiful offerings."

"Right," Owen snickered. "That's why your ass is at Gabe's house or mine, mooching meals damn near every night."

"Like I said, living my best life."

Oh, yeah, it was good to be home. Which meant it sucked I had to end the bantering.

288

"What's going on with the rocks? Did you get anything from the letter that was sent?"

"Christ, the mere fact you're asking about *rocks* being thrown makes me want to punch a damn wall," Zane irately barked. "Letter was the same as the first. Postmarked from Canada and prints belonging to Bronson Williams. Now that you and Kevin are home, after our meeting next week with President Graham I'm going to Canada to have a chat."

Shit.

"*You're* going?"

"Either he's the fucker who's been fucking with us or he knows who it is because he's been mailing fucking letters for him. So, yes, I'm going to personally deliver my own message."

I looked at Kevin and Kevin shook his head.

Yeah, that wasn't going to happen. Zane uncaged and unattended could be anything. If Zane was going we were all going. The reality was, if Zane blew, it would take the whole team to contain the blast.

"Where's the meeting, here or the White House?"

"White House," Zane griped.

"Did Graham elaborate?"

"The only thing I know is a DoD contractor reported something to Graham and whatever that something was made him reach out to me. It's the first time since he's been in office that he's made a call to us so my guess is he really didn't like it."

None of that sounded good. None of it I wanted to think about right then. Monday morning would roll around soon enough. I was taking the rest of my vacation days before I had to deal with the next trauma.

"I'm heading out," I announced.

"I don't blame you." Kevin smiled.

"I'll be back to work Monday," I told Zane.

"Would you come in tomorrow to do the job I pay you to do if I told you I was gonna fire your ass?"

"Nope."

"Figures."

"Dinner at my place tonight?" Gabe asked.

"Yeah."

"Brave man, not checking with your woman first." Owen chuckled.

Shit. What did that mean?

"Am I supposed to do that?"

Six assholes laughed at me.

What they didn't do was answer my question.

So, I amended my reply, "I'll check with Delilah and text you."

"Smart choice," he muttered.

We were going to be late for dinner at Evette and Gabe's but I didn't have the heart to rush Delilah off the phone. She'd been on with my mom coming up on two hours and before that, she chatted with my dad for twenty minutes. This was after I told them about Delilah. You would've thought by my mother's reaction to the news I'd "finally settled down"—her words—that I was a sixty-year-old confirmed bachelor. My dad asked to speak to Delilah privately, which didn't come as a surprise because I'd told them the whole story including the part about her being kidnapped. My dad was all about family and protection; I knew he wanted to make sure she was okay.

I figured my mom was planning our wedding, which I was more than okay with.

I was coming out of the bedroom and stopped dead when I heard Delilah speaking softly.

"Okay, Mom, I'll tell him. And I'll ask about a trip to Colorado." There was a brief pause then even softer, "Yeah, me, too. I'll call you soon."

Mom?

There it was—my mom taking Delilah under her wing.

"I take it we're going to Colorado soon."

Delilah craned her neck and looked over the back of the couch.

"I love your mom. And your dad, too."

"Good."

"She wants us to come out soon."

"We'll make that happen."

"You were right. I talked your mom out of getting on a flight tonight. I think the only reason she conceded was because she's due in court Monday morning and she needs the weekend to prepare."

My mother didn't need to prepare, she'd also taught me never to procrastinate. She was giving Delilah time to adjust.

"Ready to go?"

"Yep."

She jumped off the couch and skip-walked over to me.

Skip-walked.

Fuck, yeah.

When she got close she rolled up on her toes and kissed me.

Fucking brilliant.

* * *

"Then Gabe's all…she threatened my butthole." Evette tossed herself back on the couch and roared with laughter.

She was telling the ex-lax story.

It was safe to say Evette fit right in, but the best part was how happy my friend looked. After the shit-childhood he had, he deserved this, all of it. The big waterfront house, his fancy cars, toys, but mostly he deserved the woman who was hysterically laughing on their couch.

I glanced at Delilah and watched her laugh right along with Evette and Nat.

In no time at all, Evette and Nat had become tight, and tonight showed they were pulling Delilah into the fold.

"Laugh it up," Gabe invited even though they already were.

I caught my friend's eye and there was nothing but happiness shining back.

"You good, brother?" he asked.

"Never better."

* * *

"Gabe and Evette's house is amazing," Delilah told me on our way home.

It was a kickass house.

"Do you like the water?" I asked.

"I can take it or leave it."

"Me, too."

"Tomorrow can you take me to get a new phone? I might have to borrow money—"

"Yes, we'll go get you a phone. No, you're not borrowing money."

"I still don't have my debit or credit cards and the severance—"

She said severance like it was a dirty word.

She also misunderstood me so I cut her off and asked, "Are we together?"

Delilah shifted in her seat to look at me.

"Yes."

"Are we planning a life together?"

"Yes."

"Right. So, there's no borrowing money. You need something, you buy it. And just in case you're worried about it, I have money."

"I wasn't worried about it." She rushed out. "But I don't want you to think I'm a freeloader."

"Relationships are about give and take. Not about money and freeloading. It's about what you give the other person, and what you get in return."

"I want to pitch in," she whispered.

I was treading on thin ice with this topic—her mother was a man-eating freeloader.

"So pitch in. Or don't. You do what makes you comfortable just as long as you understand I don't want repayment for the things I give you."

"Thank you for understanding."

She was killing me.

"Do you understand you're not Venessa?"

There were a few beats of weighty silence before she said, "Yes, I understand I'm not her."

293

"Good. We'll get you a phone and whatever else you need tomorrow."

"Okay."

Christ.

Easy.

CHAPTER 25

I was on my knees and pressure was building. Myles was behind me, one hand cupping my breast pinching my nipple, the other was between my legs and he was alternating finger fucking me and rolling his thumb on my clit. It was arguable which felt better. And he was taking my ass.

"More," I groaned.

"Jesus," he grunted.

His thumb did this magical press and roll and my neck could no longer hold my head up so my forehead hit the bed.

I was closer than he was, I knew it when my thighs started shaking and my empty pussy clenched.

"I can't hold it."

"Wait for me, baby."

"Can't."

I was coming apart at the seams. Every part of me tingled. I was hot all over and there was nothing I could do to stop it.

My climax hit and I went down on my forearms and started floating while he drove into my ass harder.

"Jesus fuck," he roared with his cock planted deep.

His big body shook over mine, his rough groan sounded in my ear, his breath fanned over my neck.

Connected.

Moments later, he pulled out and tapped my hip.

"On your side, Delilah."

His voice was rougher than normal, edgier, more commanding. The sound of it gave me chills. I fell to my side and watched Myles walk into the bathroom. A few minutes later he returned and scooped me up. Which was a good thing because it was doubtful I could've made it on my own.

Myles stepped into the bathtub and set me on my feet, then helped me sit and slid in behind me, his long legs cocked and bracketing me in. The warm water felt like heaven over my sensitized skin.

I felt Myles shift behind me and brush my hair off my shoulder. With his mouth near my ear, he asked, "How do you feel?"

"Taken."

His body went solid.

"Claimed."

I heard him draw in a breath.

"Loved."

He exhaled and wrapped his arms around me and I gave him the rest of my weight and settled against him.

There I was sitting in a bath in a townhouse in Maryland, my big strong man's arms wrapped around me after he spent months searching for me.

I had it all.

I had everything my mother had ever wanted but never could figure out she was searching for the wrong thing.

And suddenly I felt sorry for her. She'd never be loved. She'd never be connected, taken, or claimed. She'd never know this feeling of complete wholeness. The peace and security that comes with it. She'd never have forever or the love of a man that was pure and good and right.

"Maybe I should buy a Bronco. We can have matching his and hers."

"Baby, a Bronco is a man's car."

"It is not."

"Okay it's not, but it would be a bitch to get car seats in and out of it."

I stopped thinking about what kind of car I wanted to buy and focused on car seats.

"Car seats?" I breathed.

"Car seats," he affirmed.

"If we have a boy I want to name him Cornelis Archer."

I felt Myles's body shaking behind mine.

"Hard no."

"Okay, but if we have a girl can we name her Irene Flora?"

"That's also a hard pass."

"Do I get to name our children?" I huffed.

"Sure, as long as I like the name."

That sounded like he had veto power.

"Do *I* get to like the names? Say, if you suggested one and I didn't like it do I get a hard pass?"

There was a stretch of silence before Myles declared, "Elise Monroe if we have a girl first. Deacon Monroe if we have a boy first. Whichever way it goes we'll switch it up—Elise Skye or Deacon Reid."

Deacon was his dad's name, so that was an awesome obvious choice.

"Monroe?"

"Kevin's last name."

"Willow Monroe or Willow Elise."

"Done."

I stared at the water coming out of the tap and smiled.

We'd decided on our children's names.

"Are we gonna get married or have these children out of wedlock?"

"Getting hitched as soon as I can go out and buy you a ring."

"Engaged or hitched?"

"Engaged. When we go to Colorado we'll get married unless you want something big," he told me.

"Small. But what about your friends?"

"We'll have a party when we get back."

That totally worked for me.

"Okay."

"Easy," he whispered.

"What?"

"Easy. You knew naming my boy after my dad meant something to me and you gave it to me. You asked about Monroe, knew that meant something to me, too, and gave it without thought. Earlier about money, I gave you what you needed and you gave it back to me agreeing we're not getting into the cycle of borrowing and paying back. And before that, when we were at the office, you found out I had a talk with Tamir that I didn't tell you about and you gave me that, too. You didn't have to ask; you knew I would've told you if it was worth repeating. Easy."

I didn't quibble about the names because Deacon was a great name and Monroe was just as cool. Which got me thinking.

"Would I still be easy if I told you I think I like Monroe for a first name? Maybe for a girl, Monroe Elise and you pick a new middle name for Deacon."

"Yeah, baby, you'd still be easy."

"And would I still be easy if I told you I didn't ask about your talk with Tamir because I knew if it was important I knew you would've told me, and since you didn't I knew you were keeping it to yourself to protect me because you knew whatever conversation you had with him would likely freak me out and I'm grateful you didn't tell me?"

"You'd still be easy," he confirmed, humor clearly evident in his tone.

"Good."

"Now, how are you really feeling? Sore?"

"A little," I admitted and leaned forward to turn off the tap.

The room was plunged into silence now that the water had stopped. So when I leaned back and turned my head to rest my cheek on Myles's chest I could hear the steady rhythm of his heartbeat. Something I'd heard every night since we'd been home. A sound that never failed to lull me to sleep. A few minutes later with a smile on my face, happy we'd managed to sort out our kids' names and plan our wedding, my eyelids were getting heavy and I was fading fast.

"You gonna pass out on me or are you up for another go?"

More proof my man couldn't get enough of me.

My eyes popped open and my smile was still firmly on my face when I asked, "Are you threatening my butthole?"

It took two seconds—and yes I counted—for Myles's laughter to fill the bathroom. It bounced off the walls, ricocheted off the title, and fill me up to bursting.

Yep. I had everything.

Lucky for me, Myles loved me, so he gave me more.

In record time he was on his feet, I was in his arms, and soaking wet he carried me to the bed.

Then he commenced the more portion of our night.

CHAPTER 26

Kevin Monroe

I could spot a liar from a mile away.

A well-trained government liar—they were even easier.

And the woman sitting across from me in the White House briefing room was a well-trained government liar.

A drop-dead-smokin' hot liar with arresting eyes and pouty lips.

I could spot 'em but my boss could sniff 'em out, which was something Zane did the moment we walked into the room and he caught a whiff of her expensive perfume.

President Graham was at the head of the table, Zane at the other end. Owen, Gabe, Myles, Cooper, and I filled in the seats between them.

And Layla—the professional liar—was directly across from me.

"Thank you for joining us," President Graham started.

"With all due respect, Mr. President, I don't work with the CIA."

Layla didn't blink. She didn't flinch, her nose didn't even twitch.

"I don't understand, we're not dealing with the CIA on this op."

"I thought Tom briefed you before he left office," Zane went on.

"Indeed he did."

Still no signs of discomfort.

"Then I'm positive he told you I'm out of the spy game. Moving on from that I'm sure he told you I don't like to be lied to and most of all I don't like my time wasted."

The woman almost had a bored expression on her face as she listened.

"And I'm quite sure I haven't lied to you, and moving on from *that*, I don't appreciate the insinuation that I have."

"Then what's she doing here?"

Layla's eyes went hard and they sliced to Zane.

"Layla Cunnings is a DoD civilian contractor. She works in intelligence."

"What region?" Zane asked.

"Southwest Asia," Layla answered.

"Turkey, Armenia, Georgia, and Azerbaijan," Zane quickly rattled off the countries.

"Impressive, Mr. Lewis, you know your combatant commands."

She was a spunky liar.

"What's more impressive is you managed to get Graham's ear and arrange this meeting."

"I have connections and—"

"I bet you do," Zane cut her off. "I don't work with the CIA."

Layla's cheek jumped—the first sign she was getting flustered. She got a pass on the hardening and narrowing of her eyes. I was chalking that up to Zane being Zane which translated to rude. But he had not lied, he hated his time being wasted and after his last run-in with the CIA he vowed never to work an op with them again.

"I'm not with the CIA," Layla spat.

"Right, you're a civilian contractor for the DoD. And when I worked for the CIA I was an escalator repairman. You cannot imagine the access you get to buildings using that cover. I was also a limo driver, a great one, too. It's amazing the shit people say when they think that partition is soundproof. I had lots of different *jobs* when I worked with the CIA. Yet I only had one, to gather intel by any means necessary. I'm clear of that and my men are clear of it."

"Theo Jackson," Layla said.

I didn't need to be looking at Zane to know she'd dropped a bomb.

"You know that name, yet you expect me to believe you don't work for the CIA."

"He's the reason I left. I disagreed with the way the agency wanted to handle him."

"Handle him?" Zane's voice turned abrasive and menacing.

Handle him was CIA lingo for a kill order.

At the sound of his tone, I went on high-alert. I shifted my gaze to my teammates and they, too, were alert and ready.

Layla had no reaction to Zane's clipped question.

I took in her crisp white button-down shirt, the diamond studs in her ears, the Tag Heuer watch on her wrist and figured her jewelry alone would cost a whack. Couple that with the designer outfit, heels, perfectly styled hair, and makeup, the woman screamed high maintenance.

Her demeanor remained professional and detached when she addressed Zane.

"After he left you and your platoon in Egypt he followed the intel you helped him find and went to Spain. He found his target. The problem was Langley doesn't like egg on its face and the HVT ended up being an asset that had been on the CIA's payroll for years. Theo was told to bury the intel and was given a new assignment. Theo didn't feel like burying the fact that the CIA had been paying a top Al-Qaeda leader for false intel and the money he'd been paid aided a terrorist organization's quest to kill U.S. service members. Theo wanted an investigation. Langley disagreed. Theo wouldn't back down and was fired. I didn't agree with my boss's assessment of the situation. I thought an investigation was in order, for no other reason than to ensure something like that never occurred again. A few weeks later I was called to the seventh floor and handed my walking papers. Of course, it was a carefully worded resignation I didn't write but was told to sign. Then I was reminded of the oath I took and the NDAs I signed and how both were in effect in perpetuity and was asked to leave."

For some unexplainable reason, I wanted Layla rattled. I wanted the professional façade dropped. I wanted the perfection that was sitting across from me mussed up and the real woman she kept hidden to come out. I wanted to see the fire she kept at bay burn.

It was all there, simmering under the surface. The question was, how far would I have to push before it sparked to life?

"Seems to me you need another reminder," I started, and she turned her attention to me. "Unless, of course, we're at the end of days and that NDA is about to expire."

"Are you going to turn me in?"

I couldn't help but smile at her quick comeback.

"It's possible." I shrugged. "Though you just broke your oath in front of the president so I'm thinking I don't have to call the CIA hotline and report a security breach."

Layla calmly placed her palms on the table and leaned forward.

"The oath I took was the same one you took, Special Operator Monroe. *I will bear true faith and allegiance.* My allegiance has never wavered—not from my country or my brothers and sisters in the field. I've been assured your team can be trusted with—"

Seems she'd done her homework and looked us up. My service in the Navy was easily accessible and my time spent on the Teams wouldn't be hard to find.

"Can you be trusted?" I cut her off.

Her eyes narrowed and I noticed they weren't the hazel I'd originally thought they were. They were green, and the fire was beginning to flash.

"Tell me about Theo," Zane demanded.

"According to public record, he died in a plane crash ten years ago."

Bronson Williams's half-brother died in a plane crash ten years ago minutes after it took off from Cyprus. Everyone aboard that flight was reported deceased.

Bronson Williams was throwing stones—or more accurately pebbles—and making veiled threats against Zane.

The room went deadly silent.

The air grew heavy.

The fuse had been lit.

"Aaron Cardon," Zane growled.

"Theo Jackson's real name," Layla confirmed.

There it was—the connection we couldn't find.

"We need your help locating him," Graham interjected.

Zane's angry stare transferred to the president.

"I don't work with the CIA."

Layla's control finally snapped and her fist slammed down on the table.

"For the last time, I don't work for the goddamn CIA," she seethed. "Theo trusts me. Lucas Grant told me I could trust *you.* The last time I heard from Theo he was following a lead in Armenia. He's been dark for over two months. Our deal was sixty days, no more, between contact. Ten years without fail, every sixty days he's made contact. Now it's been seventy days and no check-in. Lucas said your teams are the best. That you're the only man I can trust with this information."

Lucas Grant was a former SEAL. He was now serving as the president's personal bodyguard. Another piece of the puzzle clicked into place; that was how she got a meeting with Graham.

"Myles?" Zane called. "It's your team. Your call."

"She's got twenty-four hours to convince Kevin why we should get involved," Myles replied.

"A man's life is in danger," Layla hissed. "And you want me to convince you to help me?"

"Not me, Miss Cunnings, Kevin," Myles returned. "You're worried about one life, and I'm worried about fourteen men and their families and how us getting involved is going to put us further in danger. Theo's brother, Aaron, seems to have a personal grudge against Zane, and while right now he's a nuisance, that can escalate in the blink of an eye. So before I send my team to Armenia to search for Theo you need to convince Kevin it's worth the risk."

Layla looked beyond pissed.

The professionalism had slipped and the fire was ablaze.

Her gaze skated around the table, then it landed on me and our eyes locked.

Determined, intelligent, shrewd eyes that edged on the side of battle-hardened. And suddenly I wanted to know where she'd been and what she'd done to make her pretty green eyes so wary. How had she come about her strength, was it learned or was she born with steel in her veins? I wanted to know if there was more fire in her and how much more it would take before she combusted

It felt like eternity before she finally said, "Let's go."

Layla stood and motioned for me to do the same.

"Hurry up," she bossed. "We've got ten years' worth of intel to go over."

Damn, the woman was bossy *and* spunky—a deadly combination.

I hoped like fuck she could convince me to take the risk.

* * *

Oooooh, Layla and Kevin have some serious SPARKS going on between them…sparks we all know will turn to some serious flame! Pick up the next book in the Blue team series, *Kevin*, now!

Tarnished

Tainted

Takeback

Dangerous Love

Dangerous Rescue

Delta Team Three

Hope's Delta

Gemini Group

Nixon's Promise

Jameson's Salvation

Weston's Treasure

Alec's Dream

Chasin's Surrender

Holden's Resurrection

Jonny's Redemption

The 707 Freedom Series

Free

Freeing Jasper

Finally Free

Freedom

The Next Generation

Saving Meadow

Chasing Honor

Finding Mercy

Claiming Tuesday

Adoring Delaney

Keeping Quinn

Taking Liberty

The Masters Collection

The Awakening

The Collective

Unbroken 1 & 2 – Season One

Trust – Season Two

Standalone

Romancing Rayne

Falling for the Delta

ABOUT THE AUTHOR

Riley Edwards is a bestselling multi-genre author, wife, and military mom. Riley was born and raised in Los Angeles but now resides on the east coast with her fantastic husband and children.

Riley writes heart-stopping romance with sexy alpha heroes and even stronger heroines. Riley's favorite genres to write are romantic suspense and military romance.

Don't forget to sign up for Riley's newsletter and never miss another release, sale, or exclusive bonus material. https://www.subscribepage.com/RRsignup

Facebook Fan Group

www.rileyedwardsromance.com

facebook.com/Novelist.Riley.Edwards
twitter.com/rileyedwardsrom
instagram.com/rileyedwardsromance
bookbub.com/authors/riley-edwards
amazon.com/author/rileyedwards

There are many more books in this fan fiction world than listed here, for an up-to-date list go to www.AcesPress.com

You can also visit our Amazon page at:
http://www.amazon.com/author/operationalpha

Special Forces: Operation Alpha World

Christie Adams: Charity's Heart
Denise Agnew: Dangerous to Hold
Shauna Allen: Awakening Aubrey
Brynne Asher: Blackburn
Linzi Baxter: Unlocking Dreams
Jennifer Becker: Hiding Catherine
Alice Bello: Shadowing Milly
Heather Blair: Rescue Me
Misha Blake: Flash
Anna Blakely: Rescuing Gracelynn
Julia Bright: Saving Lorelei
Cara Carnes: Protecting Mari
Kendra Mei Chailyn: Beast
Melissa Kay Clarke: Rescuing Annabeth
Samantha A. Cole: Handling Haven
Sue Coletta: Hacked
Melissa Combs: Gallant
Lorelei Confer: Protecting Sara
Anne Conley: Redemption for Misty
KaLyn Cooper: Rescuing Melina
Janie Crouch: Storm
Liz Crowe: Marking Mariah
Sarah Curtis: Securing the Odds
Jordan Dane: Redemption for Avery

Tarina Deaton: Found in the Lost
Aspen Drake, Intense
KL Donn: Unraveling Love
Riley Edwards: Protecting Olivia
PJ Fiala: Defending Sophie
Nicole Flockton: Protecting Maria
Alexa Gregory: Backdraft
Michele Gwynn: Rescuing Emma
Casey Hagen: Shielding Nebraska
Desiree Holt: Protecting Maddie
Kathy Ivan: Saving Sarah
Kris Jacen, Be With Me
Jesse Jacobson: Protecting Honor
Silver James: Rescue Moon
Becca Jameson: Saving Sofia
Kate Kinsley: Protecting Ava
Rayne Lewis: Justice for Mary
Heather Long: Securing Arizona
Gennita Low: No Protection
Kirsten Lynn: Joining Forces for Jesse
Margaret Madigan: Bang for the Buck
Trish McCallan: Hero Under Fire
Kimberly McGath: The Predecessor
Rachel McNeely: The SEAL's Surprise Baby
KD Michaels: Saving Laura
Lynn Michaels: Rescuing Kyle
Olivia Michaels: Protecting Harper
Wren Michaels: The Fox & The Hound
Annie Miller: Securing Willow
Kat Mizera: Protecting Bobbi
Keira Montclair, Wolf and the Wild Scots
Mary B Moore: Force Protection

LeTeisha Newton: Protecting Butterfly
Angela Nicole: Protecting the Donna
MJ Nightingale: Protecting Beauty
Sarah O'Rourke: Saving Liberty
Victoria Paige: Reclaiming Izabel
Anne L. Parks: Mason
Debra Parmley: Protecting Pippa
Lainey Reese: Protecting New York
KeKe Renée: Protecting Bria
TL Reeve and Michele Ryan: Extracting Mateo
Elena M. Reyes: Keeping Ava
Deanna L. Rowley: Saving Veronica
Angela Rush: Charlotte
Rose Smith: Saving Satin
Jenika Snow: Protecting Lily
Lynne St. James: SEAL's Spitfire
Dee Stewart: Conner
Harley Stone: Rescuing Mercy
Sarah Stone: Shielding Grace
Jen Talty: Burning Desire
Reina Torres, Rescuing Hi'ilani
Savvi V: Loving Lex
Megan Vernon: Protecting Us
LJ Vickery: Circus Comes to Town
Rachel Young: Because of Marissa
R. C. Wynne: Shadows Renewed

Delta Team Three Series
Lori Ryan: Nori's Delta
Becca Jameson: Destiny's Delta
Lynne St James, Gwen's Delta
Elle James: Ivy's Delta

Riley Edwards: Hope's Delta

Police and Fire: Operation Alpha World
Freya Barker: Burning for Autumn
B.P. Beth: Scott
Jane Blythe: Salvaging Marigold
Julia Bright, Justice for Amber
Anna Brooks, Guarding Georgia
KaLyn Cooper: Justice for Gwen
Aspen Drake: Sheltering Emma
Emily Gray: Shelter for Allegra
Alexa Gregory: Backdraft
Deanndra Hall: Shelter for Sharla
Barb Han: Kace
EM Hayes: Gambling for Ashleigh
India Kells: Shadow Killer
CM Steele: Guarding Hope
Reina Torres: Justice for Sloane
Aubree Valentine, Justice for Danielle
Maddie Wade: Finding English
Stacey Wilk: Stage Fright
Laine Vess: Justice for Lauren

Tarpley VFD Series
Silver James, Fighting for Elena
Deanndra Hall, Fighting for Carly
Haven Rose, Fighting for Calliope
MJ Nightingale, Fighting for Jemma
TL Reeve, Fighting for Brittney
Nicole Flockton, Fighting for Nadia

As you know, this book included at least one character from Susan Stoker's books. To check out more, see below.

SEAL Team Hawaii Series

Finding Elodie
Finding Lexie
Finding Kenna (Oct 2021)
Finding Monica (May 2022)
Finding Carly (TBA)
Finding Ashlyn (TBA)
Finding Jodelle (TBA)

Eagle Point Search & Rescue

Searching for Lilly (Mar 2022)
Searching for Elsie (Jun 2022)
Searching for Bristol (Nov 2022)
Searching for Caryn (TBA)
Searching for Finley (TBA)
Searching for Heather (TBA)
Searching for Khloe (TBA)

The Refuge Series

Deserving Alaska (Aug 2022)
Deserving Henley (Jan 2023)
Deserving Reese (TBA)
Deserving Cora (TBA)
Deserving Lara (TBA)
Deserving Maisy (TBA)
Deserving Ryleigh (TBA)

Delta Team Two Series

Shielding Gillian
Shielding Kinley
Shielding Aspen
Shielding Jayme (novella)
Shielding Riley
Shielding Devyn
Shielding Ember
Shielding Sierra (Jan 2022)

SEAL of Protection: Legacy Series
Securing Caite (FREE!)
Securing Brenae (novella)
Securing Sidney
Securing Piper
Securing Zoey
Securing Avery
Securing Kalee
Securing Jane

Delta Force Heroes Series
Rescuing Rayne (FREE!)
Rescuing Aimee (novella)
Rescuing Emily
Rescuing Harley
Marrying Emily (novella)
Rescuing Kassie
Rescuing Bryn
Rescuing Casey
Rescuing Sadie (novella)
Rescuing Wendy
Rescuing Mary
Rescuing Macie (novella)

Rescuing Annie (Feb 2022)

Badge of Honor: Texas Heroes Series
Justice for Mackenzie (FREE!)
Justice for Mickie
Justice for Corrie
Justice for Laine (novella)
Shelter for Elizabeth
Justice for Boone
Shelter for Adeline
Shelter for Sophie
Justice for Erin
Justice for Milena
Shelter for Blythe
Justice for Hope
Shelter for Quinn
Shelter for Koren
Shelter for Penelope

SEAL of Protection Series
Protecting Caroline (FREE!)
Protecting Alabama
Protecting Fiona
Marrying Caroline (novella)
Protecting Summer
Protecting Cheyenne
Protecting Jessyka
Protecting Julie (novella)
Protecting Melody
Protecting the Future
Protecting Kiera (novella)
Protecting Alabama's Kids (novella)

Protecting Dakota

New York Times, USA Today and *Wall Street Journal* Bestselling Author Susan Stoker has a heart as big as the state of Tennessee where she lives, but this all American girl has also spent the last fourteen years living in Missouri, California, Colorado, Indiana, and Texas. She's married to a retired Army man who now gets to follow *her* around the country.

www.stokeraces.com
www.AcesPress.com
susan@stokeraces.com

Made in United States
North Haven, CT
25 July 2022

21777036R00180